★ "Guerrero touches on many topics—anxiety, fostering, friendship, family, selective mutism, and more—seamlessly weaving them all together to create a strong, moving narrative . . . A heartbreaking, heartwarming, powerful debut novel."
— *Kirkus Reviews*, starred review

"A story for anyone who's ever asked where—and what—home is."
— **Jack Cheng**,
author of *See You in the Cosmos*

"*How to Make Friends with the Sea* is a heartwarming story about family, friendship, identity, and finding courage within our own hearts. I know readers will have as much fun cheering for Pablo as I did."
— **Dan Gemeinhart**,
author of *The Remarkable Journey of Coyote Sunrise*

"Touching and sweet, Tanya Guerrero's debut *How to Make Friends with the Sea* is a multilayered story with heaps of heart. Readers will root for Pablo as he finds his courage, voice, and family on this journey to self-acceptance."
— **Elly Swartz**,
author of *Finding Perfect* and *Give and Take*

"Atmospheric and moving, *How to Make Friends with the Sea* is an impressive debut. The friendship between Pablo and Chiqui completely captured my heart."
— **Jasmine Warga**,
author of *Other Words for Home*

ALSO BY TANYA GUERRERO

All You Knead Is Love

How to Make Friends with the Sea

Tanya Guerrero

How to Make Friends with the Sea

SQUARE
FISH

Farrar Straus Giroux

New York

SQUARE
FISH

An imprint of Macmillan Publishing Group, LLC
120 Broadway, New York, NY 10271
mackids.com

Our books may be purchased in bulk for promotional, educational, or business use.
Please contact your local bookseller or the Macmillan Corporate and Premium
Sales Department at (800) 221-7945 ext. 5442 or by email at
MacmillanSpecialMarkets@macmillan.com.

Library of Congress Cataloging-in-Publication Data is available.
ISBN 978-1-250-76327-3 (paperback)

Originally published in the United States by Farrar Straus Giroux
First Square Fish edition, 2021
Book designed by Aram Kim
Square Fish logo designed by Filomena Tuosto

1   3   5   7   9   10   8   6   4   2

LEXILE: 510L

For Violet

How to Make Friends with the Sea

ONE

I studied the grains of rice on my plate, separating them into neat little piles with a fork.

Thirty-one grains. Exactly one month since we moved to the Philippines.

Five grains. Five years had passed since the last time my father kissed me good night.

Twelve grains. I would be turning twelve in just three days.

"Pablo—" Mamá's voice buzzed in my ear like a pesky mosquito. Her breath was shallow, the way she breathed when she was trying not to lose her patience. "Por favor, Pablo. Eat. Lentils *and* rice."

I didn't look at her. Instead, I eyed the small bowl of lentils with ten spoons lined up beside it. At least she'd finally gotten it right. Sauce didn't have any business touching rice. And once my teaspoon was soiled, I would need another clean one to keep on eating.

The pile with thirty-one grains disappeared into my mouth, and then I took a bite of lentils with the first spoon. Mamá exhaled. "So, I was thinking. Maybe we could invite some of the neighborhood kids for cake and ice cream for your birthday? Just a couple?" she asked.

There was a moment of silence. I glared at the twelve grains. I hated birthdays. I hated crowds. I hated messes. I hated noises. And most of all, I hated parties. Those grimy neighborhood kids—I could already picture them leaving fingerprints on every square inch of the house, rearranging everything I'd so carefully arranged, while ice cream dribbled from their chins.

"If it's all the same, I'd rather it just be the two of us," I muttered.

I looked up from my plate, parting my lips as I wracked my brain for a good reason.

I'm not in the mood.

Nope.

I'm tired.

Nope.

What's the point?

Nope.

Truth was, I'd run out of good reasons.

All I managed was a weak smile. The color of her eyes went from a sharp green to a soft hazel. "All right, then . . .

Shall I make Abuelita's orange almond cake? I know it's your favorite."

The sound of a shrieking parrot echoed from the living room. Ordinarily, Mamá ignored her cell phone during mealtimes, but the parrot ringtone was her boss, Miguel, the founder of El Lado Salvaje sanctuary—which in Spanish meant "the Wild Side."

"I'll be back. Keep on eating," she said, speed-walking to the hallway. "Hola, Miguel. Good evening," I heard her say. She paced and listened and paced and listened, uttering an "Uh-huh" now and then. After a few seconds she halted. I knew she was about to lose it by the way her arms suddenly thrust out. "Qué? So what do you expect me to do?" After that, she switched to all Spanish, which I usually understood. But her words were just too fast. Instead, I watched her body do the talking. Her shoulders and hips popped. Her chin jutted out. Her head bobbed from side to side.

As soon as Mamá hung up, she inhaled deep. It was the kind of inhaling that was supposed to blow away her anger from the inside out. I knew it well, because she was the sort of woman people called "fiery." Hot-blooded. Short-tempered. Spirited.

She came back into the kitchen holding a rose quartz crystal in her hand—one of her calming stones. "That was Miguel . . ."

I glanced up at her. "Another abused animal, huh?"

"No. Not quite." Mamá gripped the crystal even tighter. "Miguel's friend, the man who donated the land where the sanctuary is on . . . He's asking for a favor. A big favor. Seems nobody else is willing to help. Help a girl . . . an orphaned girl."

For a second I thought I'd misheard. But then I saw the signs—a quivering lip, flushed cheeks, eyes glossy with emotion. It was the same expression she had *every* single time she got suckered into helping some poor, helpless animal.

Except this time it was a girl. Mamá was going to rescue a girl. Not a wild animal. A girl.

TWO

"A girl?"

My head felt like a can of soda about to explode. Mamá's mouth moved. But her voice was muted. Then it was as if she was screaming in my ear. "YES, PABLO. A GIRL... I don't really have that many details. I don't even know what really happened to her. All I know is that she needs help," she said.

I slumped in my seat. My eyes hopscotched around Mamá's face. Her freckles were oddly comforting. But then I stumbled on a new one—a tiny freckle near the bridge of her nose.

It was weird—the freckle and this girl.

I was horrified and fascinated at the same time.

"So, what are you supposed to do? It's not like you're some orphan-girl expert or anything," I finally replied.

She began clearing dishes. "I have no choice, Pablo...

When I needed a fresh start, a new job, Miguel was there to help me. Now it's my turn to pay it forward."

That was that. Her mind was made up. She had no choice. Of course she didn't. It was something she *had* to do. One more life to save and several months later, we'd be off somewhere else.

Another country. Another adventure. Another place I'd have to get used to.

Costa Rica, Brazil, India, Kenya, Indonesia, the Philippines.

Where to next?

"I think I'll go to sleep now. Good night," I grumbled.

Mamá looked up from the sink full of dishes. "Good night, mi amor."

Eighteen steps and twenty-four terra-cotta tiles later, I was in my room with my bed and its crisp white sheets, with my alphabetized bookshelf, with my plain blue curtains that hung just right. Everything was in order—at least for now.

"Pablo . . . Pablito. Wake up."

I blinked. Mamá hovered over my bed in all black— black tank top, black shorts, black onyx bead bracelet. That bracelet had been on her wrist ever since my father left. She claimed those beads were supposed to help her release negative emotions. But I wasn't so sure they were working.

"Grace can't come today. Her daughter has a fever," she said with the slightest of frowns.

My body tensed. I didn't like sudden changes. Ms. Grace, my homeschool teacher, was supposed to come Monday to Fridays at 9:00 A.M. sharp.

"Oh. Okay," I said.

Mamá bounced off my bed and opened my dresser drawer. Her Doc Martens boots, also black, made squishy sounds against her ankles. There was dirt on them—just a smudge of dried mud near the soles. I held my breath, looking away as I counted to ten.

One. Two. Three. Four . . .

She turned around and held up an orange T-shirt and some cargo shorts. "So. You can either stay at Ate Lucinda's or come with me."

"Ate" meant "big sister" in Tagalog, and for some strange reason everyone in the Philippines called one another "Ate" or "Kuya" or "Manang" or "Manong" or "Tita" or "Tito," even though they weren't always related to one another. When we arrived exactly thirty-two days ago, Mamá had explained that most Filipinos spoke English *and* Tagalog, and sometimes even Taglish—a combination of both. Supposedly, this whole "Ate" so-and-so business was a way of respecting your elders. But to me, it was just confusing and unsettling. Our neighbor Ate Lucinda was most definitely *not* my big sister. And I didn't want to have anything to do with her four kids, ever since they came over and left cracker crumbs everywhere.

I sat up and winced at the orange T-shirt. "I guess I'll tag along, then."

Mamá sighed. I had no idea why it was so hard for her to remember my color-coordinated clothes. She went back to my dresser and searched for the white T-shirt that was supposed to go with those shorts. Deep down, though, I could see she was grinning. I knew she was pleased that I'd decided to join her mission.

Pablito, mi amor. Real-life experiences are the best school of all. You'll see.

She'd been telling me that ever since she pulled me out of school in the second grade. But as I got dressed, I couldn't help wondering, *What can I possibly learn from some random orphaned girl?*

THREE

A sleek white truck with black tinted windows pulled up to our house. Miguel's SUV was almost embarrassing in the way it stood out, as if it were a sparkly unicorn galloping down the street. Nearly all the houses in Mt. Makiling Heights Subdivision were old-fashioned bungalows with Spanish tiled roofs, rusted metal gates, and tiny pocket gardens. Mamá said the neighborhood had "character" and that the houses were "quaint." But I knew that was her fancy way of saying "affordable."

Ate Lucinda's four kids, Jem, Happy, and the twins, Bing and Lito, stopped their game—flinging flip-flops at one another—long enough to stare. I stood by the front door, hoping they wouldn't run over.

"Good morning, Ma'am Carmen and Sir Pablo," said Zeus, Miguel's smiling chauffeur—*or rather, as Miguel* liked to call him, his "right-hand man." Zeus was the first person who'd greeted us at the airport. That day he'd called me "sir," which, to me, made no sense whatsoever. Why was *he* addressing *me*—a puny eleven-year-old kid—as a knight?

There was nothing knight-like about me.

Not my skinny legs *or* my even skinnier arms.

Not my dirty-blond hair, which got dirtier every year, making it pretty much just a dull brown.

Not my freckles, which made my face look all smudgy no matter how many times I washed it.

Sir Pablo sounded ridiculous.

"Hola, Zeus. You are looking very handsome this morning," joked Mamá as she climbed into the truck.

Zeus's smile got even wider. He held his hand out to help me. But there was dirt under his fingernails. And to make matters worse, his pinkie nail was long and sharp. "No, thanks. I got it," I said politely.

He chuckled. "I think you have gotten taller, Sir Pablo!"

To be honest, having Zeus around used to bug me at first. I didn't get why we needed some dude driving us around, when we used to get by just fine on our own. But then Mamá explained that chauffeurs were pretty common in the Philippines, and that Zeus was really more like Miguel's personal assistant and all-around confidante. He was one of the good guys. Trustworthy. Reliable. Kind.

After a couple of weeks, I sort of got used to him.

I slid onto the leather upholstery. Zeus closed the door. Inside it was better. Nobody could see us, and Zeus *was* good about keeping the interior squeaky clean. It even smelled like oranges.

The engine rumbled. I could still see Zeus's smile from the rearview mirror as we drove off with all four kids chasing us down the road. After a while, they disappeared. Zeus managed to dodge every single vehicle in his way—illegally parked motorbikes in various colors, rusty tricycles, which were basically motorbikes with passenger sidecars, and jeepneys, weird-looking mini-buses covered in so many decorations that they could have easily passed for tacky carnival rides. Even though it was early morning, the neighborhood was already too chaotic.

Mamá leaned closer to the driver's seat. "How long will it take to get to Santa Aurora?"

"Four, maybe five hours if we are lucky," said Zeus.

I did the math in my head. That was 240 or 300 minutes. Santa Aurora was clearly in the middle of nowhere. There would be too many trees, too many mountains, too much dirt and mud and whatever else. But there was no point in worrying. Not yet. I looked out the window, searching for something, anything that wasn't speeding by too fast. Only the clouds seemed to be still. So I traced their shapes and counted each and every one to pass the time.

... *twelve, thirteen, fourteen, fifteen, sixteen, seventeen, eighteen* ...

FOUR

. . . two thousand two, two thousand three . . .

Suddenly, the clouds vanished.

All I saw were mountains covered with bright green jungles. It seemed impossible that there were even people living out there.

"We are near," said Zeus, turning onto a smaller dirt road.

Mamá craned her neck, exploring the trees with her eyes. It was her superpower—spotting that elusive monkey, or bird, or insect camouflaged among the leaves. "Hmm . . . I don't see any houses," she murmured under her breath.

The road twisted and turned exactly eleven more times before the truck halted.

Zeus scratched his head and peered at the GPS screen. "I guess this must be it, Ma'am Carmen."

We looked around. But there was really nothing to look

at except for a wooden sign hanging crooked by the side of the road, with hand-painted red letters that read FRESH CHICKEN + EGG 4 SALE.

Mamá squinted. "Wait. There's a path over there," she said, pointing at something that resembled a path, but not really. I wasn't even sure Miguel's tank of a truck would fit.

Zeus turned the truck slowly, inching between two massive tree trunks. I started to panic. My heart banged against my chest, and there were beads of sweat on my forehead. "Um. Are you sure about this?" I asked.

"Do not worry, Sir Pablo. I am a professional." For some reason, though, Zeus's proclamation didn't reassure me. I closed my eyes and held my breath, waiting for the sound of scraping metal. But there was no such sound.

"Bravo, Zeus!" Mamá cheered.

I opened my eyes just as a structure appeared. It was a house—well, more of a shack, really—a patchwork of corrugated metal, wood, and wire mesh where the windows were supposed to be. Beside it, under the shade of a leafy tree, was a half-falling-down chicken coop. It was about as big as a one-car garage, walls splintered and holey, roof rusted, leaning in such a way that a strong gust of wind could probably blow it right off. I remembered the sign advertising fresh chickens and eggs. But that couldn't possibly be the place.

There was nothing fresh about it.

My skin itched at the sight of all the rust and dirt and debris. "I think I'll stay in the car."

"Might be for the best," Mamá replied with a nod. Zeus opened the door for her, and she hopped out.

For a few moments they wandered, with Zeus hollering, "Tao po! Tao po!"

Whatever he was saying must have worked, because a man wearing a white T-shirt and yellow basketball shorts finally emerged from the chicken coop. Even from a distance I could tell he was happy and relieved to see them. There was a bunch of greeting and pacing and pointing and sighing. With every second that passed, Mamá's gestures got more dramatic. Eventually, though, she clenched her jaw and nodded. They all did, before disappearing into the supposed chicken coop.

I was torn.

Everything outside the car disgusted me. My skin, my scalp, even the flesh beneath my fingernails itched. But I wanted so badly to see what was going on. I inhaled as deeply as I could and opened the door.

FIVE

It was unusually dark inside the chicken coop.

But then golden laser beams sliced through the bamboo wall slats; the sunlight made it brighter. Mamá, Zeus, and Basketball Shorts Man were completely still—so still, dust particles and feathers swirled in the air around them.

I tried not to breathe. I tried not to touch anything as I tiptoed forward. Mamá was up ahead. I reached for her hand. She flinched. As soon as she realized who it was, though, she held on tight.

There were no sounds at first. It was weird. Then Mamá heaved, and Zeus shuffled his feet, and Basketball Shorts Man cleared his throat.

Bock. Bock. Bock. BOCK! BOCK! BOCK!

I blinked. That's when I saw them—a wall of chickens. No, more like a fortress of chickens huddled in the corner.

They puffed their feathers and flapped their wings and stomped around and around.

BOCK! BOCK! BOCK!

The clucking got even louder, as if they were warning us to stay away.

Basketball Shorts Man pointed at the irate birds. "The girl . . . She want stay with the chickens . . . Her lolo, um . . . her grandfather dic, already two days, ma'am. She not eat. She sleep and cry . . . only sleep and cry," he stammered in broken English.

The girl?

I stood on my tiptoes so I could see past the feathered fortress. There she was, against a wall—a tangle of black hair tucked in between a pair of skinny, mosquito-bitten legs. She could have been anywhere from four to six years old.

My skin itched. Even the insides of my nose itched. I wanted to scratch myself all over, but I didn't want to let go of Mamá's hand.

"What's her name?" she finally asked.

Basketball Shorts Man shrugged. "Hindi ko alam . . . Sorry, ma'am. I do not know. The people sa baryo—in the village . . . they not talk so much. They afraid, ma'am. The girl, her lolo was NPA, the New People's Army—communist guerrillas."

"They must have told you *something*," Mamá said, raising her voice.

BOCK! BOCK! BOCK!

The chickens crowded around the girl, closer and closer—so close I could no longer see her. But I could hear her whimpering.

The dust. The feathers. The whimpering. The *BOCK, BOCK, BOCK*ing wouldn't stop. I couldn't breathe all of a sudden. I pulled Mamá's hand, but she yanked it away. She glared at Basketball Shorts Man as if she were an angry bull about to charge.

"Well? Do you know something or not?"

Basketball Shorts Man pulled out a handkerchief from his pocket and wiped his sweaty forehead. "Ma'am, they talk, konti lang. Small talk. The girl not go to school, not go to town so much, because her face . . . She stay home, sa bahay. She help with work. Take care of chicken, sell egg, look after her lolo."

Mamá frowned. She smoothed the stray hairs from her temples and pulled her shoulders back. Her hand, she squeezed it, as if to grip one of her calming crystals. I knew she was about to do something.

My itchiness suddenly went away. Only prickles remained—prickles of excitement. I watched her approach the girl.

Squish. Squish. Squish.

The sound of Mamá's boots spooked the chickens; they scattered in different directions.

BOCK! BOCK! BOCK!

And then it got quiet. Only gecko feet pitter-pattered on the walls and the roof above us. The girl seemed even smaller without the fortress of chickens around her. Even though she was huddled into a ball, I could make out a pair of pink shorts with faded stripes, an inside-out T-shirt, and flip-flops a couple of sizes too big.

Mamá kneeled on the floor. "Shh . . . ," she whispered. "It's all right. I'm not going to hurt you."

The girl twitched. Clumps of her black hair moved, revealing one eye and a cheek streaked with tears. Mamá moved toward her. The girl's body tensed.

"Shh . . . ," Mamá whispered again, and then she reached her arms out.

The girl stopped whimpering. She wiped the tears from her eyes.

Her face. I could see it. All of it.

I sucked my breath and looked away. But the image was still there. I couldn't stop seeing it—the crack from her lip to her nostril, like a crack in a rock, or a cracked vase with a missing piece. Her teeth and gums were partially exposed, and there was a dark hole that seemed to go deep into her head.

"It's all right. You're going to be all right."

I peeked. The girl flinched. Yet despite her stiffness, she was able to sort of, kind of lean into the space near Mamá's shoulder.

The crack was gone. Not really gone, but gone so I couldn't see it anymore.

Phew.

Mamá hovered by the girl for a long time. As if she was trying to reassure her, make her feel safe. Eventually, though, she turned and glared at Basketball Shorts Man. "But where is her mother? Her father? All her other relatives?" she asked with a croaky voice.

Basketball Shorts Man shook his head. "The record, sa munisipyo. It say her nanay, her mother, die of dengue, already two years. We not find other relatives, ma'am," he said.

"And the government? Social Services? Aren't there orphanages for children like her?"

He exhaled. "Opo, ma'am. But the owner of the land, Sir Luis, he not want the government, the pulis. He want private. No questions . . . That why you here, ma'am."

I glanced at Mamá. There were tears dropping down her cheeks, perfectly round, glistening tears that reminded me of her favorite moonstone earrings. "How about doctors? Has she seen a doctor yet?"

"No, ma'am. I not think so."

"I guess we'll start there, then . . . the hospital. After that, I'll have to figure the rest out," Mamá said softly.

I stood there not knowing what to do. Not knowing if I should move, or say anything, or say nothing at all.

But one thing was for certain—I *believed* her.

I believed Mamá was going to figure it out.

And I wasn't quite sure how I felt about it.

SIX

On the way to the hospital, I sat in the front seat. I *had* to.

The girl smelled like barnyard—like chicken feed, manure, straw, dirt, and whatever else that made barnyards stink. But Mamá didn't seem to mind. She held her on her lap the entire time, whispering, "Pobrecita, chiquita."

Poor little girl.

She certainly was a little girl. Skinny too. Not lanky skinny, but the kind of skinny that made someone look frail and unhealthy. To be honest, I was kind of relieved she was behind me. I didn't want to stare. I didn't want her to notice me trying *not* to stare either.

That crack on her lip wasn't like anything I'd ever seen before. Normally, I couldn't stop myself from tracing shapes and patterns, following lines, analyzing cracks to see if they could somehow be fixed.

But this was different.

There was nothing I could do. No amount of superglue or grout or putty could fix what was wrong with her.

When we finally got to the Southern Luzon Medical Center, I stood at the entrance. Petrified. The itchiness was back. Not only that, but my throat was throbbing. It felt like hundreds of invisible insects were crawling all over me. Hospitals were the *worst*. They were illusions of cleanliness. All that sterilization was to fool people into thinking there weren't any germs. But there were. How could there not be, with so many sick people inside?

Mamá carried the girl so close, so tight, it appeared as if she had a giant tumor growing out of her. She paused and looked at me with tired eyes. "It's almost dinnertime. You must be hungry, mi amor. Why don't you and Zeus get something to eat at the hospital food court?"

"A food court *in* the hospital?" I croaked.

"Yes. It's just through the doors, next to the reception area," said Mamá, gesturing at the sign by the entrance with her chin.

I glanced through the floor-to-ceiling windows. My vision blurred, but still, I could see a green Starbucks sign. Frappuccinos. Germs. They didn't belong together. Not one bit. I froze. My insides convulsed. My ears got hot. My tongue felt like it had swelled out of my mouth. I was sweating *everywhere*.

Mamá had no idea.

But it wasn't her fault.

It was mine. I hadn't told her yet about the dirt and germs and viruses. About how they made me want to stay in my room and hide. Most of the time.

But the right moment had never come. She was always *so* busy, *so* tired, *so* stressed out.

"Um . . . I'd like to walk, actually. My legs are kind of stiff from the long car ride. Maybe there's something nearby," I mumbled.

"There is a Pizza Hut around the corner," said Zeus.

Mamá leaned to one side, adjusting the half-asleep girl on her hip. "Perfect. I'll see you later, then."

I nodded and watched her and the girl disappear through the revolving doors.

We were at the Pizza Hut and I *still* couldn't get over it.

Food courts in *hospitals*.

"But why wouldn't a hospital have a food court? Filipinos love to eat!" said Zeus.

I sat there in shock, as if Zeus has just told me the world was about to end. Food courts had zero business being anywhere near hospitals, but apparently in the Philippines, hospitals might as well be malls.

Geez.

I spotted a glass jar of red pepper flakes.

One, two, three, four, five...

Zeus started tapping the table with his long pinkie nail.

Don't say anything. Shut your trap, Pablo, I told myself.

The last thing I wanted was for him to think I was weirder than I already was.

Laughter—I heard laughter nearby. I squirmed and looked around. A group of teenage girls, two tables away, was staring at me with their hands covering their mouths.

Was it my pointy nose?

My big feet?

My unusually large earlobes?

Mamá said it was because I was a guapito—a handsome kid. But I wasn't so sure that was it. In fact, I was quite certain that wasn't it.

"Your mother is an amazing lady, Sir Pablo," said Zeus out of the blue.

"Thanks."

There was an awkward silence. I think he was waiting for me to say something else. Something meaningful. But all I wanted was to eat and go home.

"Yeah. My mom . . . she's like the Wonder Woman of animal rescuers," I said. "She just *loves* saving the day."

Zeus nodded in agreement. "She *is* a superhero. You are a very, very lucky boy . . . to have a mother like her."

I stared at the table, not wanting him to see the disappointment in my eyes. Because the truth was, I didn't really feel all that lucky. Sometimes I wished I was an injured bird or a deer with a broken leg. Then, maybe, Mamá would come and save me too.

"You do not need to worry." Zeus leaned over, so close I could see his nose hairs. "I think the girl will be okay. Her life has been *very* hard. But with you and your mother helping her, for sure she will be better soon."

I coughed. "Um. Uh. I hope so." The words stumbled out of my mouth. Zeus smiled. I guess my vague reply fooled him.

Then the pizza arrived. Thank god. No more talking. Just eating.

"Sarap. Looks delicious," said Zeus as he grabbed a slice.

I stared at the cheese pizza. I mean, how could they have possibly screwed up the simplest item on the menu? The crust was stained with tomato sauce and it was baked in such a way that only half the slices browned. Not only that, but the six slices weren't evenly cut at all. It was pretty much the saddest pizza I'd ever seen.

Sad. Wrong. Pathetic.

The girls laughed again.

But I kept on staring at the monstrosity.

"Sir Pablo?"

That pizza was like a mirror. I was staring at myself.

Sad. Wrong. Pathetic.

SEVEN

After our so-called dinner at Pizza Hut, we swung by the hospital to fetch Mamá. Apparently, the girl was extremely dehydrated, so she would have to be confined for a day or two.

Phew.

I was relieved.

On our way home, I passed out. I must have been exhausted because I couldn't even remember how I got into my bedroom, much less how I got into my bed fully clothed.

I bolted awake in a sweaty panic. My pajamas. Where were my pajamas? It was Thursday—spaceships and aliens' day. I shuffled toward my dresser. But then I noticed a faint light streaming in through the bottom of the door. There was a sound. Something clinked from the kitchen.

Mamá was still up.

I couldn't sleep. Not anymore. I tiptoed down the hall. But it took a while because I had to stop and count the shadows—the zebra-striped ones—zigzagging across the walls. There were 108 striped shadows. Each set of window blinds cast thirty-six lines. It was actually kind of mesmerizing.

In the kitchen, Mamá was stirring her tea in a trance. I could tell from the aroma that she was drinking the Ajiri black tea she'd hoarded in Kenya. It seemed like eons ago that we'd lived there. But it wasn't. I was eleven, same as I was now. In just one year we'd moved from Kenya to Indonesia to the Philippines.

"You're awake." She patted the seat next to hers. "Come. I'll make you some warm milk and honey."

I sat and watched her heat the milk on the stove the old-fashioned way. We didn't own a microwave. Mamá said they were useless pieces of junk. I was glad about it anyhow. The last thing I wanted was food nuked with radiation in a plastic box teeming with germs.

Once the milk was steaming, she poured it into my favorite cup, the one with a smiling moon and sixteen stars. Then stirred in a few teaspoons of Manuka honey. She sat back down and handed it to me.

"I couldn't sleep. I just can't stop thinking about the girl . . . How hard it must have been for her when her mother died, when her grandfather died. Being alone with no friends. All she had were those chickens . . . Poor Chiqui," she said, shaking her head.

"Chiqui?"

"I'm sorry. I forgot to mention it. The hospital needed a patient name, and since she still won't speak, I made one up. Chiquita . . . Chiqui. It's the only thing I could think of."

Small. Tiny. Little girl.

"Oh," I replied.

Mamá sipped her tea, fiddling with the teaspoon on her saucer. "Like I told you earlier, she's going to have to stay in the hospital for a couple of days. But then—"

"But then what?" I said, sitting up straighter.

Clink. Clink. Clink.

She kept fiddling with the teaspoon.

I knew she was thinking. She had this look on her face—the same one she had every time she was hatching a plan.

"We were supposed to talk about it tomorrow. Since you're awake, though . . . we might as well discuss it now."

"Discuss what?"

The teaspoon finally stopped clinking. Mamá gazed at me. I gazed at her. It felt like I was staring at two giant green peas. "Chiqui is going to have to be in and out of the hospital. She has what's called a complete unilateral cleft lip.

The doctors want to do the first corrective surgery as soon as possible. But she's got some malnutrition-related deficiencies. They want her to go to a home first . . . to get stronger. They feel she'll heal faster, mentally and physically, if she's with a family."

"A family? Like a foster family?" I asked.

For some reason, our neighbor Ate Lucinda and her four kids popped into my head.

A family.

Mamá nodded. "Yes. Exactly. I thought, well, maybe she could stay here . . . just until we figure out a more permanent solution."

"You want *her* to stay here . . . with *us*?" I gasped.

It was as if the air in the room were being suctioned out by a vacuum cleaner. It was hard to breathe. My skin tingled and the tips of my fingers and toes were numb.

Mamá smiled and caressed my hand with hers. "Miguel has offered to sponsor all of Chiqui's medical needs. He thought it would be for the best if we could keep an eye on her. It's not as if it's forever. It'll be like that time we had Milo in the house with us."

I coughed.

Milo—the orphaned sun bear Mamá rescued in Indonesia. I couldn't believe she was making the comparison.

"Milo was a bear," I said flat out.

"I *know* that."

"But she's a girl. A child. Not a bear," I said.

Mamá's smile was gone. "Of course. Don't you think I know the difference? Don't you think I've tried to think of another way?" She stood and placed her teacup in the sink. "It's all set . . . I'm sorry, Pablo."

I'm sorry. I'm sorry. I'm sorry.

Over the years, I'd lost track of all her *I'm sorry*s.

And even though I'd come to expect them, every single time she uttered another *I'm sorry*, it felt like she was punching me in the gut all over again.

I couldn't breathe. I couldn't speak. The room was spinning slowly.

Talk to her, Pablo!

I wanted to. I really wanted to.

But it just wasn't the right time. The right moment.

Not yet.

"Good night, Pablo. Try to get some sleep." Mamá disappeared through the doorway.

I closed my eyes so the spinning would stop. In my mind I pictured the creamy-colored tiles beneath my feet. I knew exactly how many there were—ninety-six tiles, six of them cracked.

But it wasn't those cracks I was worried about.

Chiqui.

Mamá.

Me.

The tiles.

I arranged them row by row, one by one until it was still again.

EIGHT

By the time I dragged myself out of bed the next morning, Mamá was already gone. In the kitchen I found a foil-wrapped plate with a note on it.

> Pablo, I left early so I could visit Chiqui at the hospital. Grace will be here at her usual time.
> If you need anything, just call. Love, Mamá.

Chiqui. I almost forgot.

I slumped into a chair. My stomach growled. Breakfast. I needed food. Underneath the foil I found a big piece of tortilla de patata and a slice of crusty bread with a smear of tomato and olive oil. It was my favorite. I could eat potato-and-onion omelet all day, every day.

The utensils were arranged and there was a napkin folded just right. Mamá was doing her best. But it didn't even matter. I was so hungry, I didn't care. The food got into my mouth somehow. Fork. Knife. Hands. Everything was soiled, smeared, crumbs everywhere by the time I was done. I never felt more satisfied, more disgusted. I cleaned up the mess and washed my hands three times just to be sure. I needed to get out of the kitchen. I needed fresh air.

I stumbled outside and sat on the front steps. It was already too hot and too humid. All the houses looked as if they were huddled together under the shade of the massive narra trees. Even the birds didn't seem to be singing. The only thing I could hear was music—a cheesy-sounding Filipino ballad, coming from somewhere across the street.

"Taho! Taho!" It was the Taho guy. Every day he would walk down our street carrying a stick with two metal buckets across his shoulders. Ms. Grace always got super excited, dashing out with an empty coffee mug and then coming back with what resembled a steaming cup of tofu snot and jelly boogers in brown sugar syrup. Gross. I had no idea why she would drink something so revolting.

Ms. Grace. Where *was* Ms. Grace anyway? How could she be late for our last lesson before summer break?

Sweep. Sweep. Sweep.

Across the road, Happy was sweeping leaves off the sidewalk. She was the second-oldest of Ate Lucinda's kids, maybe twelve or thirteen years old. It was hard to tell, though, because she was so petite.

Sweep. Sweep.

Inhale. Exhale.

It was like my breathing and her sweeping were in sync.

Sweep. Breathe. *Sweep.* Breathe.

She looked up and smiled at me. My breath halted. I coughed and looked away. But I could still feel her eyes on me.

Ms. Grace was late. I wished she would hurry already.

"Hi."

I couldn't ignore her. Happy was in front of me, holding the broom. It was like a witch's broom without a handle. She must have noticed I was ogling it because she held it up. "It's a walis tingting. A broom for sweeping outside," she explained.

"But why? I mean, why wouldn't it have a handle? Wouldn't it make it easier *and* more hygienic?" I asked.

Happy shrugged. Her blue-black hair slid past her shoulders. "I don't know. It's just the way it is."

"Huh." I felt stupid all of a sudden, caring about the broom and its lack of a handle.

"So . . . I heard about the girl," said Happy, stepping closer.

My cheeks sizzled. I looked at my pajama legs, at the spaceships and Martians and planets.

Oh god. I'm still in my pajamas. Will she laugh if I run back into the house?

Probably.

I coughed. "Um. The girl? You mean Chiqui?"

"Yes, Chiqui. Your mom asked my mom if she could borrow some of Bing's clothes . . . They must be around the same size?" said Happy, stepping even closer.

"I guess. Sort of. I'm not really sure."

Happy plopped down next to me. It felt weird having her there. I wasn't used to such closeness. Especially from someone I barely knew. The broom rested between her feet. I began counting its twigs to distract myself.

One. Two. Three . . .

"Is it true?" she asked, leaning toward me with big eyes.

I frowned. "Is what true?"

"That she doesn't speak, and that she had chickens for friends . . . and . . . and . . . uh, that there's something wrong, something wrong with her face." Happy scrunched her nose. "I'm sorry. I don't mean to be so chismosa, I mean gossipy. It's just nothing interesting ever happens around here. Well, not until you and your mom moved in," she added with a grin.

I laughed nervously and then focused on the broom again. "No, it's okay. I get it." She scooched over until her hair grazed my shoulder. "It's not *that* bad. Her face . . . Anyways, you'll see for yourself soon enough. Chiqui's coming to live here . . . for a while."

"Here? In your house? With you?"

I finally looked at her. Really, really looked at her—from her slightly raised eyebrows to her button nose, down to her glossy pink lips. This intense feeling rushed through my brain to my stomach, hurling my thoughts, my feelings out. I wanted to talk. Have a real conversation for once.

"Yeah. She—"

There was a loud screeching sound. Ms. Grace pulled up on her motorbike.

"Well, I better get back to my sweeping. The leaves, you know, they just keep on falling." Happy picked up her broom and waved. "See you later, Pablo."

I waved back and watched her cross the road.

It was true. The leaves fell no matter what.

I stood and turned around so I wouldn't have to count all those leaves she was sweeping.

NINE

I twiddled my thumbs while Ms. Grace checked my math worksheet. There was a red pen poised in her hand. She wouldn't need it, though. There would be no mistakes. Math was my thing. It was logical. Unlike life. Life made no sense—at least 99.9 percent of the time.

"Well, you did it again, Pablo. Good job," she said, writing a one hundred and a big smiley face at the top of the paper with her other pen. It was purple and smelled like grape-flavored chewing gum, or grape soda, or medicine that was supposed to taste like grapes.

"Thanks."

Ms. Grace shuffled through my textbooks. I couldn't help tracing the line her bob haircut made on her jaw—so straight, so precise, I wondered if the barber used a ruler. "So, shall we move on to science? We can review the phases of the moon," she said, opening the book to a two-page illustration.

I fiddled with the pencil in my hand and glanced at the various moon stages. Ms. Grace smiled encouragingly. Of all the homeschool teachers I've had—nine in total—she was definitely the most patient and the most cheerful. When she smiled, her entire face smiled along.

"Uh. Actually, I was wondering about something," I mumbled.

"Sure. Anything," said Ms. Grace.

"Chickens. You know, like the kinds that lay eggs."

It sounded stupid after I'd said it, but in my mind it had seemed like a good way to start the conversation.

"Chickens? Ah. Yes, of course. I grew up in the province, the countryside. We had lots of chickens," she said, tilting her head. "What would you like to know?"

"Well, I was kind of curious if chickens talked . . . I mean, I know they cluck and all, and roosters do that cock-a-doodle-doo thing. But do they actually have conversations? Do they understand one another? Do they understand people?"

Ms. Grace giggled softly. Not the kind of giggle that was meant to poke fun. But the kind that was bubbly and bouncy, as if she thought what I'd said was the cutest thing ever. "Why not? It would be rather ignorant of us to assume humans were the only ones who could communicate, don't you think?"

"I suppose."

She knew I wasn't convinced. But Ms. Grace wasn't one to give up on a tough subject. She stared off into the air. A few seconds went by, and then she clapped her hands. I could practically see the lightbulb illuminating over her head. "Like I said, we had a lot of chickens, right?" I nodded. "Well, not only did they speak to one another, but there were times when I *swore* they were speaking to us. We had this one fat hen named Barbie, short for Barbecue. I know, I know . . . Anyways, Barbie was our most reliable layer. She would lay one egg daily. Without fail. And every day after she'd lay that egg, she would strut over to our kitchen and cluck, and keep on clucking until finally my mother would have no choice but to follow her into the henhouse and thank her for that egg . . . So you see, chickens most definitely have personalities *and* they most definitely talk."

"Huh." I tried to picture Chiqui having a conversation with a happy clucking hen. But I just couldn't picture it. I looked at Ms. Grace. There was this momentary shadow on her face as if a passing gray cloud had darkened her cheer.

Busted.

It was obvious she knew *exactly* why I was asking about the chickens.

She breathed deep and exhaled. "Chiqui has had a rough life, Pablo. She didn't have a lot of the same opportunities other kids have. She didn't go to school. She didn't have her family there all the time. She didn't have any friends either. I mean, not that we know of. There's just so much that we don't know about her . . . It's going to be challenging. You're going to have to be patient and understanding . . . But I know you can do it, Pablo. I have faith in you."

I fiddled with the pages of my textbook, and then I met her gaze. "I'll try my best."

Her eyes brightened. "Great. Is there anything else you want to talk about?"

"Um. Just one more thing." I gazed down at the table. "Chiqui's face . . . Mamá told me about the cleft lip and how she's going to need a bunch of surgeries to get it fixed . . . But how come it's like that? Did something happen to her?"

Ms. Grace sat up straight, like she always did before a lecture. "Ah, well, I'm glad you asked, Pablo. The explanation is related to science *and* economics. You see, in countries like the Philippines, many women cannot afford doctors, nutritious food, or prenatal vitamins. Because of that, birth defects of the heart, spine, limbs, and face aren't all that uncommon. What Chiqui has is a type of birth defect. She's been that way her entire life. But there's nothing to worry about. Right now, she might look a bit different, but after her surgeries, her smile is going to be as bright and wide as any other little girl's."

"So is that why she can't talk? Because of her cleft lip?"

"Hmm..." Ms. Grace scrunched her mouth to the side. "Well, I'm not really sure. There could be several reasons why she's not speaking. Maybe she's still traumatized. Maybe she has a speech impediment. Maybe she can't understand English... In fact, I'm quite sure she doesn't. It's pretty common for Filipinos from rural areas not to know much English."

I nodded.

It was *a lot* to absorb.

But I smiled—smiled like it was all good.

I hoped Ms. Grace wouldn't see through my pretense, because in reality, it wasn't Chiqui that worried me. I was worried for myself.

I wasn't really ready for the challenge.

I didn't want to try my best.

I wasn't sure I wanted Chiqui in our house, in our lives. I wasn't sure I wanted her anywhere near me.

TEN

I could still remember when there were three of us—Mamá, my father, and me. Then my father left when I was seven. Mamá said he *needed* his freedom. That he *needed* to chase the ocean. But I knew the truth. It came out one night after she had one too many sangrias. I could hear her in the other room, whining, shrieking, and screaming at her friend Maria. *"Well, he can run away with that woman if he wants! I'm better off without him. She can take him. She can take all of him!"*

After that, it was only the two of us.

Now all of a sudden, there would be three of us once again.

It was my twelfth birthday and, ready or not, Chiqui was coming home.

Mamá stood in the middle of her bedroom looking somewhat lost. Cleaning and organizing were definitely not her strengths. Give her some hiking boots, a machete, and a compass and she could take you on a tour of the Amazon jungle. But give her a broom, a mop, and a bucket and she wouldn't know where to start. She swatted a cobweb away from her face and spotted me. "Pablo. There you are."

I fidgeted in the doorway. For a moment we stared at each other without speaking. Then it hit her. Mamá covered her mouth with her hand and turned bright pink. "Happy birthday, mi amor! Look at you, almost a teenager! How did this happen?" she said, shaking her head like she couldn't believe it.

I exhaled. She hadn't forgotten after all. "Thanks, Mamá."

"Un abrazo! Come here and give me a hug," she said.

I rushed over and allowed her to embrace me like a human pretzel even though her T-shirt smelled of dust and her skin was moist with sweat. It felt good to forget. To let go of the things that bothered me. But there was only so much I could take. As soon as Mamá's unwashed hair grazed my cheek, I pulled away. I breathed. Relieved. And she sighed, throwing her arms into the air at the sight of the mess she'd created. "Madre mía! I've been trying to make space in here for Chiqui's cot, but I just can't make the two beds fit. I've rearranged everything a million times. Still, it's hopeless."

The room *was* a disaster. But to me it looked more like a two-thousand-piece puzzle scattered on the floor. If I moved everything around, if I searched for the blank spaces, studied the shapes, then I could make it all fit.

"I can do it," I said.

Her body relaxed. "Really? Are you sure?"

"Yes. It's fine."

"Okay. I'll go make breakfast, then. What does the birthday boy want?" she asked with a grin.

I thought about it. With everything so chaotic, so uncertain, so unpredictable, I needed order. I craved something comforting, something perfectly round.

"Pancakes. A stack of three, please."

"All right. Pancakes it is," she said, disappearing down the hallway.

As soon as she was gone, I began moving aside the smaller objects—chairs, side tables, lamps, potted plants, stacks of books, sculptures, and way too many knick-knacks. Mamá was a collector—my polite term for hoarder. Everywhere we went, she just had to bring home some sort of remembrance. I didn't see the point in it. Anything that really mattered was stored away in your brain anyway. Stuff just collected dust, and half the time, maybe even most of the time, nobody bothered looking at it.

When the room was mostly clear, I was left with two beds and a desk. Mamá's bed was full-size, the wrought iron kind, and the smaller one, the one Chiqui was supposed to sleep in, was more like a foldaway cot for guests. I guess it would do. She *was* small and she *was* a guest after all.

It was temporary.

I dragged Mamá's bed from one side of the room to the other, which wasn't much work since the space wasn't too big anyway. Then I placed the desk right next to it, so it could also double as a side table. The rug went in the middle, and then I tucked a chair in the corner with a lamp beside it for reading. The only spot left for the cot was on the opposite wall. It was ideal. Mamá could keep an eye on Chiqui, and there was a window—a sunny window overlooking the street.

I paused mid-motion and thought about Chiqui in that chicken coop. About what a lonely place it must have been after her grandfather died. She was all alone. In the dark. No windows. Not even a single lightbulb.

"Pancakes are ready!" Mamá shouted from the kitchen.

I bent down and took hold of the cot, pushing it toward the window. Pushing until the shadows started to fade. Pushing until every inch of it was bathed in sunlight.

ELEVEN

There was a slice of park by the hospital. It wasn't much of a park. More of a block of concrete and stone, with holes for trees and planters filled with manicured bushes. I sat on a bench trying not to touch anything with my bare hands. Surely there were loads of residual germs, not to mention the bird poop—lots of it.

"So. Twelve, huh?" said Miguel, who lounged beside me as if he were at a pool with a piña colada in his hand. "That sucks. But you'll get through it," he added with a smirk.

I glared at him. "Thanks for the pep talk."

He laughed so hard I could see his pearly-white teeth and tonsils. Miguel was Mamá's boss, but really he was more like her sarcastic little brother. She'd once told me he was a black sheep. He came from a rich Filipino family who'd made their fortune in mining and palm oil plantations. Basically destroying nature for profit. So at twenty-one, when he got his trust fund, he left the family business and decided saving wild animals was his calling.

"But seriously, Pablo. Being a little man is tough. If you ever need anything, if there's a problem your mom can't help you with . . . I'm here. Anytime. Okay?" he said, lifting his sunglasses.

"Okay."

I diverted my gaze, tracing the square tiles with my eyes in an effort to numb what I was feeling. What Miguel said, the way he'd said it, reminded me of how much I missed having a father around. I loved Mamá. But sometimes I just needed someone else.

"So, this whole thing with Chiqui. You okay with it?" Miguel suddenly asked.

I squirmed. "Yeah. Sure. It's fine."

The spaces between us felt kind of awkward.

"Look. There they are," he said, pointing toward the entrance of the hospital.

I followed his finger, breathing as calmly as I could. Zeus appeared first, carrying a small duffel bag, a pillow, and a blanket. Mamá wasn't far behind. Chiqui's legs were wrapped around her like a squirrel clinging to a tree. Even from a distance I could see how scared she still was. How she hid her face and cowered with every sound, every movement.

My breaths weren't so calm anymore. Even Miguel, whose tan never seemed to fade, was three shades paler. He gripped my shoulder and whispered, "C'mon, Pablo. Let's put up a brave front."

He stood, and I stood too. They were right there. Chiqui's back was to me, but there was a hint of an eyeball peeking through her thick hair.

"Well, that was exhausting. I've never had to do so much paperwork in my life," said Mamá.

Zeus gestured to the parking garage. "Ma'am, sirs, I will go get the car."

"Yes, it's quite hot. Thank you, Zeus," said Miguel.

Mamá sat on the bench and exhaled. "She's actually heavier than she looks," she said, meeting my gaze. "Pablo, come. Sit."

I stared at the empty space beside her, and then looked at Miguel, wondering if he could save me somehow. But he only smiled.

The bench. Focus on the bench.

I counted its six metal slats and walked over.

Sit. Just sit.

So I did. Chiqui twitched and buried her face deeper into Mamá's shoulder. "*Shh* . . . it's okay, Chiqui. That's your kuya Pablo, and over there, that's Tito Miguel," she said gently.

"Big brother" and "Uncle," that's who we were supposed

to be. I glimpsed at Miguel to see if he was as uncomfortable as I was. But I couldn't really tell. His sunglasses were too dark, and he just stood there as if he were waiting for the bus or something. I cleared my throat and slid two inches closer. Mamá's eyes jumped from me to Chiqui back to me. "Um. Hi, Chiqui . . . Uh. It's nice to meet you," I croaked.

She turned slightly. The eyeball was back, glistening like a glob of Nutella.

At least she didn't smell like a barnyard anymore. *Thank god.* She also looked cleaner. Like they'd given her a bath. Though the faint odor of hospital disinfectant was still there.

Eeww.

Beep. Beep.

Miguel's truck pulled up.

The eye was gone again. I sighed. It was going to be a *long* ride home.

TWELVE

Chiqui slept in the car. The whole ordeal must have been too much for her. When we arrived home, she was still slumped over like a rag doll. Miguel carried her to bed, while Mamá popped open a bottle of Spanish wine.

"Thank god. My arms were starting to go numb," she mumbled to herself.

Glug, glug, glug.

She poured herself a glass, and then she settled on the sofa with a sigh.

I crept away slowly. Really, really slowly. The last thing I wanted was to keep on talking about poor little Chiqui.

Ugh.

Miguel's footsteps echoed down the hallway.

I snuck into my room and closed the door before he could see me.

Breathe, Pablo. Breathe.

He would call. My father *would* call. It was my birthday.

I opened my laptop and stared at the video chat screen, adjusting the volume, checking the Wi-Fi signal, waiting, waiting, and waiting. The silence hummed, taunting me. Twenty, maybe thirty minutes went by and my eyes started to burn. I allowed the screensaver to burst and bounce into a prism of colors. The only thing I could do to pass the time, to stop myself from losing it, was to stare at my bedspread. The plaid pattern turned into roads, highways, trails, and pathways as if I were following a map to nowhere. I wasn't really sure how much time had passed. It could have been several minutes. It could have been hours. But finally my laptop dinged. I fumbled with the keyboard and clicked "Accept."

"Hello?"

My father materialized, shirtless and tanned with the endless blue sky above him. "Hey! Happy birthday, man!"

"Thanks . . . thanks for calling." I could feel the warmth spread from my cheeks to my ears and neck.

"So, you got something exciting planned? Trekking in the jungle with your friends? Camping on the beach with your girlfriend?" he said with a wink.

My entire face was on fire. "Um. Yeah. Something like that . . . I haven't really decided yet."

"Well, you're almost a man. You better enjoy it before

you become an old fart like me." He guffawed. I laughed along, but it sounded like I was trying too hard. "Oh. I almost forgot," he said, pulling something out of his pocket, something triangular and white. "Check it out. It's a shark tooth from a great white. I found it on our dive yesterday. I'm going to send it to you so you can wear it around your neck and show it off to the girls."

I studied the sharp tooth. In the background, my father smiled. He was so rugged, so carefree. I could see why Mamá had fallen for him—why all the other women had fallen for him too.

"Hey, Cal!" someone shouted off camera.

He put the tooth away and stood. "I have to go. We've got Nat Geo with us. They're doing a show on the sharks of South Africa . . . Anyways, you have a good birthday, all right, Pablo? Say hi to your mom for me."

I nodded. My lips parted. My tongue moved as if to speak. But no words came out. My father waved. "Talk to you soon, okay?" And then he was gone.

I was embarrassed. Humiliated. Stunned. There was this bitterness at the back of my throat. *Is that what lies taste like?* If only he knew the truth. What a loser, what a freak I really was. The majority of my time was spent inside the house obsessing over numbers and patterns and shapes and germs and dirt and dust and every little thing that bothered me. There were no jungle treks with friends, no camping on the beach with girls. In fact, there weren't even any friends *or* girls to speak of.

It was a joke. My twelve years of life were a joke.

THIRTEEN

There wasn't supposed to be a party, just dinner at home, cake, and presents. But that was planned days ago.

A lot had changed since then.

Zeus, Ms. Grace, Miguel, Mamá, and Chiqui gathered around me. It had gone from a party of two, to a party of three, to a party of six. *Whoop-de-doo.* Once again, Mamá had managed to convince me. She said we had *so* much more to celebrate now.

As if my birthday wasn't enough.

I sat at the head of the table. Once in a while, I'd glance over at Chiqui. She had on one of Bing's hand-me-downs—a purple T-shirt dress with lime-green polka dots. But as ugly as the dress was, and it *was* pretty ugly, it was her eyes that bothered me. They were too big and too round; for some reason they made me nervous. I looked away. Instead tapping my fingers as I counted the spaghetti remnants in the serving bowl. With the sauce congealed and the herbs dried out, the strings of pasta resembled dead earthworms. I shuddered.

"I'll start clearing the dishes," said Mamá, hurrying into the kitchen. She wasn't fooling anyone, especially me. Every year on my birthday she'd make some flimsy excuse to sneak away and get my cake.

"Sir Pablo," Zeus said, pulling his chair closer to mine. "It is good your mother made spaghetti to celebrate. You know why?"

I shook my head. "No."

He grabbed a fork and twirled the leftover noodles, slurping them so globs of sauce clung to his chin. I leaned back. But what I really wanted to do was drag my chair to the other side of the room. "Because it is good fortune to eat long noodles on your birthday. Long noodles equal long life," he explained.

I wanted to frown. I wanted to raise an eyebrow and say, *Huh? So how exactly are noodles supposed to make you live longer?* But I just smiled, not really wanting to engage in a conversation with a tomato-stained chin. But then Ms. Grace swooped over. "This is a good history lesson, Pablo! Long-life noodles are a tradition that Filipinos adopted from Chinese merchants who traveled to the Philippines as early as the ninth century. Of course, they weren't eating spaghetti back then. But rather thin rice noodles, which evolved to what we know as pancit today," she said in her teacher-y voice.

I knew I was supposed to be fascinated by the historical significance of noodles in the Philippines. But I didn't care. Not one bit. What I cared about was Chiqui inching closer. Though her chin wasn't stained, it slithered at the edge of the table, picking up germs along the way.

Just ignore her.

I stared at my lap and tapped my fingers again.

One. Two. Three. Repeat.

But then something touched me. I jumped. The crack— Chiqui's cleft lip. I saw it up close, for an instant. And then it blurred as she scurried away under the table.

"Happy birthday to you! Happy birthday to you!" Mamá emerged from the kitchen holding a cake with twelve candles. *Ugh.* The singing. I was panicked all of a sudden. Cornered. But they were doing it for me. I couldn't possibly run away and hide.

Miguel slapped my back. "Go on, little man. Blow out your candles."

"And make a wish," said Mamá.

It felt like I was in one of those nightmares where faces were distorted and voices were low and slow. I tried to drown them all out. Instead focusing on Abuelita's orange almond

60

cake, which was pretty much the best cake ever—clean and simple and devoid of any goopy frosting.

Whoosh.

I blew the candles out.

Clap. Clap. Clap.

For a moment I was trapped in a vortex of hugs and kisses and handshakes. "Thanks. Thanks so much," I gasped and then held my breath until everyone backed off.

But then somehow, the candles lit up again. I frowned.

"I think you need to blow a bit harder, Pablo. C'mon, take a deep breath and give it another go," said Miguel with a grin.

Whooooooshhhhhh!

I blew them out. Nobody clapped. They just gawked at me, and held their breath.

The candles lit up again, the flames wiggling as if they were mocking me. I glared at Miguel, and then at Mamá, whose eyes looked as if a bunch of confetti was about to explode out of them.

Whoooooooooooshhhhhhhhhh!

I blew them out. One. More. Time.

The candles lit up. *Again.*

Mamá giggled. "I'm sorry, Pablito. The trick candles were Miguel's idea," she said, elbowing him.

"Blasphemy!" Miguel raised his hands as if to protest.

Zeus and Ms. Grace laughed.

Humph.

I crossed my arms and stared at my stupid cake. Through the burning candles, I spotted Chiqui. She glowed, the flames reflected in her eyes. I caught her gaze and she caught mine. For a second, maybe more like a millisecond, she smiled. It was lopsided. It wasn't very pretty. But it was a smile. It really *was* a smile.

And then it was gone.

Chiqui covered her mouth with her hand and quickly ducked under the table.

FOURTEEN

After my torturous birthday celebration, I retreated to my bedroom. I needed my safe space. I needed my rituals to relax. I showered, washing my hair, then rinsing the shampoo and conditioner residue off my skin with black charcoal soap. Next, I brushed my teeth for exactly three minutes and gargled six times. I washed my hands again just to be sure, and dried them with a fresh hand towel before getting into my pajamas—the ones with airplanes, trains, and automobiles on them.

I laid in bed staring at the ceiling. Staring at nothing at first. But the more I stared, the more I started seeing things. Shadows that moved and shifted like flying birds. Peeling paint the same shape as the sun. A water stain that was eerily fish-like.

Fish. Birds. Sunshine. All those things reminded me of when I was a little kid in California. Mamá was still working at the World Wildlife Fund, and my father was a consultant at the Monterey Bay Aquarium. On my fourth birthday, my father had come home all excited, his eyes shimmering as he pulled a gift from behind his back. I glanced at the package wrapped with sea-creature-themed paper. *"What is it?"* I asked.

My father grinned so wide, his suntanned skin crinkled. *"You'll see! Come. I'll show you,"* he said, leading me to my bedroom. He placed the gift on my bed. *"Go ahead, Pablo. Open it up."*

I began unwrapping the package carefully.

Don't rip the paper, Pablo, I said to myself.

My fingers slid in between the seams, searching for the pieces of tape.

Don't rip the paper. Don't rip the paper. Don't rip . . .

"C'mon, Pablo. Just rip the paper already." My father reached out, tearing off the paper in one go.

I flinched. My vision hazed.

"Isn't it cool? I wish I'd had one of these when I was a kid," said my father. He opened the box, fumbling with plastic and paper and batteries and switches. I had no idea what the gift was, much less what he was doing with it. *"Okay. You ready?"* he said with his hand on the light switch.

I nodded. I didn't really know why I nodded.

My room went dark.

"*Ta-da!*" My father's voice sounded like a hokey magician's.

All of a sudden, there were fish and dolphins and sharks swimming on the walls and ceiling. The lights changed colors every so often.

Blue fish.

Green dolphins.

Red sharks.

My heart was beating too fast. I was scared. I wasn't sure why. But I was scared.

"*Well? Isn't it awesome?*"

I wanted so badly to say, *Thanks, Dad! It* is *awesome. Best gift ever!*

But I couldn't. My tongue was stuck to the roof of my mouth.

Click. He turned the machine off—the fish and dolphins and sharks were gone.

It was bright again. My father stood there, squinting at me, squinting at the tears in my eyes. He looked so disappointed. No words were spoken. All he did was stuff my gift back into its box, leaving only the shreds of paper behind.

I blinked.

My father vanished.

My bedroom vanished.

My four-year-old self vanished.

I was staring at the water stain on my ceiling. It was just a water stain. A stupid water stain. I looked away and stared at the airplane on my cuff instead, stared and stared and stared until my eyelids drooped.

Creak.

What was that noise?

I opened my eyes.

Creak.

My bed groaned.

Creak.

It groaned again. But I hadn't moved at all. I bolted from my pillow, eyes adjusting to the darkness. There was something—no, some*one*—there. Maybe I was dreaming. It looked like Chiqui . . . It *was* Chiqui. She was crouched at the foot of my bed watching me.

I screamed.

FIFTEEN

After I screamed, Mamá burst through the door holding a kitchen knife.

She looked panicked.

Chiqui looked panicked.

I *was* panicked.

"Que pasó? What's going on?" she managed to say in between breaths.

I pointed toward Chiqui but she was already gone; her tiny footsteps were echoing down the hallway. "She—she was watching me. From over there."

Mamá put the knife down and exhaled. "I'm sorry you've had a fright, Pablo . . . I'm sure Chiqui was just curious, that's all. Now try and go back to sleep. I'm going to go find her and make sure she's okay." She blew me a kiss and closed the door.

Make sure *she's* okay?

Really?

Ugh.

After that, I most definitely couldn't go back to sleep. My room was contaminated.

Germs.

I couldn't see them but I knew they were there.

I pulled off the bedspread and put it in the hamper. And then I wiped the wooden footboard and the doorknob on both sides with 70 percent alcohol. The finishing touch was a couple of spritzes of lavender-scented Febreze. I inspected everything one last time to make sure it was all spick-and-span.

"Chiqui! Don't hide... Please," said Mamá from somewhere outside my room.

I could hear more footsteps and scurrying. I quickly locked my door. There was no way she was getting back in. Not that night. Not ever.

Finally, it was safe again. I huddled in bed trying to forget about what had happened. But it was impossible. Chiqui's eyes kept on watching me. As if she were still there. Through the shadows, the crack on her lip twitched and quivered like she wanted to say something.

Yet all I could hear was silence.

Bang.

Plonk.

Wumpth.

It was morning. I was on the sofa trying to read a book. Trying but failing. Chiqui was turning the house upside down with her stomping and jumping and grabbing and dropping and door slamming. Stuff was toppling all over the house.

Crash.

"Oh, Chiqui . . ." Mamá sighed from the kitchen. "That *was* Abuelita's cazuela."

I doubted Chiqui understood the significance of an heirloom earthenware serving dish.

Zoom.

Chiqui ran into the living room. She snatched the throw pillow by my feet and threw it up into the air.

Thud.

It landed on the carpet. She picked it up as if to throw it again, but stopped when she saw a frazzled-looking Mamá by the doorway. Her hair was a mess, her upper lip sweaty, her shirt buttoned in the wrong holes. "*Chiqui . . .*" Her voice was a few octaves lower than normal. "Those are throw pillows, but they aren't for throwing. Okay?"

At first Chiqui didn't react.

Maybe it was because she hadn't understood a word of what Mamá had said.

"PIL-LOW. NO throwing. Huwag...No. No. No,"
Mamá said more slowly.

I was actually impressed that Mamá had managed to
squeeze in some Tagalog in between all the noes. But it
didn't seem to make much of a difference, really.

I closed my book, sat up, and held my breath.

Was Chiqui going to cry?

Throw a fit?

Crumple on the floor and pound her fists on the carpet?

Instead, though, she grabbed the pillow and hurled it
into the air. Again. It hit Mamá on the hip, before landing
with another *thud*.

I looked at Chiqui. I looked at Mamá. It was tense and
quiet, like in those old Western movies, when the two gun-
men were about to have a standoff.

"Umm..." I stood and tiptoed around them. "I think I'll
go outside for some fresh air," I mumbled.

Neither of them seemed to hear me.

Phew.

I was out on the stoop. It felt safer.

Chiqui.

Ugh.

The last thing I wanted was to be in the middle of *that*
disaster zone.

I hopped down the stone steps. It was early morning, but

it was already too hot and too humid. Everything seemed to steam and sizzle. The only shade within a twenty-foot radius was under the big narra tree where Mamá had placed a rusty white garden set. I stared at the patches of rust, which looked like some sort of flesh-eating bacteria.

"Are you going to sit or just stand there?"

Happy appeared in all her Hello Kitty glory—gray leggings with thousands of miniature Hello Kitties, an aqua colored T-shirt with a winking Hello Kitty, and flip-flops with a Hello Kitty in between her big toe and the one next to it.

"Um. I don't know. Do you think it's safe?" I replied.

Happy plopped down on the rustiest chair. "Safe from what?"

"Safe. You know, like from germs and stuff."

There was a slight crease on her forehead. "It's a chair, Pablo. I think it's safe to sit on it."

I sat. I guess she had a point.

Happy smiled a dimply smile. She placed a closed hand on the table. "I heard it was your birthday. Catch," she said, tossing something toward me.

I reached out clumsily and caught it. The object was a small cube, sort of like origami but made out of leaves. I'd never seen anything like it. "What is it?" I asked.

"It's something we play with. A toy made out of palm leaves." Happy got up and plucked the cube from my hand.

Then she slipped her flip-flops off. "Like this." She lifted her foot to the side and bounce-kicked the cube as if it were a mini soccer ball.

To be honest, the sight of her dirty, bare feet grossed me out. Like *really* grossed me out. But I didn't want to hurt her feelings. So I faked a smile and said, "Oh. Wow."

Happy plopped the cube on the table and glanced at the house. "Chiqui—"

"Yeah, Chiqui's inside. That's why I'm out here," I replied with a sigh.

"No. I mean she's over there," she said, pointing at the window nearest to us.

I turned around. Happy was right. Chiqui was staring at us with her nose smooshed on the glass. She looked ridiculous. My cheeks were burning. I was not only embarrassed—I was embarrassed about being embarrassed. "I'm sorry. She's just . . . getting used to everything, I suppose."

But then something strange happened. Something unexpected. Happy waved at Chiqui, and Chiqui waved back. Like they were friends or something.

"She's cute," said Happy.

"I guess." What else could I say?

Happy dragged her chair so it was in front of mine. I cringed. She was *way* too close. Her dirty, bare feet were right there.

Ugh.

"So," she said.

"So," I said back.

She leaned forward.

Too close. Too close. Too close.

Her eyes sparkled. "Well, since it's summer break, I was thinking maybe we could hang out. Me and you and Chiqui. I'm really good with kids. I watch them all the time . . ."

Happy was so still. It was as if her breathing were on hold.

She wanted to hang out with *me*.

Me the germaphobe.

Me the obsessive-compulsive weirdo.

Me the awkward kid.

"Um, sure. Why not?" I replied.

Things seemed to be looking up.

I might *actually* be making a friend.

How did that happen?

SIXTEEN

Mamá was thrilled. Beyond thrilled, actually. I'd never seen her so surprised. Maybe flabbergasted was a better word for it. Her freckles practically leaped off her face when I mentioned Happy and her suggestion.

"Pablo. This is wonderful!" she exclaimed.

"So you think it's okay? I mean, having her around Chiqui and the house and stuff?"

Mamá sipped her tea and sank deeper into the sofa. I hadn't noticed until then how exhausted she looked. "Of course. I'll take all the help I can get. To be honest, I'm feeling a bit overwhelmed."

Of course you're overwhelmed.

What were you thinking?

Those thoughts somehow made me feel dirty. I fidgeted and glanced at my socks, counting the navy blue and red stripes. The stripes had warped at my ankles. As much as

I wanted to reach down and straighten them out, I didn't. I deserved to suffer.

"I'm sorry, Mamá . . . I'm sorry if you're overwhelmed. I'll try not to make things harder on you," I finally said without looking at her.

"Gracias, Pablo. But really, it has nothing to do with you. Being a single mother isn't easy, mi amor. It isn't easy on anyone. Now that Chiqui's here, I'm going to need all of you to pitch in. I've asked Grace to help out through the summer, and Zeus and Miguel will come by when they can."

I nodded. "All right."

There was this lump in my throat. It was big and solid and throbbed as if I'd puked up my heart. Mamá placed her teacup on the table. "I'd better go see what she's up to . . ." She cupped my chin with her hand and then took off in search of Chiqui.

The scents of chai tea, coconuts, and soap lingered. Despite the pleasant smells, something about the living room was making me feel sick. Maybe it was the old furniture, or the smudgy walls, or the dusty curtains. I wasn't sure what it was exactly, but whatever it was made me choke.

"*It has nothing to do with you.*" Mamá tried so hard to reassure me.

But she was wrong. It had *everything* to do with me.

She just couldn't see it because she loved me too much.

My father, though, he'd figured it out a long time ago. Once, when I was five, he brought me to work for Parent-Child Day. At first everything seemed fine. He gave me a quick tour of the aquarium. We saw all the exhibits—the colorful tropical fish, the alien-like jellies, the scary-looking sharks. Every so often he'd stop to greet a coworker. He would ruffle my hair and say something like, "*This is my son, Pablo. He might just work here one day. What do you think, kiddo?*" I always nodded because more than anything I wanted so badly to please him.

By the time we got to the touch pools, I was tired and hungry. But I didn't complain. My father wasn't fond of whining. We stood at the edge of the bat ray pool. The water was clear and shallow. But there was something about it I didn't like. There wasn't a sheet of glass separating me from them. The bat rays glided past us. They were like flat-headed monsters with wings and dangerous-looking tails. My father stuck his hand in the water and gazed at me. "*You can touch them, Pablo. They won't hurt you,*" he said.

As much as I wanted to, I couldn't do it. The water. What was underneath it scared me. My father frowned. He reached for my hand and tried to pull me over. "*C'mon, Pablo. You can do it.*"

I resisted, yanking my hand away. He let go. I fell backward. Tears dribbled down my face. Everything was blurry.

But there was one thing in the room that was crisp, clear, and painfully sharp. My father's eyes, filled with disappointment.

He sighed. *"I'll bring you home now,"* he said.

And that was the first and last time he ever brought me to Parent-Child Day.

That day, I also began to suspect something. Maybe my fears and worries and anxieties weren't at all normal. Maybe there *was* something wrong with me.

SEVENTEEN

If there was one thing I hated . . . Well, okay, I hated *lots* of things. But shopping *had* to be in the top three.

The smells.

The sounds.

The crowds.

The stuff.

Too. Much. Stuff.

Ugh.

In an effort to be helpful, I'd agreed to accompany Mamá to shop for Chiqui.

What was I thinking?

I was already sweating. Miguel's SUV was freezing, like Antarctic-level freezing, but still the sweat kept on coming. I scooched closer to the window, hoping nobody would notice. Mamá was staring off into the air. Thinking. Maybe she was thinking about how annoying it was having Chiqui burrowed in her armpit.

"Mahal . . . Mahal kita . . . ," sang Zeus from the driver's seat.

Ugh.

I was seriously starting to regret it.

The SUV cruised past the exit of our subdivision. Almost immediately, the narra trees disappeared. Without the shade, the streets and sidewalks seemed too bright, too dirty, too loud. There were the unhygienic food carts on wheels, selling snacks I wouldn't eat in a billion years. There were the stores for *everything*—convenience stores jam-packed with you-name-it-they-had-it, tiny bakeries with colorful breads and pastries, used-tire shops, which looked more like sidewalk junkyards, fruit and vegetable vendors selling their wilted produce from plastic tarps on the ground. There were the cars, the tricycles, the jeepneys double, triple, quadruple parked on the sidewalks. Traffic. *Beep. Beep. Honk. Honk.* There were the throngs of people jaywalking right and left. The assault on my eyes went on and on and on.

I looked away.

I *had* to look away.

Chiqui burrowed deeper into Mamá's armpit.

"We are here, Ma'am Carmen." Zeus maneuvered the truck into the entrance of the SM Mall. It wasn't my first time visiting that atrocious place. Ms. Grace had brought me there to buy school supplies, and on that day, she gave me all the nitty-gritty details about the place, how it was *the* largest chain of malls in the Philippines. And that back in the day, it was called Shoe-Mart, but when they expanded to selling everything under the sun, their name changed to SM.

Mamá glanced at the building, which resembled a ginormous tombstone with lights and billboards. Her shoulders drooped; she inhaled and exhaled as if preparing herself for the inevitable.

"Okay. Let's get this over with," she said.

At least I wasn't the *only* one who hated the mall.

Mamá had told me on numerous occasions that malls were the epitome of consumerism. *But* from time to time they were a necessary evil.

We hopped out of the truck. It was pretty challenging, considering Chiqui wouldn't unglue herself from Mamá's leg. And every time she tried to make a move toward the entrance, Chiqui would pull in the opposite direction and shake her head. It was quite the scene. Passersby were eyeing Mamá suspiciously as if she were some child abuser or something. I could tell Mamá was trying to keep her cool, but her cheeks were turning pinker and pinker, and her sweat was sticking to her flyaway hair in a way that made it look like someone had poured a bucket of water on her.

"Chiqui, *please*," she kept on repeating.

But still, she wouldn't budge.

That is, until Zeus stepped in. He kneeled in front of her. "Huwag kang mag-alala, Chiqui. Punong-puno ng magagandang damit at sapatos ang mga tindahan dito . . . Lalabas kang isang prinsesa!" he said with a chuckle.

Whatever he'd said was totally alien to me. There was one word, though, one word I recognized.

Prinsesa. It sounded just like the Spanish word for "princess."

Slowly, really slowly, Chiqui's grip on Mamá loosened. Then, she let go. I could see her eyes starting to glimmer. I could see the faintest hint of a smile appearing on her face.

Mamá touched Zeus's shoulder. "Thank you, Zeus."

He stood and shrugged like it was nothing. "Just call me when you need me, ma'am. Sir," he said with a wave.

I watched him get into the white truck as if it were a white stallion. As if he were a knight riding off into the sunset after saving the day.

Sir.

Maybe *I* should have been the one calling him "sir" all along.

Sir Zeus.

"We've . . . got . . . it . . . all . . . for . . . you!"

That was the catchphrase of the SM Department Store jingle. It was playing on a loop, driving me up the wall, while Mamá and Chiqui browsed the never-ending racks of clothing. It might as well have been a maze of cotton and polyester and rayon. I got dizzy after a while, the vomit-fest of colors making my eyes hurt.

"Chiqui. DR-ESSS . . . BLUE DR-ESSS . . ." I heard Mamá's exaggerated talking from somewhere behind me.

I turned around. Chiqui was shaking her head from side to side. I guess she wasn't a fan of pastel-blue frills. She yanked a party dress with silvery sequined stars from the rack closest to her and held it up.

Mamá's hairy eyebrow caterpillars danced on her forehead. "Really?"

Chiqui held it up even higher.

"Okay. Okay. I guess every girl needs a party dress." She tossed the sequined monstrosity into the shopping cart and started browsing again.

I groaned. "Mamá. I'm tired."

"We're almost done, mi amor . . ."

She said that an hour ago.

Maybe I could find a quiet spot to escape to. I looked around, but the only remotely quiet spot was a small bench in the nearby shoe section.

Good enough.

I made my way there, collapsing with a sigh and a groan and whatever other self-pitying sound I could muster. From where I was seated, I could still see Mamá and Chiqui holding items of clothing up to each other. Once in a while, a smiling saleslady would make her approach. Each and every one would flinch at the sight of Chiqui's face. Each and every one would try not to show it. And then inevitably, each and every one of their smiles would fade as they made some pathetic excuse to run off. At first Chiqui didn't seem to notice. But after the fourth and fifth and sixth time, she caught on. As soon as she spotted a navy blue saleslady uniform she would hide among the clothes.

I felt sick all of a sudden. Like someone had simultaneously stomped on my guts and slapped the back of my head. It only got worse when a couple of little girls, not much older than Chiqui, started giggling and pointing at her. Mamá was a few aisles away inspecting a pile of jeans.

I stood on jiggly legs.

What was I supposed to do?

Should I go get Mamá?

Should I run over and tell those girls to stop?

Should I jump in the way and shield her with my body?

Should I get the manager and file a complaint?

All those questions. All those scenarios were running in

my head, in circles. Running. Running. Running. Meanwhile, Chiqui kept on burrowing deeper into the clothing racks. She peeped out and made eye contact with me. There were tears streaming down her face.

Pablo. Please, help!

I could hear her screaming loud and clear, even though her lips hadn't moved.

Still, my jiggly legs wouldn't budge.

Sir Pablo.

What a joke.

There was most definitely nothing knight-like about me.

Suddenly, Mamá appeared out of nowhere. Her feathers were ruffled; I mean, she didn't actually *have* any feathers. *Duh.* But if she'd had them, they would have been standing up and puffy. I held my breath waiting for her to lash out. But she didn't. What she did was breathe deep, bend down, and speak calmly to those girls. They nodded, as if they'd understood exactly what she'd said. And then they walked away. Just like that.

It had been so easy. So effortless. Yet I'd done nothing. Absolutely *nothing.*

Mamá crept into the rack of clothing and reached out to hug Chiqui. But Chiqui was inconsolable. Her arms swung all over; it almost seemed like she was fighting with every item of clothing in her way. As the seconds went by, she got more and more tangled; hangers were dropping to the floor right and left.

It was quite the scene.

Yet again.

Except Sir Zeus was nowhere in sight.

It was just me and them.

And the only thing I did was stand there and watch them like a useless mannequin.

EIGHTEEN

The sun glared from a cloudless sky. There was this moody kind of gust that swirled around, so dirt, dust, and debris blew everywhere. It was the kind of day I hated. All I wanted to do was hide in my bedroom. Take refuge. Especially after what had happened at the mall the day before.

I was dejected.

Sad. Depressed. Dispirited.

But the more I sulked, the more I got to thinking. I didn't want to be that boy anymore—that useless mannequin. I wanted to help out.

Do my part.

Be the *very* best Pablo I could be.

I climbed out of my nest of pillows and sheets, and then dashed out of my room. But then, I stalled by the door as soon as I heard Mamá and Ms. Grace speaking in hushed voices. They were in the entryway. Instinctively, I crept back and flattened my body against the wall. At first I felt like a bumbling secret agent. As the hushed voices became louder, though, I felt braver, cooler, much more James Bond–like.

"Grace, you should have seen her . . . It took me nearly half an hour just to get her out of the clothing rack," said Mamá.

"Did she say anything?" asked Ms. Grace.

"No. That's the thing. She wouldn't speak at all. Not even in Tagalog. Not even in the car when Zeus was trying to calm her down . . . I'm worried, Grace."

"Hmm . . ." I could picture Ms. Grace thinking the way she did when her head was tilted to the side. "What did the doctors at the hospital tell you?" she finally asked.

"Not much. They gave me referrals for a child psychologist and speech therapist . . . I'm going to have to take some time off from work just to bring her to see them." Mamá sighed.

"I can help. If you need me here at the house . . ."

"Thank you. You're a lifesaver, Grace . . . Maybe, when you're alone with Chiqui, you can try and get her to open up to you? Perhaps she'll talk to someone more . . . familiar," said Mamá.

"Of course," said Ms. Grace.

I leaned forward just a bit and saw Mamá hug Ms. Grace.

"I have to go. I'm already running late. Thanks for *everything*, Grace."

The door opened and closed. A minute later, I heard the *cring-cring-cring*ing of Mamá's bicycle bell. Ms. Grace breathed deep, and then she walked toward the living room. That's when I counted Mississippi ten times, to make sure Ms. Grace wouldn't suspect I was eavesdropping.

Okay, just act normal, Pablo.

I strode into the living room like I was shooting the breeze or something.

Ms. Grace and Chiqui were on the floor playing Legos.

"Good job, Chiqui! Ang ganda ng bahay mo!" said Ms. Grace.

I glanced at Chiqui. She was fiddling with her hair, avoiding Ms. Grace's gaze. Yet still, Ms. Grace persisted. "Ano ang paborito mong kulay, Chiqui?" she said, pointing to the different colored Legos.

Silence.

Chiqui didn't utter a single peep.

That's when I kneeled down and gawked at her Lego house as if it were the most amazing thing in the world. "Wow. This is like *the* coolest house I've *ever* seen!"

Suddenly, Chiqui beamed. It was obvious that she was proud of the lopsided, multicolored house she'd built.

But still, she didn't utter a single peep.

Never mind. It was progress, nonetheless.

Ms. Grace placed her hand on my back, looking just like one of the smiley faces she drew on my test papers.

One hundred percent.

I was kicking butt.

I cleared my throat.

Ahem.

"So . . . anyone up for some fresh air? How about we go for a walk? Chiqui might enjoy a visit to the sanctuary," I suggested.

Chiqui fiddled with the Lego in her grasp, her eyes bouncing from Ms. Grace to me to Ms. Grace to me.

"I think that's a fantastic idea, Pablo!" said Ms. Grace.

"Awesome. I'll go get ready." I hurried to my room. So fast, I didn't even stop to count the window-blind shadows on the wall.

I was pleased with myself.

From then on, I was going to do everything within my power to make it up to Chiqui.

She was going to *love* the sanctuary. There were hardly any people around, and the animals, well, the animals didn't care one bit about how you looked. Maybe that's why she adored those chickens so much.

I put on a pair of cargo pants and a T-shirt, and then slathered my skin with citronella oil until I reeked. As bad as I smelled, it was still better than being eaten alive by mutant mosquitoes. I'd seen a lot of mosquitoes in my lifetime. But nothing compared to the ones in the Philippines. They were huge, thirsty, and practically indestructible.

Before leaving the room, I stuffed wet wipes, tissues, and hand sanitizer spray into my pockets. I was ready. Or at least I thought I was.

Ms. Grace and Chiqui were already outside. Chiqui had on this big, floppy hat, a bubble-gum-pink dress and rain boots with rainbow hearts on them. She was gnawing on her hair, so her face was half covered.

She was nervous.

She didn't want anyone staring at her.

She just wanted to hide.

I couldn't blame her. Most of the time that's how I felt too.

Ms. Grace took her hand and held it. "Let's go, Pablo, Chiqui. I've got bottled water and snacks for all of us," she said.

Except when Ms. Grace took a step forward, Chiqui wouldn't budge. It was as if her rain boots were glued to the concrete. Ms. Grace frowned. Then she bent down and said, "Takot ka ba?"

But still, Chiqui didn't utter a single peep.

Ms. Grace bent down even more, so she was eye to eye with her. "Maniwala ka sa akin, Chiqui." Her tone was so gentle, so patient.

But still, Chiqui didn't utter a single peep.

She did, however, unglue herself from the concrete, taking a cautious stride.

Ms. Grace stood. "Come on, Pablo."

I skipped down the steps and followed them down the street. We walked single file because the sidewalk was way too narrow. There were also these humongous tree roots busting through the concrete so we had to make sure not to trip on them. After a few minutes, I got this weird feeling. Like we were being watched. I stopped and looked over my shoulder. Jem, Happy, Bing, and Lito crashed into me.

"Ouch," I said, touching the spot on my forehead where Jem's head bumped into mine. "What are you doing?" I asked.

"We're walking. Same as you," said Jem with a scowl. She was kind of intimidating. Like a bigger, tougher version of Happy with much shorter hair.

"Well, I *know* that. But right behind us?"

Happy stepped in front of Jem. The Hello Kitties were

gone. Instead, she was decked out in Disney princesses. "I thought I'd tag along in case you needed help."

"Yeah, okay. But all four of you?" I said.

I could hear Ms. Grace chuckling behind me. "It's fine. The more the merrier."

I breathed deep.

The more *wasn't* the merrier.

I thought about those little girls at the mall. Those salesladies. All those people.

Chiqui didn't need *more* people to stare at her, to laugh and make her cry.

But how was I supposed to tell them without hurting their feelings?

Ugh.

Just roll with it, Pablo.

I glanced at Chiqui. Her face was covered by the brim of her hat, but otherwise she seemed fine.

Phew.

We continued our walk through the neighborhood, passing one old house after another. They were so desperately in need of a fresh coat of paint. Some had cracked walls, missing tiles and shingles, broken gates, and rusted fences. Fixer-uppers is what Mamá liked to call them. But I kind of thought they needed more than just fixing. Bulldozing, maybe. Perhaps that would get rid of all the clutter too. The garages with piles of junk. The patios with too many potted plants. Most especially, the never-ending lines of laundry drying under the sun—bras, briefs, and panties galore. How could they just leave them out like that for everyone to see?

Then there were the sounds—dogs barking, cats yowling, roosters crowing. There were also the tricycles sputtering by, the vendors hollering, and the distant sounds of karaoke.

It was by far the crummiest neighborhood we'd ever lived in.

Sigh.

Eventually we reached the far end of the subdivision where there were hardly any houses. There was a dead end, which wasn't really a dead end because there was a small pathway hidden behind some shrubbery. We halted. Jem, Happy, Bing, and Lito side-eyed one another.

"What's the matter?" I asked.

Ms. Grace waved and went ahead with Chiqui. "Just catch up when you're done talking!"

Jem nudged Happy with her elbow and Happy nudged her back. "The people around here are scared of this place."

"Scared? Scared of what?" I glanced at the thick canopy of trees and orchids. It was wild and jungle-y. Sure, I was scared of it. But I suspected it was for an altogether different reason.

Happy pointed at the shrubbery and treetops. "They

believe there are duwendes and kapres in there. Evil dwarves and giants."

I was kind of shocked, to be honest. There I was worried about germs and dirt and mutant mosquitoes. But my fears seemed completely normal all of a sudden. They stared, waiting for me to say something. I stood taller and puffed my chest out, imagining I was an explorer with a big machete in my hand.

Be brave, Pablo. You can do it.

"It's okay. I come here all the time. I promise there aren't any dwarves or giants," I told them. It was a lie, of course, but a harmless one. Truth was, I'd only been to the sanctuary a few times. There were too many feathers and too much fur and hay and poop there for my liking.

I gazed ahead at the pathway. It was like we were entering another world, another dimension. The edge stood beneath my feet. As soon as I stepped forward, I could be that other boy.

That other Pablo I so wanted to be.

NINETEEN

We reached the hand-carved wooden sign that read:

EL LADO SALVAJE SANCTUARY
WILDERNESS ZONE
NO ENTRY BEYOND THIS POINT

Jem eyed the sign suspiciously. "Are you sure it's safe in there? Because I'm responsible for my brother and sisters. *Especially* those two," she said, pointing at Bing and Lito, who were launching helicopter-shaped seedpods into the air.

Luckily, we hadn't come across any dwarves or giants. Otherwise my credibility would have totally been shot. I glanced at the sign like no biggie. "Yeah. Don't worry. You won't get eaten by a lion or anything."

Happy covered her mouth and giggled. "Well, *that's* good."

The security guard, Mang Wily, who looked like he could have been over a hundred years old, opened the gate. "Magandang umaga, Sir Pablo!" he said with a salute. When I first met him, I thought his first name was actually Mang. But then Mamá explained that it was actually Wily. The Mang was short for Manong—a respectful way to address an older person.

I nodded. "Hey, Mang Wily."

Then I noticed the badge on his chest was terribly askew, like leaning all the way on its side. I wanted so badly to straighten it out.

Forget it, Pablo.

I walked away.

The twins ran ahead. Jem and Happy bolted after them. But then they came to a sudden halt.

Happy gasped. "Wow."

I guess it *was* pretty amazing. Mamá said the sanctuary's goal was to mimic a natural habitat. There were hardly any cages, and if there were any, they were more like giant enclosures with jungly-looking plants and strategically placed logs. It really was wild looking. There were ancient trees with vines thick enough to swing on, flowers as big as your head, and even a small waterfall with mossy rocks and a freshwater pool.

We wandered for a while. It seemed most of the animals were in hiding until three peacocks strutted in front of us. They each gave us a look of superiority. Then two of them fanned out their tail feathers as if they were showing off.

"What a surprise!" I heard Mamá's voice before she appeared from behind some ferns. She was kind of dirty. Her cargo pants were smudged with mud, her T-shirt smeared with god knows what, and her ponytail was littered with twigs and leaves. "What are you doing here?" she asked.

"We just came for a visit," I said with a shrug.

All of a sudden, Chiqui came running down the pathway. Her hat flew off.

"Dahan dahan, Chiqui!" said Ms. Grace from behind.

Chiqui ran even faster.

"Go! Go! Go!" cheered Bing and Lito.

Slam!

It was as if Chiqui had stomped on the brakes.

She half-turned, covering her face with her hair again.

Awkward...

I sidled over and shielded her body with mine. "Um. So...maybe you can, like, give us the official tour?" I said to Mamá.

"Well, of course," she replied.

Bing and Lito jumped up and down, chanting, "Tour! Tour! Tour!"

Phew.

Mamá led us through a super green and lush maze. Here and there, flowers jutted out in various shades of pink and yellow and red and orange. Happy walked beside me looking like one of the flowers herself. A pink one, *obviously*.

"Your mom is pretty cool," she blurted out.

"Yeah. I suppose."

She moved closer so our arms almost rubbed each other. "The most exciting part of *my* mom's day is using fabric softener in the laundry," she said with a smirk.

I chuckled. "I'm sure you're exaggerating."

"No. Not really. Well . . . maybe just a bit."

I thought about Ate Lucinda and how she was always there doing chores, hollering at one of the kids about something or other. She seemed content living in their little old house with her children and her collection of potted plants. I hardly ever saw Happy's father because he worked nights and slept most of the day. But at least he was there. I was sort of jealous, actually.

Finally, we stopped at a muddy pit with several muddy beasts.

"Kalabaw! Kalabaw!" shouted the twins.

Mamá and Ms. Grace laughed, and everyone else watched the beasts wallow in mud as if it were the most normal thing.

"These kalabaw, or water buffalos as they're known in other parts of the world, were rescued from situations where they were overworked and starved. Some were scheduled for slaughter," Mamá explained.

My skin itched just looking at all that mud. I shuddered, and Happy raised her eyebrow. "What's the matter?" she whispered.

"Nothing . . . just mosquitoes," I whispered back.

We moved on. I was glad to get as far away from the mud as possible. The trees got even bigger, shielding us from the sun. *Thank god.* The shade made it less hot and humid. More bearable. But still, sweat trickled down my neck and back.

Screech! Screech! Screech!

"Monkeys!" said Ms. Grace, pointing up at the trees.

There were a dozen or so grayish-brown creatures. Some were chilling, picking things out of one another's fur. *Gross.* The rest were jumping and swinging from branch to branch. The twins, Bing and Lito, were at it again, chanting, "Unggoy! Unggoy!" which I guessed was "monkey" in Tagalog.

"And here we've got eighteen Philippine long-tailed macaques, which were rescued from small cages and chains.

Some were injured by cruel people throwing rocks at them, or electrocuted by live wires. As much as we'd like to rehabilitate and return them to the wild, the species is now in serious threat and practically extinct in some parts of the country." Mamá reached into her pocket, retrieving a handful of red hairy fruit. She tossed them up one by one, and the monkeys expertly caught them.

"Ohh. Rambutan! My favorite," said Happy.

I looked at her kind of funny. "You eat those?"

"Yes, they're delicious."

I tried not to make an icky face. But I couldn't help it. The skin on the fruit could have been from alien armpits. I even gagged a bit. It seemed Happy was catching on because she raised her eyebrow again, parting her lips like she was going to say something. I wouldn't let her, though. I pretended to be interested in what the monkeys were doing, moving closer to the tree they were on, moving closer to Ms. Grace and Chiqui.

Phew.

The last thing I wanted was for Happy to figure out how utterly weird I was.

Ms. Grace was fiddling with her tote bag, pulling out bottles of water and handing them out. Chiqui had her floppy hat back on. But the breeze ruffled the brim, so I could see her face. I watched her watch the monkeys. I'd never seen so much wonder. Her eyes were like fried eggs with glossy yolks. I tried to see what she was seeing. But to me they were just monkeys. Nothing more.

Then I flinched. Something touched me. I looked down. Chiqui's fingers were just inches away. She wasn't staring at the monkeys anymore. Her glossy eyes were on mine. Everything blurred. Her mouth moved. I heard something. A whisper. I crouched. Then I heard it again. "Pabo," she whispered. "Pabo."

Chiqui was trying to say my name.

For a second I wanted to tell everyone. I wanted Mamá to know what she'd said. But then she reached out and squeezed my finger. It was as if she were telling me she wasn't ready.

It was our little secret.

TWENTY

I didn't get malaria from mutant mosquitoes, or get bitten by rabid animals, or get tetanus from rusty nails. I didn't even get all that dirty. Maybe a bit sweaty, but I would definitely survive.

When we finally got home from a long day of animal watching and feeding, and lazing by the waterfall, Mamá announced that Miguel was coming over to cook dinner. I thought it was strange because one, I wasn't aware that Miguel knew how to cook, and two, it was totally out of the blue. He'd never offered to help out like that before. Not that I was complaining. Miguel was cool. He didn't really bother me much.

By the time I was properly disinfected and dressed, Miguel had already arrived. He was in the kitchen cooking up a storm in his pink tie-dyed T-shirt with his sunglasses perched on his head. "Hey, little man. Hope you're hungry for some veggie burgers," he said, twirling a spatula.

I glanced at the patties sizzling in the cast-iron pan. "Sure. They look good."

Pop!

Mamá came out of the pantry with a newly opened bottle of wine. It was one of her special bottles from a small winery in Asturias, the part of northern Spain where she grew up. She handed Miguel a glass and poured one for herself. Her hair was pulled into a loose bun and she had on a tank top and her pants from India that made her look like a genie.

"Pablo, why don't you set the table?" she asked.

"Okay." But I didn't move. For a few seconds I watched Mamá and Miguel dodge each other in the small kitchen, flipping patties, slicing buns, washing lettuce, cutting cheese and tomatoes. It was weird how choreographed it all was.

Suddenly, I felt a tug on my shirt. I turned. Chiqui stood there holding a pile of napkins. "Oh. You want to help?" I whispered to her.

She didn't answer. Instead, placing them on the table one by one. I grabbed the cutlery from the drawer and she took those too, arranging the forks and knives out of place. It took every ounce of self-control for me not to freak out.

My muscles jerked.

My fingers tapped.

My toes curled.

I wanted so badly to reach out and fix it. To straighten the napkins, rearrange the cutlery until they were perfect. But I couldn't. Through Chiqui's curtain of hair, I spotted a sort of cracked smile.

My muscles stopped jerking.

My fingers stopped tapping.

My toes stopped curling.

All I could do was smile back and whisper, "Good job, Chiqui."

Mamá gazed at the table, sweeping her arms out dramatically. "It looks beautiful! Well done, Pablo and Chiqui."

Miguel appeared from behind, placing the platter of veggie burgers and French fries at the center of the table. He bent down next to Chiqui and said, "Siguradong gusto mo ng French fries, noh?"

Silence.

The spotlight was on Chiqui.

But she didn't utter a single peep.

I hadn't really understood what Miguel had said, other than the French fries part. It was probably nothing. Yet Chiqui was panicked nonetheless. I brushed the table so that one of the napkins fell on the floor. Almost immediately, she ducked under to retrieve it.

"*Speaking* of French fries . . . these are just spectacular, Miguel. I mean, they're perfect! How do you cut them so even . . . so straight?" I said a tad too loudly.

Miguel chuckled. "It's all in the wrist, little man. I'll teach you one of these days."

"Okay, everyone. Enough with the chitchat. Let's eat before the food gets cold," said Mamá.

She had a point. I *was* hungry.

Mamá tried to help Chiqui into her seat, but it was useless. Chiqui squirmed and scowled and then climbed into the seat all by herself. For a split second, I thought Mamá was going to lose it. Her freckles were darker, huddling around her nose like a freckle army. The split second passed, though. All she did was exhale and sit calmly. Really, really calmly. "Gracias, Miguel. This all looks so delicious," she said.

Miguel shrugged like it was nothing. "It's no big deal. Just trying to be helpful."

He might have thought it was no big deal, but it was actually kind of glorious. The burgers were round, not too thick, not too thin, and the fries, my goodness, I still couldn't get over those fries. I'd never seen hand-cut fries so symmetrical. There were also pickles, lettuce, tomatoes, and slices of Manchego cheese to go with the burgers. Even the buns, which were clearly store-bought, were still the right ones. Not the ones with sesame seeds that reminded me of crawling larvae. They were the soft type of buns with flecks of oatmeal on top.

There was this moment of commotion—the clinking of forks and knives, the scraping of plates, arms moving, hands grabbing, mouths chewing. It was then that I noticed something was wrong. I only had one fork and one knife. I would need at least nine more of each to finish eating.

My ears buzzed. My temples prickled. My fingers and toes went numb.

But as much as it bothered me—and it really, truly did—I didn't want to be the odd man out. Chiqui had somehow loosened up; her hair was finally off her face, and she was eating with gusto even though Miguel was there, right next to her, with his ridiculous jokes. And Mamá was laughing, the most I'd seen her laugh in a long while.

If I'd gone to the cutlery drawer. If I'd taken out nine more forks and nine more knives. If I'd placed them on the table with absolute precision. If I'd cut my burger into perfect little squares . . . Then the lighthearted mood would have been ruined.

Suck it up, Pablo.

I gripped the fork and knife and cut into my burger. One bite. Two bites. Three bites. Four. Nobody noticed how uncomfortable I was. Not even Mamá, who was too busy chatting and making sure Chiqui was eating properly. Each bite became harder and harder, and slower and slower. After a while, I stopped eating altogether and just pushed my food from side to side. Once again, nobody noticed. At least I didn't think anyone had. Except someone *had* noticed.

Chiqui was watching me.

It took me forever to fall asleep. Mamá and Miguel were talking and laughing in the living room like there was some kind of party or something. Thankfully, my bedroom was far enough away so their voices were muffled. Too muffled. I was itchy with curiosity. What were they laughing at? Was it something I did? Something I said?

Eventually, though, my head got heavier and the voices faded. I passed out. It was one of those velvety kinds of sleep—soft, comforting, and cozy. There were no dreams. Only fleeting images of peacock feathers, muddy beasts, hairy armpit fruit, and Chiqui. I could even hear her cookie munching as if she were right there with me.

I opened my eyes.

Munch. Crunch. Munch. Crunch.

Chiqui *was* there with me. She was at the foot of my bed with a pack of cookies in her grasp. There were crumbs everywhere. I gasped. It was like stumbling across a bloody crime scene. That's what it seemed like in my head, in my heart, in my stomach. I didn't scream. I wanted to. But I didn't.

The bed bounced as Chiqui crept closer, her bare feet smashing cookie crumbs along the way. I winced. She bit into another cookie and then handed me the rest of it. "Pabo," she mumbled. For a moment I thought I saw the beginnings of an impish smile. But then she covered her mouth with her hand.

The cookie dangled under my chin. I thought about her saliva and the germs under her nails. The cookie. That particular cookie was the last thing I wanted to eat.

My stomach grumbled.

I *was* hungry.

She mumbled again, "Pabo," nudging the cookie toward me.

I took it. I didn't pause. I didn't think. I just stuffed it into my mouth and swallowed.

TWENTY-ONE

Mamá kept on yawning. There were shadows under her eyes and her hair was flat on one side and frizzy on the other. Her silk robe swayed as she poured herself a cup of strong Spanish coffee.

"Cereal?" She held up the box of Cheerios.

I didn't really feel like eating cereal but I shrugged and took the box anyway. Maybe I could escape into a bowl of perfect little circles. Chiqui stared while I poured the cereal, pointing her finger like she wanted to spear the falling Os. I grabbed a bowl and gave her some, and then she proceeded to do just that.

"So . . . ," Mamá said.

I held my spoon in midair. I didn't like it when her sentences started with "So."

"Miguel and I were talking last night. About summer break—"

"What about summer break?" I said, putting my spoon down.

She sipped her coffee, avoiding my eyes. "It's just that you . . . I mean, we. We're always cooped up in this house. We haven't even gone anywhere since we've been here. And now that Chiqui's with us, it might be nice to take a trip so we can all get to know one another. Have some fresh air and do something fun together."

Fresh air? Fun? What was she talking about? She *knew* I hated traveling—road trips, airports, airplanes, buses, trains. She *knew* I wasn't exactly the let's-go-on-an-adventure kind of guy.

But what she didn't know . . . what I'd been keeping from her . . . was *how* triggered I really was by travel. Just the idea of it made my skin crawl. There were endless amounts of chaos, dirt, and germs involved. And the sleeping somewhere new was the worst. What if the sheets were scratchy? What if there were bedbugs? What if the bathroom wasn't clean enough?

"Is it really necessary?" I finally replied.

"No. It's not *really* necessary. But I think it would be nice. Miguel's friend is hosting a surf competition in Baler over the weekend. It might be exciting. Don't you think?"

Surfing. That meant the sea would be right there, near me. My face burned. If I stared at my cereal any harder, my eyeballs might actually plop into the bowl. "In . . . in two days?" I said with a high-pitched voice.

"Yes. There's a nice resort there. It's brand-new. Miguel already booked us some rooms. You'll be fine, Pablo. I promise." Mamá tried to reassure me with a smile.

But there was nothing she could do to reassure me.

My mind was elsewhere.

The sea.

The beach.

California.

I was zapped back in time.

To the aquarium. My father looked straight at me. He blinked. The color in his irises sort of faded, as if I were watching a green leaf drying out, curling, and then turning into a crunchy brown. It was the color of disappointment. I'd seen it so many times. I didn't want to disappoint Mamá too.

I inhaled and stared at my cereal again. It was already soggy. Heavy. Drowning in milk.

"Okay. I'll go."

I was curled up on the couch, sulking. My body felt heavy—so heavy that every time I breathed, it was like I was sinking, like I was being swallowed up by a piece of furniture. I'd been there since after breakfast, trying not to think about the upcoming beach trip, trying not to kick myself for not speaking up. Why was it so hard for me to say something? Anything?

For years, I'd rehearsed it in my head—*exactly* what I was going to say.

"Mamá, I have something to tell you."

"What is it, mi amor?"

Long pause.

"Ever since we started moving around so much . . . things have just gotten worse for me. It's not only the forks and spoons and knives, and how my food is, and how my clothes need to be. There's so much more that bothers me now. Dirt and germs. All the bacteria everywhere. The air and the dust that's in it. The noises and smells and crowds make me want to stay in my room. All the time . . . And sometimes I'm scared. I'm scared of the sea, of what's in it, and what's underneath it. I'm scared of losing you, just like I lost Dad . . . I'm sorry, Mamá. I'm sorry I didn't tell you sooner. It's just . . . I was embarrassed. Ashamed."

"Oh, Pablito. There is absolutely nothing to be ashamed of! I'll help you. I'll help you get through this. Okay? I'm your mother. I love you no matter what."

Mamá would embrace me. I would be relieved. Everything would be fine.

That's how I'd envisioned it. I knew all the words. I knew what we would wear, how our bodies would move, how our facial expressions would change with every emotion.

But no matter how hard I tried. I just couldn't say those words in real life. They'd been bottled up for too long. How was I supposed to get them out?

I mean, a kid should be able to confide in his parents, right?

Yet I couldn't.

My father was Cal Jones, world-famous marine biologist. He was all about being a man, being adventurous, being brave. There was *no way* I was spilling my guts out to him.

Mamá. She loved me. I *knew* she loved me. But she was just too busy saving every living creature on the planet. And when she wasn't busy, she was all about positive energy and natural healing and crystals. Crystals wouldn't help me one bit. There was *no way* I was spilling my guts out to her.

Then there was that time in Spain, right after my father left us. We were staying with Abuelita. She lived on a hillside fishing village in Asturias. All the houses were white with terra-cotta-tiled roofs and window shutters in different colors—Abuelita's were green, with bloodred geraniums in planters. Thankfully, hers was one of the houses closer to the top of the hill, so it wasn't too near the sea. Almost every day, Mamá would walk to the beach to swim, or go boating with Tío Ricardo, her brother. Almost every day, I would stay inside, reading book after book, taking nap after nap, helping Abuelita with the cooking and cleaning.

It was on one of those days in her rustic wood-and-stone kitchen that I sort of, kind of, almost confessed. I had been shucking fava beans for the stew. Abuelita was seated next to me cracking walnuts with an ancient-looking nutcracker.

Snap.

Crack.

She had pulled the shell apart and tossed the walnut in a bowl. Then she leaned over, squinted one eye, and stared at me with the other, as if she were looking into a crystal ball. "Pablito, escúchame. I want to tell you something," she said in Spanglish, which for whatever reason, she insisted on speaking.

I cringed and braced myself. Surely, it was going to be one of her rambling stories about the olden days.

"Sabes qué? I tell you secrets . . . Your tío Ricardo, he *very* scare of spiders. Even small ones!" She held up her thumb and index finger and pressed them together. "And your mamá . . . when she was una niñita, she cry every night because she think there is un monstruo under her bed!" She laughed. "And you remember Tía Emita? She believe the vampiros kill her! Por dios! She hang many garlic in her house, qué peste!" She held her nose and made a stinky face. "And por supuesto, there was bisabuelo, your great-grandfather Jorge. He like everything VERY clean. Todo muy limpio! Even his food. Todo perfecto!" She widened her pale green eyes.

I gulped and then fake-smiled. I wasn't quite sure I liked the direction she was heading. Abuelita squeezed my cheek and grinned. "Pero sabes qué, Pablito? Everyone scare of something. Everyone act strange sometime. Es normal! In España, we accept a todo el mundo! Everyone welcome... Okay?"

There was this echoing silence. Empty. As if it were desperate to be filled with words. I shifted in my seat.

Should I say something?

Was she expecting me to fess up?

But the more I thought about what she'd said, the more my insides shriveled. She was telling me, in a not-so-direct way, that I was normal. There was nothing wrong with me. Yet that wasn't how I felt at all. In fact, it was the complete opposite of everything I *was* feeling.

I'd cleared my throat and uttered the most casual reply I could muster. "Sabes demasiados secretos, Abuelita..."

You know too many secrets, Grandma...

She cackled and squeezed my cheek again. "Es verdad, Pablito! Is the truth."

I'd gone back to shucking the fava beans. And she went

back to cracking walnuts. She meant well. That much I knew. But as I shucked bean after bean after bean, my insides continued to shrivel.

I was disappointed. Deep down, I'd wanted Abuelita's affirmation.

I'd wanted for her to tell me that there *was* something wrong with me.

And that she would help me fix it.

After that, I made the decision. Only *I* could fix myself.

I just needed to figure out how.

TWENTY-TWO

"Pablo!"

I jumped. Or rather, I flew off the couch as if it had just spit me out.

"Uh. What . . . what happened?" I said in a daze.

Ms. Grace stood there, looking at me with her head cocked to the side. "Are you okay?"

"Yeah. I'm fine."

Pitter-patter. Pitter-patter. Pitter-patter.

Chiqui ran past the doorway with a bubble machine in her grasp.

One bubble.

Two bubbles.

Three bubbles.

Four . . .

"Anyway," Ms. Grace said with a sigh. "I think Chiqui needs to get out of the house. I'm running out of things for her to do."

"Oh," I replied, still not sure what she wanted from me.

"You want to come with us to the sanctuary? It would help if I had an extra set of hands and eyes . . . Chiqui is pretty fast these days."

"Sure."

Truth was, I really didn't want to go. What I really wanted was to sink into the couch again. But I could tell just by the sweat on her forehead, by the way her hair swished across her jaw, that she was flustered.

Thankfully, though, by the time we got to the sanctuary, Ms. Grace was back to her calm, composed self, even though Chiqui was bouncing around like a Ping-Pong ball. Maybe it was because *I* was the one doing all the chasing. No wonder Ms. Grace wanted me to go.

"Chiqui!" I shouted as she zoomed down a fern-lined path. "Slow down!"

I ran after her, spotting a blur here and there of her yellow dress. I ran past the too-big trees and the too-colorful flowers. I ran past the conceited peacocks and the muddy beasts and the hairy-fruit-eating monkeys. Once in a while, Chiqui would halt and gasp at something cool, or shriek at something amazing. But then as soon as she saw me, she would zoom off again.

"Chiqui! C'mon! Give me a break, will you?" I shouted in between labored breaths.

After a while I gave up trying to catch up to her. I stumbled along, watching the dirt smudge my shoes. The path narrowed and the trees and foliage tangled in such a way that I couldn't tell which leaf or stalk or branch belonged where.

"Pablo! Where are you?" Ms. Grace hollered from somewhere.

"Here!"

"Is Chiqui with you?"

"No." I stopped. "I mean, yes . . ."

Chiqui materialized in front of me. Completely still. Pale. Her eyes popping from their sockets.

I heard Ms. Grace gasp beside me. Then she said something in a hushed voice. "Susmaryosep . . ."

For a moment it was silent.

I stepped back and gazed higher and higher and higher. At a giant.

Oh my god. Run!

I bolted.

But then the giant spoke. "Wait!"

Chiqui ran and hid behind Ms. Grace's legs.

I froze and stared at it again. Maybe it wasn't a giant. It sounded more like a woman—a gigantic woman with brown fabric over her head and chest. There were holes cut out where her eyes blinked through. And the weirdest part of all was that her forearms and hands were covered with brown feathers.

"I'm sorry if I scared you all," the feminine-sounding voice said. The giant removed the brown fabric from its head. It actually *was* a woman. She must have been well over six feet tall. Her caramel-colored irises, the ones that had looked scary at first, were actually soft and kind.

"Um. It's okay. I guess," I said.

From the corner of my eye, I could see Chiqui covering her face with her hands, except there was a slit between her forefinger and her middle finger where she was peeking through. Ms. Grace stepped ahead of us looking like a miniature action figure. "Do you work here?" she asked suspiciously.

The giant woman didn't seem at all fazed by Ms. Grace's tone. She simply smiled and held up her feather-covered hand. "Not technically. But I *am* a volunteer. In fact, I'm on my way to feed the owls if you want to tag along."

Ms. Grace was suddenly delighted. "Oh sure! Why not? It might be a good educational experience. What do you think, Pablo?"

"Okay," I answered with a shrug.

How bad could it be, right? I mean feeding owls couldn't possibly be that gross.

So we followed the giant woman as she blabbered

nonstop. "Any*who* . . . So you must be Carmen's Pablo. She told me I might run into you one of these days. And here you are! I'm Francesca, but everyone around here just calls me Frannie. I'm what you call a birder. Not a bird-watcher, but a birder. And technically, what I'm doing here is a *big* secret. So you won't go and tell anyone, will you?"

I shook my head, because to be honest, part of me was still scared. Her eyes might have been kind, but she looked like the sort of woman who wrestled grown men with her pinkie finger. She gave me the thumbs-up with her feathery hand, and then she halted in front of a huge—a really, really huge—enclosure. It was high enough to stand in, and there were trees growing inside it, jutting from the top through strategically placed holes.

Hoohoo! Hoohoo! Hoohoo!

Chiqui swept the hair from her face, and then she stood on her tippy-toes, searching for the owls. Clearly, she was fascinated. But she wasn't the only one who was fascinated. For a split second Frannie observed Chiqui as her gaze moved from bird to bird to bird.

I panicked.

Was she going to say something about Chiqui's cleft lip?

Was she going to make an icky face?

Was she going to make some stupid excuse and run away from us?

121

Frannie did none of those things, though. She just grinned real wide and spoke to Chiqui in the gentlest of voices. "Ang ganda ng ibon, diba?"

"Ganda." I remembered Zeus telling me it meant "beautiful" in Tagalog when he pointed out a ginormous double rainbow as we were driving down the highway one day.

I had no idea what else Frannie had said. But whatever it was made Chiqui nod ever so slightly. Her eyes were still wide, but they were wide from amazement, rather than fear.

Phew.

"Any*who* . . . It's best you guys keep a distance since you're in plainclothes," said Frannie, gesturing at our outfits. "You see, this disguise of mine serves a purpose. The owls in this enclosure are being rehabilitated to go back into the wild. That's the *big* secret. Technically, we should be turning these birds over to the government. *Shh* . . . But they don't really have the birds' best interest at heart. So instead we keep them here. Part of my job is to teach them how to hunt for food . . . This outfit is so they don't get used to humans. We want them to be wary of people. That way they won't get caught or hurt after we release them."

I nodded and kept on nodding, trying to absorb everything she was telling us.

"Well, okay then. I hope none of you are squeamish,"

said Frannie, placing the brown disguise back on. She stuck her hand under the fabric of her costume and pulled something out—a clear plastic box attached to a bungee cord.

Ms. Grace squeaked and sucked her breath in. Her skin turned into a sickening shade of puke green.

What was she getting so freaked out about?

Then I saw something squirming in the box. There were at least a dozen little white mice, the kind with beady red eyes.

Frannie quickly hid the box out of sight. "I'm sorry. It's the only way to teach them. I'll understand if you don't want to watch." She grinned crookedly and then lumbered off toward the enclosure.

The part of me that was horrified wanted to hightail it out of there. But there was this other part, the maybe 1 percent of my brain that wanted to stay. My muscles twitched. My nerves rattled. Yet I didn't budge. Even Ms. Grace, who was still kind of green, stood there, gripping the fabric of her shorts until her knuckles turned white.

We watched Frannie sneak into the enclosure. She kneeled on the hay-covered ground and released the mice one by one. Slowly, she retreated, glancing at us with her finger to where her lips would have been. At first the fluffy gray owls didn't seem to react. I inhaled and exhaled, watching and waiting. And then the mice scattered. The owls became more alert. They twisted their heads around, stalking the rodents as they moved.

Swoop!

One owl, and then two, and then three, and then four—I lost count.

It was a frenzied mouse-eating party.

It was sad.

It was brutal.

It was beautiful.

I felt this sudden release. Like my chest had burst open, letting everything out all at once. Like my shoulders were lighter. Like my head finally belonged on my body.

I wasn't really sure why I was getting all emotional.

There were tears in my eyes.

I wiped them away.

And as my vision cleared, I noticed tears in Chiqui's eyes too.

Except I couldn't tell if they were the sad or happy kind.

TWENTY-THREE

I wasn't going to make a list. I wasn't going to check it twice or three times or more. What I *was* going to do was pack my bag like any normal twelve-year-old kid would.

I was in my room trying to figure it out. My blue duffel bag—the one with the reflective piping and the nice sturdy handles—was on the floor. Not on the bed, but on the floor, because despite being squeaky clean I was sure there were still microscopic bits of dirt on it.

My clothes were neatly piled into categories: underwear, socks, T-shirts (short-sleeved and long-sleeved), shorts, pants, swim trunks (believe it or not, I actually owned two pairs), and pajamas (the ones coinciding with the days we'd be in Baler).

Phew.

Maybe this wouldn't be so hard after all.

Next up were toiletries. I imagined most guys or dudes or whatever hardly gave toiletries a thought. I mean, what was so complicated about shampoo, soap, and toothpaste, right? But in my case, the decisions were never ending. What if the shampoo I packed exploded in my suitcase? What if the hotel soap was only the bar kind? What if it reeked? What if it gave me rashes? What if I somehow misplaced my bamboo toothbrush? What if I ran out of toothpaste or cotton buds or deodorant or wet wipes or hand sanitizer or alcohol or all of the above?

Would I survive?

I could go on and on and on. But I just had to deal with it. One by one, I arranged the products I thought I would need and then zipped my toiletry organizer closed. I placed it at the bottom of the duffel bag in case anything should leak. On top I packed the clothing items from larger to smaller.

Finally.

I was done. And it hadn't taken more than an hour.

Pssst!

Tap. Tap. Tap.

Happy was outside my window. On top of her head she had on one of those sleeping masks with a cat's face on it.

I opened the window.

She leaned on the sill with both her elbows. "I saw your light was still on," she said, looking into my room.

"Yup. Still on," I said, repeating her more-than-obvious statement.

She pointed at my duffel bag. "You going somewhere?"

"Baler for the weekend. You know, surf and sand and whatnot." I dragged my beanbag chair over and sat down.

"Hmm ... surfing. You don't look like a surfer," said Happy with a raised eyebrow.

"That's because I'm not. I don't even know how to swim. I mean, not really." I tried hard to sink into the beanbag even more. My skin itched and I could feel beads of sweat forming on my upper lip.

"Well, if it's any consolation, I don't know how to swim either."

I sat up. "Really?"

"Yes. Really ... I haven't even been to the beach. Weird, huh? We live on an archipelago and I've never stepped foot on the sand or the sea. Pathetic," she said.

The itching was gone.

Happy studied my room as if it were a museum exhibit, eyes sweeping from one object to another.

Was it too neat? Too empty? Too boring?

"Um. So. What are you doing up anyway? It's past eleven. Isn't everyone asleep at your house?" I said, gesturing across the street with my chin.

She made a sad face. Her body sagged over the

windowsill. "I can't sleep. It's too hot. Our air-con broke last summer and my parents never fixed it."

"Air-con?"

"You know. Air conditioning."

"Oh." I swept my hands in the air. "I don't have air-con either."

Happy perked up. "Really?"

"Yeah. My mom says it's bad for the environment. She also thinks it's unhealthy not to sweat. Something about releasing the toxins from your body," I explained with an eye roll.

"Pablo!" There were footsteps, thuds, and bags being dragged down the hallway.

Happy stepped back and waved. "I better go. Have fun and bring me pasalubong. Okay?"

"Pasalubong?" I asked.

"A gift . . . a souvenir from your travels."

I stood and leaned out the window. "Like what?"

She shrugged. "You'll know it when you see it."

I had a bunch of questions on the tip of my tongue.

What was her favorite color?

Her favorite shape?

Her favorite number?

Her favorite scent?

Her favorite food?
Her favorite animal?
But she ran off into the darkness.
I was left alone with all my unanswered questions.
Wondering.

TWENTY-FOUR

We left at midnight for the more-or-less six-hour drive. Apparently it was better to travel at night. Miguel explained it was the best way to avoid the epic Manila traffic. The added bonus was sleeping the time away and waking up at the beach, well rested.

Everybody conked out pretty fast except for Zeus, *obviously*, since he was the one driving. It took me a while, though. For the first hour I just sat there and pretended I was asleep so no one would bother me. I looked out at the blackness closing my eyes when the car was going too fast. It felt like we were driving through a never-ending dark tunnel. I had no idea what would be on the other side. My stomach fluttered. My neck throbbed. My fingers and toes were numb. I squeezed my pillow, burrowing into the pile of throw blankets around me.

Go to sleep, Pablo.

I let my mind and body go.

There was nothing left to do but hope for the best.

I was awakened by the sound of slamming car doors.

"Welcome to El Gran Pacifica Resort!" said a blurry man and woman.

I blinked and tumbled out of the truck. The blurry man and woman handed me a fruity drink with a cocktail umbrella.

"Uh. Thanks," I said, taking a sip so I wouldn't look ungrateful. The jolt of sweet mango hit me, and then everything started coming into focus.

I glanced at the man's and woman's name tags, JON-JON and RAEZEL. They were both smiling and fresh-faced, dressed in matching black-and-white sarongs. I guessed they were the resort's official welcome wagon. After they ushered us through the entrance, more black-and-white-clad staff carried our bags. We must have looked bedraggled with our crumpled clothes and slept-on hair. Mine was probably flat against my head, Mamá's was poufy, and Chiqui's was all over her half-asleep face. The only presentable one was Miguel, who was somehow uncrumpled, as if he'd slept on air.

"Why don't you guys have a look-see while I check us all in?" he said.

Mamá and Chiqui plopped down on a teal-colored sofa. Chiqui's brow was furrowed like she was in a bad mood, or maybe she was just tired; she curled away from us, sulking on the opposite side.

Mamá's sigh practically echoed through the giant reception area. I stood and walked away, not wanting to get in the middle of either of their moods. Instead, I kind of strolled in a big circle, taking it all in. The place *was* brand-new. I mean, it practically sparkled. Everything was glass, metal, and wood with pops of tropical prints—pineapples, banana leaves, and shells. Nothing was worn or scratched or faded. Nothing was crooked or out of place or askew. Nothing smelled funky or chemically or plastic-y.

As far as I could tell, it was perfect.

After a few minutes Miguel came back with a handful of key cards. "We're all set. Why don't we freshen up, and then we can have some breakfast?"

"Yes. Por favor. I need a shower and a very, very strong coffee," said Mamá.

The porter led us to an impressive glass elevator. There wasn't a single smudge; I couldn't help wondering how much glass cleaner it took to keep it that way. We got out on the top floor, where supposedly there were four suites. Ours was the first one: the Hibiscus Suite. It sounded promising. The porter tapped the key card, a green light blinked, and the door opened. I caught a whiff of sage and grapefruit and then entered.

For a second all I saw was sunlight coming through the floor-to-ceiling windows. But then it hit me like a tidal wave.

Whoosh! Whoosh! Whoosh!

The sea. The infinitely deep blue sea was right there on the other side of the glass.

I was surrounded by it.

I froze. Then every inch of my body trembled.

"Pablo? Are you all right?" asked Mamá.

"Yes. Uh. Um. I think I need to go to the bathroom."

I ran to the nearest door. It was the closet. But it was too late. I puked all over the complimentary bedroom slippers.

Thankfully, there were curtains—thick, velvety green ones that covered the entire view. I was in bed trying not to envision what was on the other side of them. It was actually a relief to be alone. I'd told Mamá I was feeling nauseated from the long car ride. She tucked me into bed, kissed me on the forehead, and went down for breakfast with Chiqui and Miguel, after I assured her I'd be okay. I was embarrassed and humiliated, especially after the nice housekeeping lady came to clean up my puke. She had rubber gloves and numerous spray bottles, plastic bags, and even a suction vacuum thingumajig that was supposed to make every trace of nastiness disappear. I was kind of impressed, even though my insides were still doing somersaults. After she was done, she smiled like it was nothing and said, "I hope you are feeling better soon." And I could tell she meant it.

Suddenly, my stomach grumbled. The door clicked open. Maybe it was Mamá with some food. But when I looked over, it was Miguel. "How you feeling, little man? I brought you some lugaw. It's like chicken soup. The chef made it vegetarian especially for you," he said, placing the steaming bowl down on a table.

I sat up. It *did* smell good—garlicky and gingery and earthy. I crawled out of bed and joined Miguel at the table. "Thanks. I am kind of hungry."

He watched me eat the first bite. It didn't even matter that I only had one spoon and one napkin. I was *that* hungry.

"So . . ." he finally said. "What's going on, Pablo? You can tell me, man-to-man."

I felt like I should have been looking him in the eye. But he had on his sunglasses. So I wussed out and just stared at the grains of rice floating in my broth. "Nothing. I must have been carsick or something," I mumbled.

"You sure?"

I peeped at him. Miraculously, his sunglasses were off. His eyes were like magnets. They drew me in. I couldn't look away. "Um. It's just. Well. I'm kind of—"

"Kind of what?" he interrupted.

Then I had that feeling again—the same feeling I'd had at the sanctuary, watching the owls feeding on the mice. A sudden release. Like my chest had burst open. Like my shoulders were lighter. Like my head finally belonged on my body.

Whoosh!

The tidal wave returned, except it was words that were hurling out of my mouth instead of puke.

"I'm scared . . . of the sea . . . Like deathly, end-of-the-world kind of scared."

Miguel frowned, but only for a split second. "Huh. I wasn't expecting that."

I had no idea why I'd decided to finally spill my guts out. Miguel was Mamá's boss. He wasn't my father or an uncle or a best friend. But maybe that was it. Maybe it was easier to talk to someone who wasn't so close.

"Does your mom know?" he asked. I could tell he was thinking by the way he fiddled with his sunglasses.

"No. Nobody knows. I guess, I was too ashamed to tell anyone . . . And now, it just feels like it's too late."

Then it occurred to me. Was he going to snitch? Spill the beans?

"You won't tell her, will you? *Please* . . . I don't want her to think I've been keeping secrets," I said, leaning forward so he could see the urgency on my face.

"But you have been, Pablo."

I looked down at my lap. "I'm sorry."

"Don't be." Miguel bent down really low, searching for my gaze. "Now, I want to know everything. How it started . . . How it makes you feel. Everything."

"I—I don't know how it started. One day it was there. The first time I really felt it was when I was at the aquarium with my father. There was this bat ray touch pool. Just looking at it made me nervous. I didn't want to be near it. The bat rays scared me. Then there was this other time we went on a sunset cruise. I was shaking the minute we stepped on board. My clothes were drenched in sweat. I couldn't look at anything. I just closed my eyes, hoping I wouldn't puke. But I did. My father, he said—" I paused, swallowing back the tears. "He said, '*It's nothing. Pablo's just going through a seasickness phase. He'll get over it.*' Thing is . . . I *never* got over it."

Silence.

I peeped at Miguel.

It seemed like it was taking him forever to reply. But finally he gripped his sunglasses, tapping his other palm on the table like he'd come up with a plan. "Okay. I won't tell her. *But* . . . I want you to promise me something."

I nodded.

"I want you to promise to let me help you. Starting today, we're going to work on it. Work on making it better. No miracles. Just better."

It was my turn for silence. Except my heart was stomping, beating, clawing its way out of my chest. I gasped and coughed. Miguel handed me a glass of water.

Glug. Glug. Glug.

I drank half the glass.

He squeezed my forearm gently. "I'm not going to force you to do anything, Pablo. I just want you to give it a shot. Maybe we can take a short stroll on the beach. And then we go from there. Okay?"

A shot.

Easier said than done. But Miguel was reaching out. He wanted to help.

Maybe I should trust him.

Or at least try.

"Okay." It came out sounding squeaky.

"Good," he replied, handing me his sunglasses. "Let's start with these. They're yours now. You'll see. *Everything* looks better with a pair of shades on."

TWENTY-FIVE

The sunglasses made me look like a total dork. At least that's what I thought. Miguel assured me I looked cool. But it seemed like a bit of a stretch. One thing was for certain, though. When I gazed through the grayish-green lenses, everything became one color, as if I were gazing at faded black-and-white photos. That was a good thing, because it gave me the illusion of being in a dream. And dreams couldn't drown you, or suck you into a current, or serve you up into the jaws of a man-eating shark. Not for real anyway.

As we strolled past the hotel swimming pool, which overlooked the stretch of beach and sea, my stomach tightened and twisted and almost somersaulted. I was okay, for now. But for how long, I wasn't sure. I had a sneaking suspicion the puke was just waiting to hurl upward at the worst possible moment.

Mamá was in the kiddie pool with Chiqui—or to be more specific, *Mamá* was in the pool, and Chiqui was nearby, hiding next to a lounge chair.

"Chiqui, come...I promise it'll be fun. Look... P-O-O-L...WA-TER," she said slowly, splashing the water with an exaggerated happy face. Chiqui shook her head and lifted her neon-green arm floaties to shield her face.

Mamá was getting nowhere.

Sigh.

Her shoulders sagged in defeat.

"Still no luck, huh?" said Miguel.

"Not yet," Mamá replied. "Pablo! Guapito. You look so handsome." She beamed as soon as she saw me. Either that, or it was the sunscreen making her skin all glowy.

She was clearly deluded.

I waved and pushed my chest out in an effort to match my eyewear. I mean, people who wore sunglasses were confident, right? Like movie stars and rock stars and rich people.

Miguel slapped my back. "We're going for a walk. To check out the surfing action."

"On the sand?" Mamá asked with a surprised frown. She knew I had a thing about getting dirt in between my toes.

"Of course on the sand," he said.

I wiggled my toes inside my canvas shoes. Thank goodness I'd packed them.

Splish-splash.

Chiqui had inched to the edge of the pool, the tip of her toes dipping in and out of the water. For a second she gawked at me. I guess she didn't think I looked cool *or* handsome.

"All right. Well, you guys have fun, then!" Mamá blew me a kiss.

I blushed.

Ugh. How embarrassing.

A dude wearing shades shouldn't have his mom blowing kisses at him, right? Luckily, I didn't think anyone noticed.

Inhale. Exhale. Inhale. Exhale.

I was stalling. Delaying the inevitable.

My feet shuffled.

Is it too late to chicken out?

Maybe I should offer to stay and help Mamá?

But I promised to give it a shot.

"C'mon, Pablo," Miguel said.

Mamá waved goodbye, and then she went back to coaxing Chiqui into the kiddie pool.

Oh well, here goes nothing!

I stumbled and caught up with Miguel. He was walking toward the beach, whistling like he didn't have a care in the world. When the pathway ended and the sand began, I closed my eyes.

Be brave, Pablo. It's sand. It's not going to kill you.

My one shoe inched forward, and then my other shoe followed. I sank a couple of inches. It was kind of bothersome. But I was fine. I opened my eyes. Miguel was right there. "C'mon," he said.

We walked on the edge of the beach, with Miguel on the side closest to the water. That way his body would block the majority of the view. It kind of worked. Once in a while, I'd see a silver-blue shimmer, the froth breaking on the shoreline, the curl of a forming wave. But it wasn't enough to freak me out.

Not completely.

It was mostly quiet. I think Miguel knew I had to focus on my feet to keep from getting nauseated. After several minutes, he halted and surveyed the distance. I was afraid to look.

"You'll be fine, Pablo. Just take a quick peek. It's awesome," said Miguel.

My eyeballs twitched. And then my gaze panned from the ground to the horizon. The sea was wild, rising and falling into perfect waves. There were at least half a dozen surfers gliding and flying as if they belonged there, as if they were in total control even though I knew they weren't. It was awesome. But it was also dizzying. I could feel my stomach churning, the puke bubbling and rising.

"I have to sit." I flopped on my butt. I didn't even care that the sand was sticking to the backs of my legs. My head dangled between my knees. I slammed my eyes shut, waiting for the world to stop spinning.

Inhale. Exhale. Repeat.

Miguel's hand rubbed my back. "You're okay. Just breathe," he said softly.

And after a minute I *was* okay. My insides were back to normal and the spinning stopped. I looked over at Miguel. "Thanks."

He smiled. "No problem, little man."

"There you are!" a voice boomed from nearby.

"Sam, you scoundrel. We were just coming to find you," Miguel replied with a chuckle.

The man with the booming voice popped out of nowhere like one of those jack-in-the-box toys. He was sunburned and mustached and dressed in linen pants, a T-shirt, and a paisley scarf, which was draped around his neck. I couldn't quite figure out why someone would wear a scarf on the beach. It was weird. Something about him reminded me of the old French films Mamá liked to watch, the ones with guys who drank too many martinis and charmed too many ladies. He and Miguel did one of those manly kinds of embraces, slamming chests and shoulders and clapping each other's backs. When they pulled apart, the man gestured at me with his thumb and made a corny-looking face. "So, who's this handsome devil you're with, mate?" he said with a thick British accent.

"Sam, this is my buddy Pablo. Pablo, this is Sam, an old friend."

Sam stuck his hand out. I didn't really want to go anywhere near his hairy knuckles but he was a friend of Miguel's, so I shook his hand, not to seem rude. "Um. It's nice to meet you," I muttered.

"Hey. Where's Lucky? I was hoping Pablo could meet him," said Miguel, combing the beach with his eyes.

Sam laughed. "That troublemaker? He went off somewhere. I can't get him out of the water these days." He took a deep breath and then whistled one of those super high-pitched whistles. For a second nobody spoke. But then Sam pointed at the shoreline and said, "There he is!"

I didn't want to look. I didn't want to get all dizzy and nauseated again. But I was curious—curious enough to risk puking. I craned my neck past Miguel's and Sam's legs. At first all I saw was splashing sea-foam. Then something big and yellow burst from a rolling wave. It was a dog. Sam kept on whistling and the dog leaped and ran through the water.

For some reason, even though I was staring straight at the sea, my stomach calmed, my nerves relaxed, my puke retreated. It was a miracle. Lucky sprinted down the beach, sand flying everywhere. With every stride, more and more sand stuck to his fur so by the time he reached us he looked as if he were coated in bread crumbs.

"Hey, boy! Long time no see," said Miguel.

Lucky wagged his tail, bouncing between Sam and Miguel. They both petted him, and then he stopped bouncing all of a sudden.

"Oh no! Duck and cover, mates!" Sam shouted.

I had no idea what he was talking about.

Lucky sneezed, and then he shook so hard, his loose skin slid back and forth. By the time I realized what was going on, it was too late. I was covered in wet sand from head to toe.

Ordinarily I would have been horrified. But something peculiar happened. I laughed. I even giggled. Sam and Miguel were laughing too.

And Lucky, well, he just stood there with the dopiest dog smile I'd ever seen.

TWENTY-SIX

It turned out Lucky was blind. I couldn't believe it. I mean, other than the fact that his eyes were really, really squinty, there was no way to tell. In fact, Sam said he didn't even have any eyeballs! It was a congenital defect—he'd been born like that. Just like Chiqui had been born with her cleft lip.

After brushing off as much of the sand as possible, all I wanted to do was go back to the hotel room, take a hot shower, and decontaminate myself. But Sam had other ideas. He invited us back to his place for a drink, a snack, and a chat. I sort of got swept into the middle, sandwiched between Miguel and Sam with Lucky right behind.

So off we went.

Woof! Woof!

Lucky barked a greeting when we got to Sam's Surf & Turf, which was a surf shop, café, and hostel all in one. It was one of those hip and homey types of places with lots of comfy seating, shelves with books and magazines, and people who hung out, drank coffee, and smiled a lot. Against the walls was a rainbow display of surfboards, and right smack in the middle of the room was a counter with a shiny espresso machine.

Miguel and Sam settled on a sofa and started talking about the "good old days," which to me basically sounded like they were reliving their youth. I couldn't even understand half the conversation. Sam kept on referring to birds, saying stuff like, "Remember that bird from Manchester? The one with the red hair?" and "Nah, mate. Not *that* bird. She was certifiably nutters." It was just plain confusing. Birds didn't have hair, as far as I knew. And what was "certifiably nutters" supposed to mean anyway?

After a while I wandered off. Maybe Lucky would be better company. I found him sitting next to the barista guy. He was completely still, except for his tail, which moved back and forth like a wriggly snake. As soon as the barista saw me, he put his finger to his lips and quietly opened a jar labeled DOG TREATS. Moving in slow motion, he carefully placed the treat on Lucky's nose. I counted five whole seconds before Lucky jerked his head so the treat bounced high into the air.

Chomp.

He caught it with his mouth and then spun around doing a sort of celebratory doggie dance. It was pretty much the most awesome thing I'd ever seen.

"Good job, Lucky! High five!" The barista guy held his hand out; Lucky lifted his paw and slapped it.

"How does he do that?" I asked.

The barista guy chuckled. "Lucky is a superhero in disguise. He even saved a kid from drowning a couple of months ago."

"For real?"

"Yeah, for real. Have a seat. You want a cookie or something?" he asked.

"Okay. Thanks," I said, hopping onto a bar stool. The barista was small and wiry with overgrown hair that was shaved at the sides. His dark skin was covered with a bunch of geometrical tattoos. I couldn't help tracing the shapes, counting the squares, triangles, and circles.

He handed me a plate with a ginormous chocolate chip cookie on it. "I'm Heinz, by the way," he said with a smile.

"Heinz like the ketchup?" I immediately felt stupid. I mean, how many people had probably asked him the same thing?

But he only laughed and made a silly face. "Yes, like the ketchup. It was the only German name my mother could think of. You see, my father was from Germany. I never got to meet him, so I guess my mother wanted me to have some sort of connection. But what I really got was a lifetime comparison to ketchup. It kind of sucks, but I'm used to it," he said.

I took a bite of my cookie. There was this lump in my throat—the same lump of phlegm that materialized every time I thought about my father. Heinz had reminded me I wasn't the only one. At least I'd had my father for seven years. Which I supposed was better than none.

Heinz placed a frosty glass of milk in front of me and then he tossed Lucky another treat. "So, tell me . . . are you a morning person?" he said.

Morning person? Why is he even asking?

"Um. I don't know. Sometimes, I guess."

He leaned on the counter real close, as if he were going to let me in on a secret. "Every day Sam lets me take Lucky out on the beach at sunrise. We run and go swimming when nobody is around. It's nice. Quiet. If you want, I can give you a quick surf lesson."

My body stiffened. I glanced at Miguel, wondering if he'd broken his promise.

Had he told everyone?

Miguel laughed.

Sam laughed.

Were they laughing at me?

But then I realized they were just laughing at themselves, at their corny jokes and ridiculous stories.

Phew.

Stop being so paranoid, Pablo.

"What do you think? You up for it?"

I breathed in and out. I tried to forget about the room and all the people in it. Heinz's tattoos—I focused on them— following the lines and shapes until I felt better. Calmer.

"But why? It's not like you know me or anything," I finally said, fidgeting in my seat.

Heinz punched me on the shoulder lightly. "Lucky told me he liked you. He's an *awesome* judge of character."

Lucky flopped on the ground, showing me his belly. I couldn't help but grin.

All of a sudden, though, I remembered something. "It's just, well, there's one thing . . . I—I can't really swim."

"It's all right, man. The lesson starts on the sand. You don't even need to get wet."

"Oh. Right. Um. I guess I'll think about it . . . I'll see what my mom says," I muttered.

Ugh. That sounded so babyish.

"No worries. We'll be out there tomorrow. Sunrise. If you decide to join us, you know where we'll be," he said, holding his fist out to me.

Miguel appeared. "We better go. Your mom is probably wondering what happened to us."

My hand was numb but somehow I managed to curl it into a limp fist. Heinz bumped his knuckles on mine. It was strange but cool. This guy—this totally amazing surfer dude—didn't think I was weird. At least I didn't think so.

I hopped off the stool and followed Miguel to the door. But before leaving, I turned and said, "I'm Pablo, by the way."

"Like Picasso?" Heinz answered with a grin.

"Yeah, like Picasso."

I was in bed. Dead-tired. I couldn't remember the last time I'd had such a challenging day—challenging yet amazing. Everything hurt and tingled, including my brain, which wouldn't turn itself off. I just kept on thinking about the beach, the sea, the sky, and the surfers. I kept on thinking about Lucky and his superhero powers. I kept on thinking about how patient Miguel had been, and how ridiculous Sam's jokes were, and how Heinz had treated me like any other guy, and how Mamá hadn't touched any of her calming stones, and how Chiqui had eventually gotten into the pool, refusing to get out until she was as wrinkled as a prune. When I was done thinking about all those things, and I finally thought my mind was calm enough to go to sleep, I started thinking about the next morning—about Heinz and Lucky. I so badly wanted to join them.

But what if?

There were always those big, fat what-ifs in the back of my mind.

What if I hurled?

What if I made a fool of myself?

What if I got sunburned?

What if? What if? What if?

I just wanted to smash every single one of those what-ifs into smithereens.

Smash! Smash! Smash!

When I mentioned it to Mamá, she'd said, "*Fantástico, mi amor! It sounds like a wonderful opportunity.*" And then Miguel had to chime in, "*Heinz is the man. You most definitely have to hang with the man!*"

How could I say no to that?

I'm not going to chicken out. I'm not going to chicken out.

"Pabo."

I sat up.

Chiqui was right there gazing at me from the edge of my bed. "Pabo. Mee. Seep," she whispered.

Am I hearing things?

I stared at her all googly-eyed.

"Pabo. Mee. Seep," she repeated.

Chiqui was talking to *me*. Like *really* trying to say something. I couldn't believe it. It was astonishing. Unexpected. Why *me*? Why not Zeus or Ms. Grace or Mamá?

I leaned over and whispered, "What?"

"Pabo. Mee. Seep." She pointed at the pillow next to mine.

Ohhh . . .

Pablo. Me. Sleep was what she was trying to say.

I looked over at the other bed. Mamá was passed out with her mouth slightly open. Chiqui must have crawled out from under the covers undetected.

"Chiqui. Go back to your bed," I said softly.

But she stayed put, blinking her puppy-dog eyes at me. "*Kuya* Pabo. Mee. Seep."

I noticed her emphasis on the *kuya*.

Big brother.

Sigh.

I pulled the covers aside. "Okay. Fine."

She crawled in and settled beside me. It was a little too close for comfort. But to be honest, it didn't bother me that much. I let her situate her body next to mine. Her head was on my pillow. Her warm breath touched my neck every time she exhaled. After a while I could tell she was asleep.

Whoosh!

I felt the breeze come in through the open window. The curtains fluttered and for a second I could see the full moon shining over the sea. The water rippled. All those ripples shimmered. And then finally, I closed my eyes and fell into a deep, deep slumber.

TWENTY-SEVEN

I almost chickened out.

But then, I thought, maybe all I needed was a little moral support. A sidekick to keep me from failing miserably.

Knock. Knock. Knock.

Miguel opened the door to his room. His eyelids were heavy. His face was unshaven. Even then, his hair was still perfect, and his T-shirt and pajama bottoms looked as if they were freshly ironed.

"Hey, Pablo . . . Up at the crack of dawn, huh?" he said groggily.

I stepped closer and gave him my most convincing gaze of desperation. "Will you go with me? To meet Heinz? Please?"

I counted his pearly white teeth, waiting for him to respond.

One. Two.

"Do you even have to ask?" he said with a wink.

The sun had barely risen. There were traces of light painting the horizon. The sea was almost visible.

Thump, thump. Thump, thump.

My heart was beating against my chest.

I put on my sunglasses. Fast. They had become a security blanket of sorts. It felt safer with the world dimmer. Less bright meant less scary.

I wasn't going to puke.

I wasn't going to make a fool of myself.

I wasn't going to run away and hide.

"Check out these coconut trees," said Miguel, tapping the trunk of a tall and spindly tree. "They're really underrated, you know. Like, nobody ever talks about how beautiful they are, because, well, they're not *that* beautiful. But they're strong. Stronger than you can ever imagine, Pablo. There could be a typhoon, a tsunami, an earthquake. Everything around them could be destroyed. But they would survive. Unscathed. As if nothing had happened."

"Huh." I stared at the tree, from its base all the way up to its green coconuts, all the way up to the tips of its leaves. "If I were a tree, that's the tree I'd want to be," I said.

Miguel chuckled. "Me too, little man. Me too."

We didn't say much after that. We didn't need to.

There were some lounge chairs nearby, so we sat and waited. Miguel watched the sky change colors. Even though I didn't want to look out in front of me, once in a while, I would peek, catching flashes of muted color through my sunglasses. It was almost like one of Miguel's tie-dyed shirts. The blues became lighter and lighter toward the water. Hints of purple appeared, and then the sun turned into an orange fireball.

My stomach was queasy.

My neck was stiff.

My arms and legs were prickly.

"Pablo Picasso! You made it!" Heinz strolled toward us with a neon-green surfboard under his arm.

"Morning, Heinz," I replied, trying to sound casual, as if I'd planned on meeting him all along.

Miguel bumped fists with him. "*The man* . . . Nice to see you again, my friend."

Lucky zoomed past us. Then he heard our voices and zoomed right back. He rubbed my legs and licked the tips of my fingers. It was kind of gross. No, actually it was really gross. I had this sudden urge to bathe in hand sanitizer. But

I inhaled and exhaled, and smiled and laughed and tried to not care so much.

"You ready?" said Heinz. He situated the surfboard so it was flat on the sand.

I glanced at Miguel and he gave me a thumbs-up.

Breathe in. Breathe out.

You can do this, Pablo.

I stood and hobbled over. "I guess."

Heinz didn't seem all that fazed by my lack of confidence. He peeled off his T-shirt and swung his arms around. "Let's start with some stretching. Just copy what I do," he instructed.

I watched him touch his toes, bend his legs, stretch to the right, to the left, and reach for the sky. His brown skin gleamed under the morning sunlight. With all his tattoos, he kind of reminded me of an ancient warrior—strong and tough and fearless. For a second it made me feel like a pip-squeak. Like I was this scared little kid without any hope in sight.

But then Heinz grinned and Lucky leaped into the surf like it was nothing and Miguel—he was there. For me. The fear and the insecurities, all the reasons holding me back were just in my head. I didn't have to feel that way. As ridiculous as I might have looked, I went ahead and did exactly what Heinz did. I stumbled. My bones creaked. At one point I got sort of dizzy. I didn't stop, though. Even when Heinz asked me to lie on the gunky surfboard without my shirt on as he instructed me to push off and stand.

"All right. You're getting the hang of it," he said.

Miguel clapped his hands. "You got it, little man!"

I wasn't even in the water. Only sand. But I was triumphant. I was doing something I'd never done before. Something my father would be proud of. I couldn't wait to tell him.

"Pablito!" Mamá popped up out of nowhere. "You're on the beach. On a surfboard!" she added, sniffing and scrunching her face as if she was about to cry.

I froze. I mean, how was I supposed to react when my mother was getting all emotional in front of Heinz, in front of Miguel, in front of *everyone*?

Then I spotted Chiqui. She smiled and waved at me from behind Mamá's leg. Her egg-yolk eyes were back—wet and glossy, almost as if she was proud of me too.

I smiled back. At Chiqui. At Mamá. At Miguel. At Heinz. Even though my cheeks must have been flaming-hot-pepper red, or ripe-tomato red, or whatever the reddest thing you could possibly imagine red.

"It's nothing. Really," I insisted.

Miguel was trying hard not to laugh; I could tell by the way his jaw wiggled. "Carmen. Why don't you go ahead to breakfast while Pablo finishes his lesson?"

"Oh, yes. Good idea," she said, nudging Chiqui away.

But then she turned around on her tiptoes. "I'll get you some waffles. Okay, mi amor?"

"Okay. Whatever. Anything." I nodded and kept on nodding until finally she was gone.

I exhaled.

"*Moms . . .*," Heinz said under his breath.

"Yeah . . . *moms*," I replied.

Miguel threw his hands up and shrugged. "Ugh, *moms . . .*"

All of a sudden, Lucky barked. *Woof! Woof! Woof!* And then he collapsed on the sand, covering his face with one of his paws, like he was agreeing with us.

That's when we stared at one another and lost it. Heinz dropped to his knees and laughed. Miguel was swaying back and forth, clutching his stomach. Lucky ran around and around, kicking up sand while I cracked up so bad my stomach hurt. It wasn't even that funny. But for some reason we got caught up in the moment—a whirlwind—a spinning, dizzying, giggling whirlwind of hilarity. Before I knew it, Lucky had clamped onto my swim trunks with his teeth. He pulled and played with me as if I were an amusing chew toy. I couldn't tell what was going on. What I was supposed to do. Where we were going. I just went along with it, chortling with happy tears rolling down my face. It was all fun and games until I realized my feet were wet. So were my ankles.

I looked down and gasped. The water was four inches deep, and I was in it.

I.

WAS.

IN.

IT.

The sea-foam bubbled and the wet sand crept between my toes.

No!

My sunglasses fell off. I tried to catch them but I was too slow. I reached for them. They floated away farther and farther, until they were just too far. "Heinz! Miguel!" I shouted, pointing at the water.

Miguel squinted in confusion. But Heinz leaped off the sand, sprinting as if he were saving a life, not a plastic accessory. It all happened in slow motion. The puke gurgled inside me.

No! No! No!

I shut my eyes.

You're NOT going to puke, Pablo.

I heard a splash.

I opened my eyes too fast. For a second everything was kind of murky. And then slowly, the water calmed and cleared. Something glimmered—something shiny and pink. Whatever it was disappeared and then reappeared. My hand lunged into the water. Searching. Fishing. Sifting. A wave trickled in. Like magic, the object landed on my palm. It was a dainty little shell—pastel pink with polka dots. It was perfect. I knew it the moment I saw it.

"I got it!" Heinz broke through the water with the sunglasses in his grasp.

"I got you!" said Miguel, grabbing hold of me.

TWENTY-EIGHT

That night, Heinz invited us to a get-together at his house. He said a bunch of his friends and surfer buddies would be there, and of course that included Lucky too. I kind of swelled up inside, fantasizing about being one of Heinz's surfer buddies.

Pablo—the surfer.

But then my cheeks got all warm. I mean, *duh*, I'd only had that one lesson, and *hello*, it was just on the sand.

Pathetic.

When we pulled up to Heinz's place it was dusk. There was this mellow, golden light still shining, as if the fading sun were kissing everything good night.

"Precioso! Isn't it beautiful?" said Mamá as she got out of the car.

I'd never seen anything like it. It was like a bamboo tree house, except it was an actual house with a huge balcony shaped like a wave. Surrounding it was a lush tropical forest. There were even banana trees with green and yellow fruit hanging in clusters. I could hear music and laughter echoing over the treetops.

"C'mon. You guys are going to love it up there," said Miguel, leading the way.

We followed him past a walkway and some stairs, which zigzagged through the foliage, higher and higher. Every now and then, Chiqui would stop, clutch at her flowery dress, and glance back at me with enormous eyes. I could tell she was nervous. Heck, I was nervous too.

"It's going to be okay, Chiqui," I mouthed to her with a thumbs-up.

She nodded and continued on her way. Mamá reached for her hand. Chiqui hesitated. Her arm went limp. And then all of a sudden, she yanked her tiny hand away as if she'd been burned.

I held my breath, wondering if Chiqui was finally going to say something.

It was quiet except for the crickets.

Chirp. Chirp. Chirp.

Miguel was nearby; it seemed his breath was on hold too.

Mamá kneeled in front of Chiqui. Her hand was on her thigh, rubbing an invisible calming stone. After a second that felt like an eternity, she leaned forward and said, "Huwag kang matatakot, Chiqui . . . Aalagaan kita."

My body stiffened. I'd never heard Mamá speak full-on Tagalog like that before. It sounded weird, with her accent and all. Even then, I was impressed. Maybe Ms. Grace had been teaching her. Or maybe Zeus.

I sidled over to Miguel and whispered, "What did she say?"

He blinked and looked down at me. "Don't be afraid, Chiqui. I will take care of you," he said with a crackly voice.

Oh.

My gaze returned to Mamá and Chiqui.

Still, Chiqui didn't utter a single peep.

Yet her pout *had* softened.

Slowly, she reached out and opened her hand. Mamá stood and then curled her fingers with Chiqui's, one by one.

I exhaled.

Phew.

I was relieved. But also, I was feeling something else. Envy. As much as I didn't want to admit it to myself, I was kind of envious that Mamá was making some sort of effort.

Get over it, Pablo. Don't be ridiculous. Chiqui's just a kid.

I inhaled and exhaled and tapped my fingers on my hip. Just a couple of times was good enough. The moment passed.

"Let's go, Pablito," Mamá said from up ahead.

We continued on. Finally, we reached an open-aired entryway with colorful paper lanterns hanging from the ceiling. When we passed that, there was a circular room with lots of floor pillows, low wooden tables, hammocks, and plants tucked into every corner. All sorts of people were lounging around, talking and laughing. Some were still wearing their trunks and swimsuits, some had shorts and T-shirts with rips and holes in them, some were dressier, in linen and cotton pants and shirts and summer dresses. *Everyone* was barefoot.

Wow.

"Hey! Pablo Picasso, Carmen, Miguel, Chiqui . . . Glad you guys could make it!" Heinz appeared from behind a bamboo divider carrying a big platter of grilled seafood. "Just in time for the Boodle Fight. Take off your shoes and come join us on the balcony," he said.

Boodle Fight?

What was he talking about?

I slipped off my canvas shoes and cringed the minute my bare feet touched the uneven bamboo flooring.

Ugh.

Creak. Creak. Creak.

The flooring groaned and squeaked as we walked. Even before we got outside, I could hear Sam's booming voice, "Another toast, mate! Another toast!"

Clink.

They were all clinking beer bottles. "Oy! Grab another beer! No, two beers! Oy, Pablo, you don't drink beer, do you?" said Sam with a wink.

I almost spat out my saliva. "Not that I know of."

There was a whole lot of hugging and fist-bumping and cheek kissing. I didn't even know whose leg or arm or shoulder belonged to whom. Through the chaos, I found Chiqui's eyes. She was hiding behind Mamá's legs, looking scared and overwhelmed. I wanted to go to her. Tell her it was going to be all right. But there were too many people in the way. So I held her gaze. It was just the two of us.

Woof! Woof!

Lucky poked his nose through the crowd, sniffing here, there, and everywhere. He stopped beside Chiqui—*sniff, sniff.* Then he sat down and leaned his head against her chest. For a second she seemed confused. It wasn't for long, though, because as soon as Lucky nuzzled her some more, she relaxed. She raised her tiny hand and stroked Lucky on the head with a sweet smile.

It was true—Lucky *was* a superhero.

"Everyone! Kain tayo! Let's eat!" announced Heinz.

The crowd parted. My breath halted.

What the . . .

I was in complete and utter shock.

There was a long and low table with sixteen floor cushions. There was no tablecloth, no place settings, no napkins, no coasters, no platters, no serving ware. Nothing. Instead, there were huge, shiny green leaves covering the table. Along the center, from one end to the other, there were mounds of food plopped directly onto the leaves—grilled meat and seafood, tomato, onion and eggplant salad, sautéed greens, boiled eggs, red and white rice, watermelon and mango slices, and little coconut bowls filled with condiments and water. I didn't see a plate or a fork or a spoon or a knife in sight.

How am I supposed to eat?

People settled onto the floor cushions, and then they dipped their hands in water before helping themselves to the food. *With. Their. Hands.* The only ones left standing were Mamá, Chiqui, and me.

Chiqui was mesmerized. She had this look of recognition in her eyes, as if what she was seeing were something familiar.

Mamá was glancing at me and the table—back and forth, with her mouth open.

I just stood there feeling helpless. Every part of me felt simultaneously itchy and numb, which I wasn't sure was even possible.

"Chiqui, why don't you go ahead and start eating?" Mamá said, pointing at the food. She ushered Chiqui to a seat next to Miguel. Almost immediately, she began grabbing pieces of food, slurping on a shrimp, smooshing rice between her fingers and shoveling it into her mouth.

It was like second nature to her. She didn't seem to care one bit that there were no utensils or glasses or plates, and that *everyone* was touching one another's food.

Mamá went over to Heinz and whispered in his ear. I knew more or less what she was saying.

"I'm sorry to bother you, Heinz. It's just that Pablo . . . He cannot eat this way."

I closed my eyes. I couldn't watch them. I couldn't watch any of it.

"Hey, Pablo Picasso."

I peered through my eyelids. Heinz was in front of me with his usual dude-like grin. Mamá, on the other hand, was pale; she was squeezing her hands, searching for her calming stones again.

"Do you want to go back to the hotel, mi amor?" she asked.

"No," I blurted out.

She reached for my arm. "I can go with you . . . It's okay."

"No." I stepped back.

I didn't want to leave.

I didn't want to be the weirdo kid anymore.

What I wanted was to be Pablo—the surfer.

Miraculously, Heinz was still grinning. "Carmen, why don't you go ahead and sit? I'll bring Pablo to the kitchen."

She hesitated, bouncing from foot to foot. "Pablito, are you sure?" she finally said.

I nodded.

"All right. I'll be out here if you need me," she said, walking away.

When she was gone, Heinz slapped my back as if nothing had happened. "Come, I just cooked up some monggo. I think you'll like it."

I was still numb and itchy, but I trailed behind him anyway, feeling kind of like a ghost. Like I didn't exist.

Pablo—the ghost.

The kitchen was small and simple, with its concrete counters, metal sink, two-burner stove, and wooden shelves. There was a table by the wall with two chairs. I somehow got my butt into one of them. Heinz grabbed a bowl, the entire cutlery tray, and a pile of napkins and placed them in front of me. He took a pot from the stove and then proceeded to ladle some sort of lentil soup into the bowl. After he put the pot away, he sat on the other chair.

"That's monggo. My mother's recipe," he said, pointing at the soup. "Usually, there's meat or seafood in it. But my mom likes it pure. Only veggies."

"Thanks." I took a spoon from the tray and scooped a

169

bite into my mouth. "Mmm. It's good," I said after swallowing.

"Of course it's good!"

I looked at Heinz, feeling kind of awkward still. My cheeks turned hot just thinking about it. "You can go back to the party. I—I can eat by myself . . . I don't mind," I mumbled.

"Nah. Don't worry about it. I see those people all the time," he replied.

I smiled at him, and then took another spoon so I could keep on eating.

Heinz leaned back on his chair all casual-like. "So, Pablo Picasso. Are you going to come back to Baler and surf with me sometime?"

"Um. I hope so."

"Good. Make sure you bring home a souvenir to remember us by. Sam has some awesome stuff at the café," he said.

That reminded me.

I stuck my hand inside my pocket and pulled out the pink shell. "I found this on the beach today. I was thinking of giving it to . . . a friend."

"Ahh." Heinz inspected it with a glint in his eye. "A friend, huh? Does she have a name?"

I coughed.

Busted.

"Happy. She's my neighbor."

Suddenly, Heinz jumped off his seat as if a firecracker had been lit underneath it. "Wait!"

He disappeared. A couple of seconds later he was back with a piece of gold twine and a small cordless drill.

"May I?" He reached for the shell in my hand.

I had no clue what he was up to, but Heinz was a cool dude. I trusted him.

"Here," I said, handing it over.

He went to the counter and put the shell on a wooden chopping board.

Reer. Reer. Reer. Reer.

The drill was super noisy. I covered my ears. Then it was quiet again. Heinz fiddled with the gold twine—pulling, tying, knotting.

He sat back down and held up the finished product. "For Happy," he said with a twinkle in his eye.

It was perfect.

TWENTY-NINE

The beach trip was like one of those unbelievably beautiful postcards. Somehow, those postcards always made the places look way better than they really were. But in my case, it really *was* that beautiful.

It seemed impossible that I had experienced any of it.

Finally, things were changing. I had some real memories. The kind I could talk about when I was a grumpy old man. I'd tell my grandkids about them and they would ask me a million and one questions. Eventually they would tire of all my stories and roll their eyes and pretend to listen.

I was contemplating those imaginary grandkids when we arrived home—to the same old, boring house. For some reason, all I felt was disappointment. Three days ago you couldn't get me anywhere near a beach. And now it was all I could think about. Maybe I did have a bit of my father's DNA somewhere inside me.

I unpacked, which took longer than expected. The dirty clothes went in the hamper, and the clean ones back in the closet. Then there were the toiletries—every item had to go back to its respective place. After that, there was the sweeping of sand that had managed to stow away in my bag. When I was done, it was as if I hadn't gone away at all. Not a speck of evidence was left. There was nothing left to do. I sat on my bed tracing the plaids on my blanket, wishing the lines could lead me back to Baler. To Sam's corny jokes and Heinz's easygoing smile and Lucky's crazy dog zooming. I even missed the kind housekeeping lady and her impressive array of cleaning supplies.

I sighed and spotted my laptop. Maybe I'd feel better after talking to my father. Maybe he'd finally be interested in what I had to say. Maybe he'd invite me to spend some time with him on one of his expeditions. Maybe. Maybe. Maybe. There were just too many maybes that needed answering.

I flung myself at my desk. My hands were kind of shaky. But eventually I managed to turn my laptop on. If he was still somewhere in South Africa, it would be after lunchtime, at least according to Google. I stared at the video-chat icon with my finger hovering over the touch pad.

Just press it, Pablo. Quit being such a scaredy-cat.

So I did.

Ding. He was online.

Ding ding. Ding ding.

"Well, *hey* there..." My father was even tanner than the last time. His blond hair and chest were wet like he'd just gotten out of the water.

"Um. Hi. Hi, Dad."

"How's it hanging, Pablo? I wasn't expecting you to call. But it's good, man. It's nice to see you," he said, flinging his head from side to side.

Beads of water must have hit the camera, because all of a sudden my father looked kind of warped and blobby.

I took a deep breath. "So I went on a trip to Baler. It's a beach, a really nice one, and I met a surfer, Heinz. He even gave me a lesson, and there was this dog, he was blind but so awesome, he could swim and everything, and there was this guy—"

"Whoa. Whoa. Whoa. Slow down," my father said.

I gulped. "Sorry."

"This guy you mentioned. Who is he? Your mom's new *boyfriend*?"

Even through the blobby image on the screen, I could tell my father was tensing his jaw like he was bothered by the idea of another man. Maybe he had some sort of amnesia. Had he forgotten that *he* was the one who left Mamá? Who left me?

"No. There's no guy. What I meant to say was Miguel; he's just Mamá's boss. It's nothing like that," I mumbled.

He snickered. "Fraternizing with the boss, huh? Well, that's convenient."

I knew what he was implying. But I couldn't believe it. My head and the back of my neck, my gut, were so hot it felt like my insides were going to burn through my skin.

"I've got to go now," I said, staring at the keyboard.

"Yeah, sure. Nice talking to you, kid . . . Keep a lookout for the UPS guy. I'm going to send you that shark tooth first chance I get."

I nodded, glancing at his blobby image one more time before pressing the "End" button.

Ding.

He was gone.

My room was swaying back and forth. I itched; it felt like I'd break out in hives at any moment. The lights were too bright, blinding almost. And the lines and patterns and shapes and shadows were jumping out at me, trying to pull me in. I couldn't breathe.

I searched for something, anything to make the swaying and brightness go away. Then I saw my sunglasses on the nightstand, the ones Miguel had given me. I stumbled toward them, trembling as I put them on. The room, the lights, the shadows, the lines, the patterns, and the shapes— they dimmed.

Breathe. Breathe. Breathe.

I needed more air. I needed something else. Something more. But I wasn't quite sure what that something was.

I sat outside on the front steps, head hunched with my sunglasses still on. It was late, so the usual noises were hushed. Once in a while I'd hear the sputtering of a tricycle or a barking dog. Even the massive narra trees above me were quiet, as if they were too tired to ruffle their leaves and creak their branches. They weren't the only ones. I was tired, but for completely different reasons. I was tired of trying to please my father. I was tired of moving around so much. I was tired of having no real friends. I was tired of all my fears and worries. I was tired of being abnormal.

And most of all, I was tired of being me.

Twelve years seemed like an awfully short time to be alive and still be so exhausted. I mean, assuming I'd even make it to the ripe old age of ninety-two, how could I possibly last eighty more years? Just the thought of it made my head want to explode.

There was a noise from across the street. A rusty gate opened and closed. Footsteps. And then a lightbulb flickered. Happy tiptoed toward me with a pair of squishy green rain boots. The closer she got, the more I noticed how big they were. So big she kind of looked like a circus clown.

She stopped right in front of me and made a funny face. "*Why* are you wearing those?" she said, pointing at my eye-wear. "They make you look suspicious."

"I thought they made me look cool."

She twisted her features into an even funnier face. "Hmm . . . Not so much," she said, plopping down on a nearby step.

Well. At least she was being honest. I took the sunglasses off and hung them on the collar of my T-shirt. She must have caught me eyeing her boots because she proceeded to stomp them on the ground. "I know. They're big and I look like a duck."

"More like a clown."

Happy slapped my leg. "They're my dad's boots. I couldn't find my slippers in the dark."

And then it was quiet for a second.

"So . . . how was the beach?"

I jerked forward like a car switching gears too fast. I wanted to tell her about Heinz and Lucky and Sam and the sunrise and the sea and the surfing. But then I slammed on the brakes. I didn't want to brag or anything. "It was okay. Kind of fun, I guess."

She raised her eyebrow. "Then why the sad face? I mean, I've been practicing my jealous look for days now."

"It's just . . ." I slumped down.

"It's just what?"

"It's just . . . a lot of stuff. I wouldn't even know where to begin," I said with a sigh.

Happy scooted closer. "I know I may talk a lot, but I'm a good listener too. So try me."

My insides knotted and unknotted and knotted and unknotted, and all of a sudden, words started flying out of my mouth again.

"It's just . . . I've always felt I was strange. Like I was different from all the other kids. I was always worried about something, scared of something. Things only got worse when my mom and dad split up, when we started moving around . . . There are days when I feel okay. Sort of . . . Then there are days where *everything* is wrong, *everything* bothers me. Germs. Dirt. Messes. Crowds. I can't stop obsessing. I can't stop it from messing with my head. And it doesn't help that I don't have any real friends. Friends who I can talk to. Friends who get it. Friends who will like me no matter what."

By the time I was done spilling my guts, there were tears in my eyes. I grabbed my sunglasses and put them back on. At the very least, I could save myself from further humiliation.

"I'm sorry," Happy said with a frown.

I didn't say anything at first. It felt like I'd run out of words. Like everything inside me—all my emotions—had been emptied out all at once.

But then her frown disappeared and her eyes sparkled. "Well, now you've got at least one friend . . . It's a start."

I nodded. But what I really wanted to do was give her a great big hug.

Happy glanced at her house. "I better go before anyone notices." She stood and moved slowly as if she didn't really want to leave, but had to.

And then I remembered something.

"Wait. Hold on." I snuck inside the house and shuffled down the hallway until I was in my room. When I found what I was looking for, I snuck back outside. Happy was waiting patiently by the curb.

"Here," I said, handing her my gift.

She took the pink shell that Heinz had turned into a necklace. "My pasalubong. It's perfect," she said with a dimpled smile.

I fidgeted in place, hoping it wasn't bright enough for her to see me blush. "You were right. I saw it, and . . . well, it made me think of you."

Happy held the shell with the tips of her fingers. Her eyes drifted closed. She brought it to her face and inhaled deep. I watched and waited, hearing nothing except my heartbeat. Then she fluttered her eyes and threw her arms around me. I gasped. Her cheek brushed against mine.

"Thank you for bringing me the sea," she whispered.

THIRTY

The next morning, I was in an unusually good mood. It felt like I'd slept on a cloud, like I was walking on marshmallows, like my fingers and toes were light as feathers. When I got to the kitchen, Mamá was already dressed in khaki shorts and one of her work shirts. She was slicing bananas ninja-fast. "Oh good. You're awake," she said, looking up at me.

I served myself some oatmeal before taking my seat. Chiqui grinned and handed me her spoon. I wasn't quite sure why, but when I saw my place setting I noticed Mamá had forgotten about all my spoons, or maybe she hadn't. Maybe she'd done it on purpose.

But Chiqui knew. She knew I could use an extra spoon—*her* spoon.

If she were tall enough, I was sure she would have reached up on the shelf and grabbed me eight more. All this time she'd been watching and learning and absorbing all these little details about us—about *me*.

Mamá gulped her orange juice and then took a deep breath. "Grace is running a bit late. But I can't stay. They're delivering a pair of Philippine eagles and I have to prepare their enclosure. Come by any time in the afternoon if you want to check it out... Invite Happy if you want."

"Thanks, I will."

"See you later," she said, kissing me on the forehead. "Oh, and Chiqui, please try and finish your bananas this time, okay? BA-NA-NAS...SA-GING." Mamá pointed at the sliced fruit in the bowl, staring at Chiqui with I-mean-business kind of eyes. "SA-GING...BA-NA-NAS," she repeated.

"What's sagging?" I asked.

Mamá sighed. "Nothing is sagging, Pablo... Saging is 'banana' in Tagalog."

"Oh." I slid down in my seat.

How was I supposed to know what saging was?

"Okay. I'm really going now." Mamá pointed at the bananas one more time and then she scrambled away.

All Chiqui did was scowl.

I could hear the door opening and closing.

I could hear the *cring-cring-cring*ing of Mamá's bicycle.

As soon as she was gone, Chiqui plucked the sliced

bananas from her oatmeal and dropped them on her napkin with an icky face. Clearly, Mamá's plea in English *and* Tagalog was a total fail.

"Yuck," I said, pointing at the offensive fruit bits. "Superduper yuck. Right?"

She giggled and made an even ickier face. "Saging. Yack. Yack. Yack."

I chuckled. "So . . . Chiqui." She stopped eating and listened. "How come you don't talk to anyone but me, huh?"

It was silent for a minute, maybe longer. Her eyes narrowed. Her lips twitched. Her head tilted to the side.

I guess she didn't quite get what I was saying.

Then it hit me.

Chiqui knew what I needed.

But I knew what she needed too.

"Chiqui," I said, leaning toward her. She gazed at me with an open mouth. "At night when Mamá falls asleep . . ." I laid my head on the back of my hand, closed my eyes, and snored. "You come to my room." I pointed at my bedroom door. "And I'll teach you, so you can understand. Okay?"

She nodded.

Had she understood? Maybe she had. Maybe she hadn't. Either way, I felt like it was my responsibility to help her.

But could I?

I was just a kid.

Not even a normal one at that.

We were at the eagle enclosure. Ms. Grace, Chiqui, Happy, and I watched from the outside. Inside were Mamá, Frannie, and a really short Filipino guy dressed like he was going on safari. Besides his weird khaki-colored ensemble, he also had on a thick leather glove on one hand, which made him kind of lopsided. It bothered me, of course. But I tried to focus on what was going on with the eagles rather than how awkward he looked. Supposedly, he was from the Philippine Eagle Foundation—a group protecting the endangered bird species.

There were two large carriers situated on tree stumps. Safari Guy opened the door of one of them and stuck his gloved hand inside. After a second or two, he pulled it out, and on it stood a ginormous bird. Its talons were practically the size of my hands. Strangely, it had a brown hood over its head and eyes so it couldn't see us. He brought the eagle to a nearby tree branch. It hopped off his arm, ruffling its brown-and-white feathers. Then he fetched the other bird, who was even more ginormous, and brought it to the same branch. He shushed everyone with his finger.

Slowly, really, really slowly, he removed their hoods.

At first the eagles seemed kind of dazed. But the confusion didn't last very long. One bird raised its crest feathers, and then the other did the same. The two of them resembled medieval knights with punk-rock hairdos. For some reason, they made me nervous—the way they glared and stared at me as if I'd done something wrong.

After a few minutes they backed out of the enclosure one by one. Safari Guy sidled over to us and whispered, "Mayari and Tala were confiscated from an illegal zoo in the province. We hope to release them after some months of rehabilitation. But we must be very careful because the last eagle we released from captivity was shot soon after. We never caught Pamana's killer."

We all gasped.

"Oh yes. I remember hearing about Pamana on the news a couple of years ago. Kawawa naman . . . Poor thing. She was a beautiful bird," said Ms. Grace.

Frannie was angry all of a sudden. Her neck, shoulder, and arm muscles rippled and bulged. "Man. If I could only get my hands on that guy, he'd be sorry, *real* sorry," she growled. Even though she didn't have on her freaky owl costume, she was still kind of scary. It didn't help that she was standing next to Safari Guy, which made her seem even huger than she already was.

Happy looked at me and I looked at her. She had this

expression that screamed, *I'm scared out of my wits*, and I must have had the same one. We kept on staring at each other, twisting our faces more and more until we cracked up. Safari Guy glared at us just as the eagles had. Maybe he'd been around them for too long. Maybe he was turning into zombie-man-eagle. We laughed even more, stumbling around like a couple of fools. Mamá shooed us away with her hands. Neither of us could stop no matter how hard we tried. So we half-ran half-walked until we were far enough not to be heard.

"I thought he was going to bite my head off," said Happy in a hushed voice.

"*Impossible*. Not with Frannie around."

She giggled and then punched the air with her fists. "*If I could only get my hands on that guy, he'd be sorry, real sorry.*" Her impression was actually pretty good, except it was kind of difficult getting past her head-to-toe sparkles—sparkly headband, sparkly pink shirt, sparkly leggings, and sparkly sandals embellished with sparkly rhinestones. I was almost blinded by her sparkly-ness.

Finally, we'd run out of laughter. It was mostly quiet except for all the birds chirping. We strolled. After a while we found ourselves back at the muddy puddles where the kalabaws lazed. It was bizarre how they enjoyed wallowing in the dark and sticky muck. But it was obvious they did. Everything about them was relaxed—from their sunken backs to their floppy ears, to their eyes with super-long lashes. They even managed to ignore the pesky black flies buzzing around them. That alone was a most formidable feat.

Suddenly, I got this feeling someone was staring. It turned out Happy wasn't at all interested in the water buffalos. Her eyes were on me. "Your face," she said, waving her hands. "You should see it. Really, you should . . . It looks like you're constipated," she said with a giggle.

Constipated?

I had no idea what she was talking about. But then I touched my face with my fingers. It was all scrunched up. It was the same icky look Chiqui had made at the bananas. "I can't help it," I said with a shrug.

"I think you can. And I think we need to work on it."

"Work on it? Like a science project?"

Happy rolled her eyes. "No, nothing like *that*. I mean, obviously this is part of you, Pablo. It's not something you can change overnight. But I think there's room for improvement. Maybe you just need to get out more? See things you're not used to seeing. You know what I mean?"

"Didn't I just come back from the beach?"

"Well, yes, but what about the everyday kind of getting

out? Like taking the tricycle to the palengke. I bet you've never even *been* to the palengke," she said, leaning forward as if to challenge me.

"The palengke?"

"See? You don't even know what it is."

"Well, why don't you show me, then?" I said, stepping forward as if to accept her challenge.

"I will."

"Good."

"It's a date."

THIRTY-ONE

I wasn't expecting Chiqui to show. But I stayed up anyway, browsing Google and YouTube for lesson plans on basic conversational English.

Ding.

My father was online.

I quit the video chat program and went back to browsing. I didn't want to see him or talk to him. I didn't even want to think about him. I was *that* mad. Then I heard something. My door creaked open and Chiqui's head popped through. Her hair was puffed in different directions, as if she'd been tossing and turning on her pillow.

She tiptoed inside. In her grasp she held a small plate of cookies. It was obvious she'd raided the pantry. There were Oreos, digestive biscuits, and Mamá's favorite Marie cookies for dunking in tea and coffee. With her messed-up hair and crumpled pajamas, she was definitely giving Cookie Monster a run for his money—or rather a run for his cookies.

Chiqui must have gotten the gist of what I'd said after all.

Good thing Mamá was a heavy sleeper.

"Come, Chiqui. I've got some stuff for you to watch," I said, tapping my desk.

She traipsed across the room and hopped on the chair. "Kuya Pabo. Kuya Pabo." Her hand danced in the air, moving like a talking mouth. It was actually pretty adorable.

I laughed. "Yes. Pablo and Chiqui are going to talk a whole lot. But first I want you to pay attention. Okay?"

I clicked play on a YouTube video titled *Speak Cartoon, Learn English for Kids*. It was pretty silly. The cartoon voices sounded like chipmunks. But Chiqui seemed to like it. She sat still except for her legs, which swung back and forth. Her hand reached for a cookie every so often.

Munch. Crunch. Munch. Munch.

I supervised from the bed. But in reality, I was doing more thinking than supervising. I thought about Chiqui and her talking and not talking. Part of me wished Mamá and everyone else could see her laugh and hear her jibber-jabbering. But the other part of me was happy to have her all to myself. It felt special somehow—to know that she trusted *me*, she had picked *me* to open up to. Besides that, I also thought about what Happy had said, about getting out more and seeing things I wouldn't ordinarily want to see. I thought about the last five years—all the countries we'd moved to and from, all the people I'd met and hadn't met, all the stuff I'd done and hadn't done. When it came down to it, there wasn't much there. My memories were mostly of the different homes we'd had, and the different teachers. But that was it.

Happy was right.

Until the last few weeks I'd hardly been living.

"Kuya." I flinched with so much force, the bed bounced. The YouTube video had finished, and Chiqui was standing there staring at me. "Hewo. I, Tintin," she said, reaching out to shake my hand.

Tintin?

I kind of frowned. And then Chiqui slapped her mouth with her hand.

"Is that your real name . . . Tintin?" I pointed my finger at her chest.

For a second she glanced down at her lap. And then slowly, she found my eyes with hers. There was fear in them. She nodded apprehensively.

I tried to smile in an effort to put her at ease. "Hello, Tintin. It's nice to meet you. I'm Pablo," I said, sticking my hand out.

She stepped back and shook her head. "Hindi! Hindi! Chiqui. I, Chiqui . . . I, Chiqui."

I dropped my hand, confused. Why wouldn't she want me to call her by her real name? Was she scared of her past? Did she want a fresh start? I opened my mouth, but I didn't know what to say. I was stupefied. All I could do was keep on watching her shake her head until tears dropped from her eyes.

"I, Chiqui," she repeated over and over again.

I had no idea why she was getting so upset.

Do something, Pablo!

I glanced around the room in desperation. My bed. My bookshelves. My dresser. My windows. My computer . . . my computer!

A-ha!

I crawled over to it and jabbed my fingers at the keyboard. The Google translate box appeared. I selected "English" to "Tagalog," and typed, "I . . . will . . . keep . . . your . . . secret."

There it was.

Success!

I grabbed a piece of paper and jotted down exactly what it said. And then I flung myself from my desk and kneeled in front of Chiqui. She was still bawling. My eyes skimmed the piece of paper a couple of times. When I had it down pat, I opened my mouth again. But this time, I had something to say.

"I-ta-ta-go . . . ko . . . ang . . . i-yong . . . li-him, Chiqui," I said.

The Tagalog words felt strange on my tongue, as if I'd just eaten some unfamiliar food and I couldn't figure out if it was good or not.

Sniff. Sniff.

Chiqui tried to breathe through her stuffed-up nose. She heaved, then wiped her eyes with the back of her hand.

"Itatago . . . ko . . . ang . . . iyong . . . lihim, Chiqui," I repeated.

"I, Chiqui," she murmured.

I nodded. "Yes, you're Chiqui."

She wiped her eyes again. Little by little, her feet inched toward me. When she was close enough, she stuck her hand out again and said, "Hewo, I, Chiqui." This time, she said it louder and clearer. With conviction.

I reached out and held her hand, even though it was wet with tears and snot and god knows what else. "Hello, Chiqui. It's nice to meet you. I'm Pablo."

And for some strange reason it felt like a pact.

She would keep my secrets.

I would keep hers.

THIRTY-TWO

We were outside readying ourselves for our daily stroll to the sanctuary, when Happy suggested we go to the palengke instead. Ms. Grace was immediately smitten with the idea. Her face lit up and she got all excited, as if we were taking a trip to Paris. "Excellent idea, Happy! We can go on a cultural food tour and have merienda," she exclaimed.

I didn't really get what the big deal was. The palengke was a market. So what?

"We're going to have to take two tricycles to get there. We can't fit the four of us in one," said Ms. Grace. She leaned into the road and stuck her hand out. Almost immediately, two tricycles pulled over and stopped.

I took a step back and shook my head. "Um. I don't think so. There aren't even any seat belts."

"Come on, Pablo. It's going to be fun. I promise," said Happy.

Why was I the only one worried about this? The tricycles were basically rusty sardine cans with wheels. On one side was a motorcycle and driver, and on the other, a decrepit-looking sidecar barely big enough for two people. Instead of doors, there were filthy pieces of plastic. And the seat was a piece of plywood covered in moldy and torn vinyl. The two guys driving had on basketball shorts and flip-flops. Not a helmet in sight.

Ms. Grace led Chiqui toward the first tricycle. "Tara, Chiqui," she said, motioning for her to get in. For a moment Chiqui paused and glanced at me; her expression was pinched with worry. She was tense. She was suspicious. She was unsure if I *really* was going to keep her secret. But as soon as she saw that my lips were sealed tight, she relaxed and ducked into the sidecar.

I must have still had a look of dread on my face, because Ms. Grace stared at me with her signature head tilt. "You know, Pablo, when I was your age, I used to take tricycles to school every day. Sure, they're a bit . . . well, unconventional. But it's just part of life here in the Philippines."

That's when Ms. Grace and Happy got into their respective sidecars. I was the only one left on the sidewalk. The tricycle guys looked up from their cell phones long enough to give me a curious sort of glance. I wondered if they thought I was a weirdo, which was bizarre, since clearly they were the weird ones.

I wanted to throw my hands up in the air and say something cool and casual like, *Why not? You only live once, right?* But truthfully, I had no words. There was this scratchy lump in my throat. My limbs were limp. Not to mention the itching, which started at the tips of my toes and spread so that even the insides of my ears felt like they were covered in mosquito bites.

"Pablo?" Happy popped her head out.

I breathed deep, but not *too* deep, because it stank of diesel exhaust. "Okay, I'm coming."

Happy's eyes almost disappeared, that's how big her smile was. She scooched to the outer seat and pulled her legs in so I could pass. "Get in. You'll feel safer on the inside seat," she said.

I didn't want to touch anything, so I kind of just shimmied through the tarp into the sardine can. Thank goodness I'd worn long pants instead of shorts, otherwise my calves would have rubbed against the dirt and rust and germs from thousands and thousands of passengers. Happy slid closer to me. Then I heard Ms. Grace shout, "Kuya, sa palengke tayo. Salamat."

My head nearly slammed on the metal awning as we lurched forward. Chiqui squealed and giggled from the other tricycle.

"You better hold on!" said Happy as she gripped a rubber handle that was hanging nearby. But I had no such handle, and even if I did, I wouldn't want to hold on to it anyway.

The tricycle zoomed over so many potholes I lost count. My butt bounced off the seat, landing hard every single time. "Ugh," I grunted. It felt like my bones had disconnected and reconnected in the wrong order. Happy laughed. There was another bump and our limbs smashed together. Her cheek pressed against my chest. All of a sudden, it got really stuffy.

"Sorry," she said as she straightened herself out.

I didn't mind, actually. The smell of strawberries from her hair somehow made the rusty sardine can more bearable.

Screeeeeech. The brakes were deafening. The fumes were making me choke. But at least we weren't moving anymore.

Happy elbowed me. "We're here!"

"Finally," I replied under my breath.

As soon as Happy got out, I practically dived from the rusty sardine can/deathtrap. For a second I checked the different parts of my body to make sure nothing was broken. Thankfully, I was intact. Then I looked around.

Big mistake.

I wanted to dive back into the rusty sardine can/deathtrap.

Except it had already gone.

The market was huge and crowded and dirty and every-thing that a market *wasn't* supposed to be. There were black flies so big I could have thrown a collar and a leash on one and walked it like a dog. And there were actual dogs and cats—skinny, mangy ones. I looked at the rows and rows of animal carcasses and meat parts hanging from metal hooks.

I would have cried, but I was too shocked.

"No. No. *No.* I'm not going in there," I said.

Happy glared at me with her hands on her hips. "But we're already here, Pablo. Just give it a chance."

Ms. Grace was already walking away, pulling Chiqui's hand. "Come on. It's better on the other side where the eat-eries are. You'll see."

I'll see? What was she talking about?

By the time I'd recovered from the shock, Ms. Grace, Chiqui, and Happy were already ahead of me. Even from behind, I could tell Chiqui's legs were too stiff, as if she was hesitating with every step. She was nervous. There were peo-ple all around, cutting ahead, falling behind, zigzagging from side to side. Thankfully, though, nobody seemed to notice her or her cleft lip. They were too preoccupied checking out all the wares and haggling. After a minute or so, her strides loosened up. She looked over her shoulder and smiled at me.

Whew.

I chased after them, skipping over bloody puddles and piles of fish guts. I was grateful for the sneakers I'd decided to wear that day. Just the thought of wearing flip-flops gave me the heebie-jeebies. At least we'd left the bloody scene of the crime behind and hit the fruit and vegetable section, which was much more like a market *should* be. There were loads of things I'd never seen or even heard of. Ms. Grace would stop every so often and point stuff out.

"These are mangosteen. They're sour and sweet and taste like heaven," she said, buying a dozen of the dark purple fruit.

"Oh, and these are the famous durian. To some, they smell and taste like perfume, but to others they stink like sewers. Go on and give it a whiff!" The vendor lady held out a piece of the cut-open fruit. Even from a distance, there was already a hint of something rotten. I covered my nose with my T-shirt, causing Chiqui to break out in a fit of giggles.

After we passed the fresh produce section, we arrived at a wide-open area with lots of stalls and communal seating. There was a sign that read KAINAN SA PALENGKE, which Ms. Grace translated as "Market Eatery."

"Yumm . . . barbecue!" Happy dragged me to the nearest stall. My eyes went wider than wide—I didn't even recognize half of what was on those little wooden sticks. Ms. Grace poked her head between our shoulders, browsing the nasty tidbits. "Adidas, Helmet, and Betamax. As you can see, Filipinos have a strange sense of humor." She chuckled.

Adidas? Helmet? Betamax? What was she talking about?

Happy laughed so hard, her ponytail swished from side to side. "Adidas are barbecued chicken feet," she said, pointing at the charred feet on sticks. "Helmet are chicken heads, and Betamax are chicken blood cakes. So which one are you going to try?"

I glared at her. "I'm vegetarian."

She frowned. "Oh. Well, then maybe you'll like the fish balls. *Everybody* likes fish balls."

I backed away from the stall. "Fish aren't vegetables."

"Come, Pablo. I know what you can have," Ms. Grace said with a sympathetic smile.

I reluctantly followed her. Happy was chomping on a stick of god-only-knows-what. Every few steps, the sauce dripped on the floor. I desperately wanted to call her attention to it. But I guess nobody really cared about messes in such a place. Besides, I didn't want to make a bigger stink than I already had.

Ms. Grace stopped at Manang Rose's Bakery stall. There was a display of desserts—little cakes with grated cheese on top, all sorts of buns and squares, some purple, some yellow and white, sticky ones coated in coconut and crunchy ones with caramelized sugar.

"Here. Try this." She handed me what looked like a crunchy egg roll, except it had a hard melted-sugar coating and sesame seeds sprinkled on top.

"What is it?" I asked.

"Turon."

"Turon?" I repeated suspiciously.

"Just trust me."

I glanced at Happy, who gave me the thumbs-up. And then at Chiqui, who was busy munching on her own piece of turon. Whatever it was, she seemed to like it.

You can do it, Pablo. It's only a pastry. It's not going to kill you.

The tips of my fingers were sticking to the sugar and grease.

Ignore it. Ignore it. Ignore it.

My head and chest leaned forward, and my hips and legs leaned back. It was my way of protecting my clean clothes from messes.

Crunch.

I took a bite, and a flurry of crumbs dropped like snowflakes.

Munch. Munch. Munch.

Swallow.

Everyone watched me, and it seemed as if their breaths were on pause.

"Well?" Happy finally asked.

"It's good!"

THIRTY-THREE

I glanced at my alarm clock: 10:37 P.M.

Ugh.

I was tired. More like comatose, really. But it was time for *Speak Cartoon, Learn English for Kids, Episode Two.*

Chiqui was sitting at my desk staring at the computer. She barely moved. It was almost like she was a sponge dressed in a striped pajama dress. If I looked hard enough, I could see the bubbles of knowledge drifting from the screen into her brain. Every once in a while she'd jam a fistful of seaweed snacks into her mouth. There were bits and pieces scattered on her dress, on the desk, on the chair, on the floor. At first I felt the telltale prickles. I twitched. The urge to clean up the mess nagged me. I imagined all those little pieces getting lodged into crevices, getting lost underneath the furniture, getting sucked into vents and holes, getting stuck on every surface in the room.

But then she would repeat a phrase from the video, something like, "I aym hungray. My I peas hab somtin to ayt?" And all of a sudden I'd forget about the prickles and twitches and crevices and holes and surfaces.

It was weird. I hadn't felt that way since we lived in California, when my parents were together and life still seemed somewhat normal. Things were calmer. Even though the twitches had always been around. In those days they were easier to ignore.

"Tenk yo. Eeet wus dewaysus!" Chiqui said to the screen.

I grinned. The prickles returned. But they were warm and fuzzy and not at all unpleasant. The video ended, and she hopped off the chair, holding the last piece of seaweed in her hand. "Dewaysus! Dewaysus!" she chanted.

I sat up and slowly mouthed, "DE-LI-CIOUS."

"DE-WI-SUS," she repeated.

"DE-LI-CIOUS."

"DE-WI-SUS."

"Okay, okay. Good enough," I said with a chuckle.

She gobbled the seaweed and crawled into my bed. Part of me wanted to send her off to the other room with Mamá. But the other part—the part that was lonely and kind of confused—wanted her to stay.

Go. Stay. Go. Stay. Go. Stay.

"Let's sleep, Chiqui. It's late," I said, patting the pillow.

She burrowed under the sheet, crumbs, seaweed grease, and all. I exhaled and laid down next to her. By then, I was too exhausted to care. Her eyelids fluttered, and she smiled sleepily. It was sweet and innocent. My heart swelled. I reached out and touched her lip with my finger.

"Smile," I said softly. "Chiqui's smile."

Her arm moved just a bit. Her brow furrowed just a little. I could tell that for a second she'd wanted to hide her mouth with her hand again. But she didn't. Instead, she smiled even more.

"Ngiti," she said, touching my lip back.

"Niti," I repeated.

Chiqui giggled. "Ngiti."

"Nigiti."

"Ngi ... ti ..."

"Ngiti."

She nodded.

Yes!

Ngiti must mean "smile" in Tagalog.

We both exhaled. And then she moved closer so her head was resting on my collarbone. "Gud nayt, Kuya Pabo," she whispered.

"Good night, Chiqui."

The warm fuzzy prickles spread. I just let myself sink into the cozy pile of sheets and blankets and pillows and Chiqui's feathery-soft hair. Everything dimmed and blurred.

The door clicked open.

Mamá.

Her smile. Ngiti.

She watched us. For a moment.

Then her smile faded.

The door closed.

Slowly.

THIRTY-FOUR

I hadn't planned on going to the hospital for Chiqui's checkup, except when it came time for them to leave, Chiqui had an epic meltdown. There weren't enough calming stones in the world to help Mamá keep her cool. How could she, with Chiqui spread out on the floor like a sack of fallen potatoes? Her arms and legs were a tangled mess, kicking and swinging and slapping the air. And her face—*geez*—it was bright red and swollen and dripping with an endless supply of tears. There were no words, only cries and shrieks and moans. Mamá would try to pick her up off the floor, but Chiqui would arch her back and wriggle out of her grasp every single time. "Shh...Shh...Shh..." she kept on repeating. But all her *shh*ing was doing nothing to help the situation. At one point, Mamá stood and stormed off into the kitchen. I heard her whispering to someone on the phone, sighing every so often.

All the while, I'd been watching from my bedroom, unsure of what to do. But there was one thing I knew for certain.

Chiqui needed me.

And so did Mamá.

I tiptoed into the hallway until I was beside her.

You can do this, Pablo.

I knelt down and captured both her hands in mine. "Chiqui," I whispered.

She stopped her squirming and stared at me through puffy eyelids. "Ayoko . . . Ayoko," she croaked.

I couldn't understand exactly what she was saying. It *was* pretty clear that she didn't want to go to her doctor's appointment, though.

"It's okay, Chiqui. I don't like hospitals either . . . But I'll go with you. I'll hold your hand." I got up and took my hoodie off the coatrack and put it on. Then I held my hand out to her. "Come. Let's be brave together."

One.

Two.

Three.

Four.

Chiqui gripped my hand and pulled herself up. She buried her sopping-wet face into my hip just as Mamá returned. She exhaled, looking all sorts of relieved.

"We're ready," I said.

Mamá mouthed, "Thank you."

Beep. Beep.

Zeus arrived just in time.

We were off to the hospital.

Great.

I was at the waiting area. I felt guilty—*really, really* guilty—for leaving Chiqui's side. When Mamá walked off with her, Chiqui's eyes drooped, and her jaw tensed. It was the look of betrayal. Disappointment. My hand twitched. I was supposed to be with her. But the nurses wouldn't let me. I had to hang out in the stupid waiting area for god knows how long. It wasn't just a standard checkup. There would be blood tests, which meant needles. According to Mamá, she was also having a dental X-ray done with a giant contraption. All of this and more, to prepare for her upcoming surgery.

I wondered if she was scared.

Of course she was.

Sigh.

Meanwhile, it was just me and the myriad floating viruses. Thankfully, I had on my sunglasses; they made the place seem less gross, less germy. Like maybe the shiny lenses had the ability to zap the viruses in their path. Even the people surrounding me seemed easier to dismiss. I kind of just stared at my lap, twiddling my fingers and fidgeting my feet. Every time the linoleum squeaked or the loudspeaker crackled, I'd jump from my seat.

After an hour or so, Mamá came back. She slid into the seat next to me. "It's going to be a while," she said.

Maybe it was the crappy hospital lighting, but suddenly, she looked drained. Her skin was sallow. Her eyes were tinged with red. Her lips were cracked and dry. Even her freckles had somehow faded.

Screech! Screech! Screech!

It was her parrot ringtone. She reached into her bag and grabbed her phone.

"Hello?"

I couldn't tell who it was, but there was a muffled voice on the other end.

Mamá exhaled. "I'm *so* sorry. I'm going to be late again . . . I won't get to the sanctuary until this afternoon . . . You'll have to call the vet and have him take a look. I *know*. I *know*. I wish I could help. But I'm tied up at the moment. Keep me updated, okay? Thanks." She hung up.

It was a work emergency. Usually when that happened, she would run off and take care of whatever it was. This time, though, she couldn't. She smoothed her hair and put her phone away, and then finally, she cleared her throat. "I wanted to thank you, Pablo. You've been so patient with Chiqui. It's been really helpful."

"It's okay. I don't mind."

She placed her arm around my shoulder and squeezed. "So. I was wondering about something . . . Has Chiqui talked to you? Has she said anything at all?" she asked.

Thump-thump. Thump-thump. Thump-thump.

My heartbeat was so loud. Could Mamá hear it? Could she feel it? I stared at my shoes. I didn't want to lie, but I didn't want to betray Chiqui either.

She trusted me.

I looked up and met Mamá's gaze. "Why?"

Answering a question with a question wasn't lying, right?

"It's just, well, the child psychologist thinks Chiqui might have what's called selective mutism . . . Because of the trauma, because of the change of environment, because she might be shy about not speaking English. She feels Chiqui *can* speak . . . She's just choosing not to."

"She's seeing a child psychologist?" I already knew Chiqui was seeing one because of my eavesdropping. But Mamá had no idea I knew what I knew, so I had to pretend to be surprised.

"Yes. Doctor Reyes came highly recommended."

"And? What else did this doctor have to say?" I asked.

Mamá fidgeted in her seat. "Well, she's only had an assessment thus far. But for now, Doctor Reyes thinks we shouldn't make a big deal of Chiqui not speaking. We need to shift the focus from the negative to the positive."

I shrugged. "Huh."

"The doctors want to schedule her corrective surgery next month. Before that happens, though, she's going to have to adjust to all the changes, physically *and* mentally. That's why it's important she sees a child psychologist besides her regular doctors. We need to figure out what's going on with her. If you know something ... anything ..."

I didn't move a muscle. I went back to staring at my shoes. Hard.

Mamá let go of my shoulder. She leaned her face closer to mine. So close I could smell the coffee on her breath. "Pablo ... mi amor. I'd *really* be grateful if you told me the truth. Knowing some of Chiqui's past history ... If she's ever seen doctors. If she can speak normally. If she has a speech impediment ... All that information could be crucial to her recovery. It's not just the one surgery. There's also the dental procedures. To be honest, I'm not really sure how many of those she'll need ... Hopefully, the family that adopts her can manage ... Miguel is pretty optimistic. He's already got some potential leads, people looking to adopt children like her." Mamá exhaled and reached for my hand.

But I didn't want to be touched. Not at that moment. I was afraid she would feel me twitching.

Family. Potential leads. Adopt. Children like her.

I didn't want to hear *any* of those words.

I didn't even care about lying to her anymore. Because Mamá didn't care about me; she didn't care about Chiqui. Not one bit. All she cared about was her stupid work. It felt like hundreds of bees were stinging me all at once. I was nauseated except I couldn't even puke, because there was this glob of something lodged in my throat. I coughed. My face and neck burned. I must have turned bright scarlet red.

Say something, Pablo. SAY SOMETHING!

I coughed again and then again. The glob wouldn't budge, so I croaked out my reply. "Does Chiqui know? Does she know she's not staying with us?"

The glob bulged to double its size. I could barely breathe.

Mamá's brow furrowed. "Well, no. Not yet. Chiqui has been through a lot, Pablo. I think it's best we let her heal first. Of course she's going to be upset . . . It's only natural. But she's young. In the long run, she'll be better off in a more stable family situation."

I heaved.

My insides were on fire. Even the glob in my throat

sizzled. I was angry. I couldn't remember the last time I'd been so mad at Mamá. She squeezed my hand. I squirmed and pulled away.

"Pablo?"

I stood.

"Pablo? What's the matter?"

I said nothing. All I could do was walk it off. I dodged nurses and doctors and visitors and patients in wheelchairs and gurneys. I counted the linoleum tiles, reaching twenty-five before they changed from lemon yellow to lime green. Then I started all over again, counting and counting and counting until I was too dizzy to continue. I stopped, leaned on a wall, and hyperventilated.

"*In the long run, she'll be better off in a more stable family situation.*"

What did *she* know about stability anyway?

Mamá had this alarm in her brain. The second we got settled in a new city, country, whatever, the alarm would go off.

Ding! Ding! Ding! Ding!

Then it was time to move again, and again, and again, and again.

I was so sick of it.

But I was too scared to tell her. I'd already lost my father. What if I lost her too? What if she sent me to live with

Abuelita in Spain? Or shipped me off to some boarding school?

I kicked the wall.

Ugh.

Why was I such a coward? I mean, what was the worst that could happen? She'd probably get pissed off. Her hair would lash out like a bunch of snakes. Her arms would swing and pound and jab the air. Her words would spew out in English and Spanish. That's exactly how she was when my father left. That version of Mamá—I didn't want to see it anymore. All I wanted was for her to be happy, even if I wasn't.

But Chiqui—*she* deserved better.

Tears dribbled down my cheeks. I felt so helpless. So tired. My back slid. I landed on the floor. There was nothing more I could do but hug my knees and cry.

THIRTY-FIVE

I was in no mood for dinner much less a dinner party at Miguel's house. But Mamá had already accepted the invitation. *"It would be awfully rude,"* she'd said to me after I asked if I could stay home.

Clearly, she didn't care that I was still upset.

Whatever.

I begrudgingly agreed. Then I moped off to change into my good jeans and a button-down shirt. I combed my hair, making sure the part was nice and straight. The final touch was my sunglasses, hung at the collar. Just in case.

By the time I was done, nobody was even ready yet. So I sat in the living room and stared out the window. Against the darkness I could see Happy's house. It almost looked like it was trapped in a snow globe, except it was covered in falling leaves instead of snow. There were lights shining inside and a flickering TV. Every so often, a shadow of someone would walk past the curtains. I imagined they were getting ready to eat soon. Happy's dad was probably drinking a beer and watching a basketball game while Jem and Happy helped cook the meal. The twins, Bing and Lito, were sitting on the floor somewhere, making a mess with their toys.

Their house was small and old and far from perfect. But it was *their* home. Mine wasn't even a home, just a crappy motel masquerading as a house. I sighed. But then I saw a set of curtains ruffle. I sat up and craned my neck. First a forehead, then a nose, then some lips and a chin, and then Happy's entire face peeked through. I could tell she was gazing at my bedroom window. For a moment she seemed kind of disappointed until her eyes moved sideways and found mine. She grinned. Even from all the way across the road, I could see her white teeth and the dimple on her cheek.

She stuck her hand out and waved.

I waved back.

Then she disappeared through the curtains. They ruffled for a split second before hanging still again.

"Ready!"

I turned around. Mamá was polished and clean. She

wasn't dressed up or anything, but something about the way she looked told me she'd taken more care than usual. Her wild hair was pulled back in a neat ponytail, which made her green eyes stand out even more, especially with the hint of eye makeup she'd applied. She was wearing black leggings, the ones that weren't as faded, an embroidered tunic shirt from India, and her nice boots. I could even smell a trace of perfumed oil, something citrusy and herby.

Chiqui tiptoed down the hallway as if she were worried the silvery stars on her dress would fall off. Every time she moved, the stars twinkled. She would stop and admire their shine. But what she didn't know was that her smile was even brighter. I got up and held her hand, trying to ignore this weird feeling in my gut.

Maybe it was fear. Maybe it was sadness. Maybe it was guilt. Maybe it was all of the above.

After the ordeal at the hospital, Mamá bought Chiqui a double scoop of ice cream, stacked on top of a chocolate-covered waffle cone with rainbow sprinkles. It was bribery. But it worked. Of course it worked. Ice cream was like a magic wand in the form of food. A parent could wave it in front of any sullen kid and *boom*—tears would vanish, frowns would vanish, pouts would vanish.

When Mamá smiled and asked me what flavor I wanted, I turned away without a word. I was too old for that kind of bribery. It would take a *whole* lot more than an ice-cream cone to make the hurt go away.

I expected Miguel to live somewhere in the city, in a mansion with an Olympic-size swimming pool. But I was wrong. His home was about an hour away in a place called Tagaytay, which, according to Zeus, was a town that overlooked a crater lake with an active volcanic island in the middle. It sounded kind of dangerous, if you asked me. Who in their right mind would want to live near a volcano that could blow up at any moment?

Miguel—that's who.

Finally, we arrived at an old wooden gate. There was a canopy of vines over it with flowers the color of raspberry sorbet. Zeus ushered us through the pedestrian entrance. On the other side I saw no house, just a twisty-looking stairway that led down a steep incline.

"It is eighty steps to the house, Ma'am Carmen. I shall carry Miss Chiqui and lead the way," said Zeus, scooping Chiqui up on his shoulders. For a second she looked unsure; she wrapped her arms around Zeus's neck and hunched over his head with bug eyes. But then he held her legs tight and said, "Huwag kang mag-alala, Miss Chiqui. Hindi kita haha-yaang mahulog. Promise."

Whatever he'd said calmed her. She stopped holding on so tight, and her eyes went back to normal.

We began our descent. I lagged behind, wanting to confirm that there were indeed eighty steps, or if Zeus was just exaggerating. It was hard keeping a precise count, though, with all our shoes stomping and clomping. In between thirty-seven and thirty-eight, I paused to catch my breath. That's when the view appeared through the trees. It was breathtaking. A full moon, probably the biggest and yellowest one I'd ever seen, shimmered over the lake. At the center there was a small cone-shaped volcano.

"Wow," I gasped. But nobody heard me.

I scrambled to catch up, trying my hardest to keep count without killing myself.

Thud.

The eightieth step was a slab of rock that looked more like the entrance to a cave. In fact, the house did actually remind me of a cave. The exterior was a grayish-blue adobe. There were pieces of old wood that served as doorways and window frames, blending in with the trees and shrubbery.

The front door opened and out waltzed Miguel, wearing a cream-colored sweater and brown corduroy pants. Anywhere else in the Philippines, that outfit would have made him sweat like a pig. But surprisingly, it was pretty chilly on that mountain.

"Hey, there you guys are. I've got the fireplace all set up, some cheese and wine... and a *big* surprise for Pablo," said Miguel with a wink.

Mamá's smile turned all wiggly. Obviously she knew what the surprise was. No wonder she'd forced me to go.

I sort of hesitated, not knowing how to react. But eventually my voice managed to squeak something out. "Surprise? What surprise?"

"You'll see. You'll see." Miguel nudged me through the doorway, and all of a sudden I was pounced on by a yellow ball of fur.

"Lucky!"

There was a burst of laughter and chatter. For some reason, my eyes were kind of teary, making the room and all the faces inside it blur. I wiped the wetness away with my sleeve. My vision cleared enough to see Zeus and Chiqui and Mamá and Miguel and Sam and Heinz and last but not least Lucky, who was busy rubbing against my legs and whacking me with his tail.

Miguel was right. It *was* a surprise.

A *really* good one.

THIRTY-SIX

I felt warm and tingly. Not just from the blazing fire and the sip of red wine Mamá allowed me to have but also from all the giggling and laughing, and Sam's corny jokes, and the overlapping conversations, which I sort of got lost in. It was easy relaxing in Miguel's house. The living room, dining room, and kitchen were in one humongous area, with a panoramic view of the volcano, the moon, and the stars. The walls were a dark cobalt blue and everything else was warm wood and stone, decorated with a bunch of stuff from his travels.

Not once did I find myself counting the tiles on the floor, or following the zigzag pattern on the sofa, or wondering when the last time something was disinfected, because it was surprisingly squeaky clean. Miguel even showed me the utensil drawer and the bin with napkins in it so I could help myself to as many as I wanted.

"Dinner is ready, guys. Come and get it!" Miguel finally announced.

I was *starving*. Mamá told me once that starving wasn't an appropriate word to use, considering there really were starving children—not just hungry, but really, really starving—all over the world. But at that moment I did feel starved. My insides practically echoed, they were so hollow.

When I got to the table, my plate was heaped with a mountain of pasta, salad, and four mini pizzas. Sam took one look at my plate and guffawed. "Ahh, to be so young again . . . When I was a lad like you, Pablo, I used to eat at least three helpings every meal. At one point I was growing so fast, my dear old mother had to buy me new pants every few months. Now, if I eat like that, the only thing that'll be growing is my belly!"

"I suspect the endless pints of beer might have something to do with it," added Miguel.

Sam made a face somewhere between a pirate and an ogre. "Oy! You just wait fifteen more years, my friend. Then let's see how pregnant *you* look!"

I cracked up with a mouthful of pasta. So did Mamá, and so did Chiqui, even though I was sure she had no idea what we were laughing at.

Heinz lifted his bottle of beer and said, "Mabuhay!"

"Hear, hear!"

"Salud!"

"Cheers!"

Woof! Woof! Lucky barked.

We toasted with our glasses of beer and wine and water and lemonade. I was happy—no, I was giddy. It was as if I'd left all my worries at home.

"So I was wondering, Pablo . . . ," Miguel said after refilling his wineglass. "If you might be interested in taking another trip."

I stopped cutting my pizza. "Another trip? Where?"

"Anywhere you want. Within reason, of course."

"Really? Like all of us? Together?"

Miguel glanced at Mamá and then Mamá glanced at me. "Well, actually, *we* were thinking it could be a boys' trip this time around. With all of Chiqui's upcoming doctor and dentist visits, I'm just going to be in and out of the hospital. It's not going to be much fun," she explained.

We? Who was "we" supposed to be?

My temples itched all of a sudden. The tips of my fingers went instantaneously numb. Everyone's eyes hit me like piercing-hot lasers.

Why did they want me out of the way?

Did it have something to do with Chiqui's adoption?

Had Mamá finally found the permanent solution she'd been looking for?

"Um. I don't know . . . Maybe I should stay. I mean, you might need my help with something," I mumbled, staring at my food, which now looked messy and gross.

"It's summer, mi amor. You should be out there enjoying yourself, not cooped up at home or in a hospital. Just think about it, okay?" Mamá reached across the table and squeezed my hand.

I squeezed back with the best pretend smile I could muster. "Okay."

"Great!" she replied with a little too much enthusiasm.

I hadn't expected Mamá to believe me. Usually she could tell when I was faking it from a mile away. When I was younger, I was convinced she had some sort of warning sound that went off in her head every time I was pulling her leg. She'd give me this squinty-eyed, head-tilted look and say, "Pablito" through her teeth so it sounded more like "Fabito."

But there was none of that. Instead, she smiled and gazed at Miguel with shiny eyes. "Let me help you with dessert," she said to him.

The whole thing just bothered me. Maybe it was all the red wine she'd had, or maybe she was tired or stressed out, or whatever. I couldn't quite put my finger on it. By the time I was done trying to figure it out, the dining table was empty. Zeus was helping to clear dishes, Sam and Chiqui were having a tickle fight on the sofa, and Heinz was strumming a guitar by the fireplace. I sat beside him, sneaking glances at Mamá and Miguel as they prepared the coffee. Mamá's cheeks were already flushed from the wine, but every time Miguel said something funny, her cheeks would get redder. Even her laughing was all wrong—too girly sounding—like she'd been body-snatched by a giggly teenager.

Where had my forty-four-year-old mother gone?

My itching worsened. I reached into the legs of my pants and scratched my calves, and then moved up my arms and neck, and scalp, and behind my ears. It was almost impossible to look away, but somehow I managed. I stared at the fire and counted the crackling sounds and the glowing embers as they flew up the chimney.

Eighteen, nineteen, twenty, twenty-one, twenty-two . . .

Lucky collapsed on my lap. He nudged my hand for a petting. But still I had to keep on counting.

Twenty-three, twenty-four, twenty-five . . .

I ran my fingers through his thick fur.

Twenty-six, twenty-seven . . .

Chiqui giggled uncontrollably.

Twenty-eight, twenty-nine . . .

Heinz began singing a lovey-dovey sort of song.

Thirty . . .

I glanced back at Mamá and Miguel.

Their eyes met.

His hand touched hers.

That's when it clicked. That's when I figured it out.

Something was going on between the two of them.

THIRTY-SEVEN

I was in no mood for *Speak Cartoon, Learn English for Kids, Episode Three*. It was late. I was tired and bothered and annoyed and angry. But when Chiqui appeared at my door, I couldn't say no. I was a pushover. A sucker. A wimp. She sashayed into my room in one of Mamá's old white T-shirts that reached past her knees.

"Aren't you tired, Chiqui?" I asked, making a sleepy face.

She shook her head and pointed at my computer. "No. Mee wats," she replied.

"WA-T-CH." I exaggerated the way my mouth moved.

"WA-T-S."

"WA-T-CH."

Chiqui twisted her face and contorted her lips. "WU-A-T-S . . ."

"Good. Much better," I said.

She blushed and grinned. I could tell she was proud of herself.

"Okay. C'mon." I set her up at the computer, and then plopped back down on my bed after pressing "Play."

Munch. Crunch. Munch.

She snacked on a bowl of Cheerios. It was loud and irritating but at least all the munching and crunching helped to drown out the cartoon voices, which were even louder and more irritating.

"This is my mother—" said an obnoxious chipmunk.

Munch. Crunch. Munch. Munch.

"This is my father—" said a cheerful flea.

Suddenly, the munching and crunching stopped.

I glanced at the computer; the video was paused.

Chiqui pushed the bowl of Cheerios away and stared at her lap.

"What's the matter?" I asked.

She didn't reply. Instead, she poked her finger on the keyboard.

"This is my mother—" repeated the obnoxious chipmunk.

"This is my father—" repeated the cheerful flea.

Ohh...

I lunged for the keyboard and stopped the video. "I'm sorry, Chiqui. I'm sorry about what happened to your mother."

She threw herself on my chest and hugged me. I could feel her warm tears dribbling on my skin. I'll admit, it bothered me. But the last thing I wanted was to push her away. So I let her cry. I let her cry until it seemed as if her tears had run dry.

After a while, Chiqui unglued herself from my shoulders. She wiped the wetness from her eyes. She brushed her hair off her face. She breathed real deep.

"You okay?" I said softly.

She nodded. And then, as if nothing had happened, she faced the computer once again and poked the keyboard.

"Sister and brother—" said the silly ducks to one another.

Sister. Brother.

Ugh.

Why was the universe messing with me?

I retreated back to the bed, hoping she wouldn't break down a second time. My own emotions were bad enough. They sucked, actually. I smashed a pillow over my head, not wanting to hear or see anything. Unfortunately, it didn't work. There was the image of Chiqui's sweet smile, her voice whispering, *"Kuya Pabo"* in my ear. There was the image of Mamá and Miguel flashing in my mind. It was like watching a cheesy TV ad for toothpaste or deodorant or some other product that was supposed to make you look or smell better.

There were too many smiles and meaningful glances and gentle touches.

Suddenly, I could hear my father's voice snickering in my ear, "*Fraternizing with the boss, huh? Well, that's convenient.*"

Oh god.

I was so mad at him for saying what he'd said.

Turned out I was wrong.

And he was right.

He was *right*.

Maybe Miguel was just buttering me up to soften the blow? Did Mamá and Miguel have a plan? Were they going to get rid of Chiqui first, then me?

I couldn't breathe. I coughed and threw the pillow off my face.

Inhale. Exhale. Inhale. Exhale. Relax, Pablo.

Calm down.

I searched for the familiar water stain over my bed and traced its shape. It was like a big tuna or a marlin or one of those silvery-blue fish that jumped out of the water. Even though the sea scared the crap out of me, I was kind of jealous of those fish. They could go whenever they wanted. Stay wherever they pleased. It was all the same to them. Their lives were less complicated. Unlike mine, which was a tangled mess—so tangled I wasn't quite sure how I was going to get myself out of it.

I bolted from my pillow. There were spots of white light in my eyes. I needed something, anything to distract me.

My plaid bedspread—I followed its pattern.

But nothing changed.

My bookshelf—I counted the books and double-checked if they were still alphabetized.

But still nothing changed.

My curtains—I skipped from one curtain ring to another, making sure the spaces in between were even.

But still nothing changed.

Chiqui looked over her shoulder. She frowned and then hopped off the chair. "Kuya," she said, reaching out to touch my hand.

I trembled and closed my eyes. There were tears. I could feel them pushing.

No. No. No. Don't cry, Pablo. Please don't cry.

I was supposed to be the strong one. The kuya—the big brother.

The bed bounced. Chiqui was beside me. Her fingers grazed my cheek. A tear snuck out. She wiped it away. I could feel her head resting near my heart. Her arms held me tight. Except this time, it was *she* who was comforting me.

"Kuya. No cwai. Chiqui wuv yo," she whispered.

My chest heaved. I tried so hard to hold it in. But the tears pushed and pushed and pushed, hitting my cheeks like rain on a windshield. It was impossible to stop. The crying. The heaving. The lump in my throat kept on growing.

It hurt so bad.

I just wanted to *be* her brother. For real.

I didn't want to leave her behind.

Not *ever*.

THIRTY-EIGHT

I was a zombie, or at least I felt like one. My arms and legs moved slowly. The rest of me seemed to be working just fine. But inside I felt heavy and hollow at the same time. I didn't even know that was possible. My brain was numb. My eyes saw nothing, even though all around me, there were a ton of things to see.

We were back at the sanctuary—Ms. Grace, Chiqui, Happy, and me. For some reason, the animals seemed livelier than usual. Maybe they sensed my unease. Maybe they were trying to scream at me.

Pablo! Wake up, Pablo! Do something!

Or maybe I was just losing it.

"Oh, look! Mayari and Tala seem so much better now!" said Happy, tugging my shirt.

I tried to focus—squinting and blinking and making my eyes as wide as they would go. The two eagles were perched on a tree branch. They did seem calmer. Their feathers were smoother. Their talons more relaxed. Their eyes were less beady.

But they still stared. In fact, it was as if they were staring right through me. Like they could see exactly what was wrong. It made me panic.

I couldn't stand it.

I stepped back in slow motion. My body twitched. My forehead, neck, and hands got all sweaty. I breathed but it felt like I was breathing in the entire world all at once, including the dirt and dust and germs and bacteria and viruses and god knows what else.

"I—I have to go," I mumbled.

Happy looked at me kind of funny.

Ms. Grace frowned. "What's the matter, Pablo?"

I took another step back.

Chiqui's eyes widened. Her lips parted. I knew she wanted to say something. But Ms. Grace and Happy were there. She glanced at them and her lips clamped shut.

That's when I ran.

"Pablo! Wait!" shouted Happy. I could hear her flip-flops slapping the soles of her feet as she ran after me. "Pablo! Pablo!" she kept shouting.

I stumbled down the pathway, nearly running into the giant trees, which seemed to be blocking me on purpose.

Even the bushes were out to get me, scratching me with their thorns and scraping me with their woody branches. I kept on running except my feet wouldn't cooperate. I lost my footing and fell to my knees.

"OMG! Pablo!"

I could hear Happy hyperventilating. She knelt beside me. Even though I didn't want to look at her, I did. Her pastel-pink ensemble was smudged with dirt and sweat, and there were twigs and leaves stuck in her hair. Ordinarily, I would have cracked a joke. But I wasn't really in a joking kind of mood.

"I'm sorry," I finally said.

She pulled a little pack of wet wipes from her pocket. "Here, take them."

"Thanks." I wiped the dirt and bits of grass off my knees. There were scrapes and a small cut on my skin. For a second I thought about flesh-eating bacteria and tetanus and legionella and leptospirosis and melioidosis. I closed my eyes.

You're being ridiculous, Pablo.

When I opened them, Happy was staring at me with crooked eyebrows and crooked pigtails.

"Are you okay now?" she asked.

"Yeah. Thanks."

"Did something happen? Whatever it is, you can tell me, Pablo."

I stared at my scrapes and cuts. Those wounds—they were on the outside. But it was the wounds inside that hurt the most. "It's just, I'm overwhelmed. That's all . . . To be honest, I'd rather not talk about it."

Happy blinked at the ground like she was thinking about what she was going to say.

One second. Two seconds. Three seconds. Four –

"I'm sorry. I'm sorry you're feeling that way . . ."

"It's fine. It's not your fault," I blurted out.

She stood and offered me a hand. "Come. I know what will make you feel better."

"What?"

"Dirty ice cream."

I took her hand and stood. "*Dirty* ice cream?"

She giggled and covered her mouth. I could still see her dimple through her fingers. "It's not *really* dirty," she explained. "We just call it dirty because they sell it on the street."

"Oh. Well. What a relief."

"Come on. Trust me," she said, pulling me along.

Once we exited the sanctuary, we walked several blocks, and then there it was on the corner—a metal cart with wheels, painted bright yellow with handwritten letters on the side that read:

DANNY'S SPECIAL SORBETES

I was dubious, but it looked pretty harmless.

"Happy! Kumusta?" said an old guy, whom I presumed to be Danny.

"Mabuti naman po, Mang Danny. Ito si Pablo," she said, gesturing at me.

"Hello," I said with a nod and a wave.

Mang Danny's face was crinkled but his eyes were full of life. He grinned a toothy grin before bending over for a cone and a napkin. Then he opened the circular hatch of his cart and scooped balls of yellow and purple ice cream.

"Danny's Special," he said, handing it to me.

"Thank you."

I waited for Happy to get hers. There was absolutely no way I was going to be the guinea pig. It may have looked like ice cream, smelled like ice cream, and melted like ice cream, but I highly doubted it had anything to do with real ice cream.

"Salamat po, Mang Danny," said Happy. She took her cone and licked it all the way around. "Let's go for a walk."

I followed her down the street, holding the cone away from my clothes. It was scorching hot, so the ice cream was already dribbling down my fingers. The purple and yellow colors were too vivid—like fresh-from-the-can paint. I wondered what kind of artificial gunk they'd used to get it that way.

"Um. So what are these flavors supposed to be anyway?" I asked.

Happy looked at me and half-rolled her eyes. "You should see your face, Pablo! It's only ice cream. But if you must know, the yellow one is cheese and the purple one is ube, a sweet yam."

"Cheese? Yam?"

"It's good! Just try it!"

I stared at the ice-cream cone. My choices were to eat it, throw it, or let it melt all over my hand.

Don't be such a wuss, Pablo.

So I went for it. I brought the ice cream to my mouth, silently hoping it wouldn't taste like dirt or give me food poisoning.

Slurp.

Oddly enough, it didn't taste like dirt. The purple one was kind of earthy, not in a bad way, and the cheese one, well, it tasted like sweet cheese.

"Not bad!" I said.

Happy punched me on the arm. "See! I told you."

We walked and ate our ice cream in relative silence, relative because it was never really completely silent. There were always motorbikes *beep-beep-beep*ing, dogs barking, roosters crowing, vendors shouting, and birds chirping loudly as if they too wanted to be heard. At the corner, Happy halted.

"Hold on. I have to buy load for my mom at the sari-sari store," she said, fumbling for her wallet.

"Sari-sari store? Load?" I repeated, trying to figure out what she was talking about.

She pointed at a hand-painted sign:

IRMA'S SARI-SARI STORE

It was basically a convenience store inside someone's home. "Sari-sari stores, you know, they sell practically everything . . . And 'load' is just another name for cell phone credits," she explained.

"Oh."

"Here, hold this," she said, handing me her ice cream.

I just stood there with the two cones drip, drip, dripping everywhere. Happy approached the counter, which had a metal grate separating her and the lady who worked inside. They chatted in Tagalog for what seemed like ages.

Meanwhile, I just gawked at all the stuff. It was an explosion of products—jam-packed from floor-to-ceiling. Everything they were selling was tiny—individual sachets of shampoo, soap, detergent, bleach, pieces of candy, gum, and chocolates in plastic jars, festive colored bags of chips hanging from the walls, and never-ending cans of tuna, sardines, and mystery meat. There was also a display of bottled sodas. Some brands I recognized, but others, like Royal Tru-Orange, Sarsi, and RC Cola, were completely foreign to me.

I had to stop myself from counting, from inspecting the rows to see if they were evenly spaced.

Ugh.

"Salamat po!" Happy waved at the lady, and then she took her ice cream back. "Let's go find somewhere shady to sit."

She took the lead, and I followed. When we reached a park with a decrepit-looking basketball court, Happy led us to an even more decrepit-looking bench. I studied it for a second, wondering about splinters and rusty nails.

"Sit," she commanded.

I knew she knew more or less what I was thinking. So I sat and hoped for the best.

"So . . . I know you'd rather not talk about it, but I'm your friend, remember? Maybe I can help," Happy blurted out.

"Uh . . ." I was kind of tongue-tied.

Happy reached out and touched my arm with her glittery nail-polished fingers.

I inhaled and exhaled, searching my mind for the best way to explain it all.

"Like I said, I'm overwhelmed. There's a lot going on right now," I said.

"Such as?"

"Well . . . for one, Chiqui's going to be adopted by someone else. Another family. Not right away, but soon. I suppose I've gotten used to having her around. She's kind of like the little sister I never had."

When I looked at Happy, her brow was furrowed. "But can't you talk to your mom or something?"

"My mom?" I huffed. "She's kind of preoccupied these days."

"Preoccupied? Like busy with work?"

"No, busy with Miguel, her boss," I said, pretend-smooching the air.

"Oh. Like *that* kind of busy."

Thump. Thump. Thump. Swoosh.

A couple of guys were playing basketball. For whatever reason, they kept on glancing at us. It made me squirmy and uncomfortable.

"Anyway, so I guess that's pretty much it . . . Of course, there's also my father forgetting I ever existed, and, you know, me being a total freak and all," I muttered, hoping the basketball guys couldn't hear.

Happy leaned toward me. "You're *not* a freak, Pablo."

I wished I believed her.

Thump. Thump. Swoosh. Thump. Thump.

I could feel the basketball guys' eyes creeping on me. They were staring. I was sure of it.

"Pablo," said Happy.

I looked up. Slowly. My gaze lingered at her neck. She was wearing the shell necklace I'd given her.

Swoosh. Swoosh. Whoosh. Whoosh.

The basketball sounds disappeared. All I could hear was the sea.

It made me tremble. It made me sick to my stomach.

But it had also made me happy.

The sea. Happy.

Bingo!

I had an idea.

THIRTY-NINE

It had been a long day—with the eagles, with the dirty ice cream, with the sari-sari store, with the basketball guys staring me down. Not to mention, my mini-breakdown and subsequent confession.

I was exhausted. Thank god dinner was over.

Chiqui was still at the kitchen table, absorbed with the *Where's Waldo?* book in front of her. She hardly moved. The plates, glasses, and cutlery clattered. I glanced at Mamá doing the dishes. I thought about how she was always laughing at Miguel's stupid jokes. She'd hardly laughed when my father was still around. Mostly they just argued. I got kind of dizzy thinking about the past and the present, one memory whirling into another and another and another. Then I glanced back at Chiqui and her book, and I thought about Waldo and his knit hat and his red-and-white-striped sweater, and how he was always lost in a crowd but not really since there were always people searching for him. I got even dizzier. So I glanced at the floor instead, counting the tiles I'd counted so many times before. The dizziness went away.

"Mi amor, can you help me dry the dishes, please?"

"Okay." I finished counting the last three tiles.

The wet dishes were laid out on several washcloths. It was a mess. Mamá really had no organizational skills whatsoever. Sometimes I wondered if she was even my mother—if I was mixed up with another baby at the hospital. But then I remembered that I wasn't born in a hospital. I popped out exactly on the date I was due in a bathtub full of water at our old house in California.

I grabbed a clean washcloth and began drying each and every item, making sure not to miss any spots or crevices or cracks.

"So, have you thought about Miguel's offer?" asked Mamá.

I let a moment pass. Then I put down the glass I was holding and looked at her. "Actually, I have."

"You have?" She turned the faucet off.

"Yeah. I was thinking about camping . . . You know, like camping on the beach."

For a second she gawked at me like I was a three-headed alien. But then she blinked and went back to normal. "Well, Pablito . . ."

I held my breath.

Please. Please. Please.

"Es fantástico! What a wonderful idea!" she finally said.

"Are you sure?"

"Of course I'm sure," said Mamá, with a reassuring smile. "Will it be much fun, though? With just you, Miguel, and Zeus?"

"It doesn't *have* to be just the three of us," I said nonchalantly.

Mamá tilted her head. "Oh, really? So what *exactly* did you have in mind?"

Busted.

My cheeks burned. I was sure they'd turned a horrendous shade of pink. But I didn't care. Not really. Maybe just a bit.

"Um . . . well . . . I was wondering if you could talk to Ate Lucinda and see if she'd let Happy go with us, because she's never been to the beach and I think it would be fun and I'd like to do something nice for her, since she's, like, the only friend I have here. Don't you think?" I gasped for air.

It was hard to tell *what* Mamá was thinking. She kind of just stood there with her arms hanging at her sides. There was this indistinguishable gleam in her eye. After a few torturous seconds, she pulled her shoulders back and tucked her hair behind her ear. "I *think* that can be arranged." She squeezed me into a hug and kissed my cheek before letting go. "I'll talk to Ate Lucinda. I'm sure it will be fine as long as Grace chaperones and Jem tags along."

I smiled the kind of smile that stretched your entire face and made your lips numb and your gums dry from being exposed to the air for too long. I was *that* happy. So happy I wasn't even mad about the Mamá-Miguel situation anymore. In fact, it reminded me of how much I loved her and of how beautiful she was, and that maybe I shouldn't have been mad at her in the first place.

Of course Miguel liked her. What wasn't there to like?

"Thank you, Mamá."

"Anytime, mi amor."

I couldn't wait for Happy to see the sea!

I was expecting the door to creak open. Chiqui would peek in with a mischievous smile and another one of her crumbly midnight snacks. But she was a no-show. All her *Where's Waldo?*-ing must have tuckered her out.

Speak Cartoon, Learn English for Kids, Episode Four would have to wait, which was fine, because if I hadn't known any better I would have said I was drunk, or at the very least tipsy. Like that time Mamá let me drink half a glass of champagne on New Year's Eve. My insides were kind of woozy and giddy and queasy and jumpy. I'd actually convinced myself that an extremely rude person had somehow stuffed cotton candy in my head and slipped firecrackers in my shoes. It was ridiculous but true.

I most definitely couldn't sleep. So I sat by my window, staring at Happy's pitch-black house. She was going to flip out when I told her. I could just picture it. Her eyes would widen like shiny new marbles, and she'd gasp, and I'd be able to count all her teeth—her smile would be *that* big.

And then one of the windows lit up. I wasn't sure which part of the house it was, since I'd only been inside once. But it seemed to be one of the bedrooms at the back. I wondered if it was Happy. Maybe she couldn't sleep either.

I just *had* to tell her.

I contemplated sneaking out through the front door, but I didn't want to risk it. So I pushed open my window and shimmied out. Hopefully, nobody was passing by, otherwise they might think I was a cat burglar or something. As soon as my feet hit the grass below, I realized I was barefoot.

Good job, Pablo.

I had two choices—crawl back up, grab my slippers, and crawl back out again, or risk permanent injury by stepping on something contaminated, rusty, or sharp.

Great.

There really was no debating it. I was *not* going to walk across the street without any shoes on. It may have looked relatively harmless. But I knew what was out there. The road between my house and Happy's was an obstacle course of grossness. There were squished cockroaches, oil slicks, globs of dried spit, bird poop, decomposing bits of food, and worst of all, pee—cat pee, dog pee, *and* people pee.

I pulled myself back up rather clumsily, since my upper body strength was virtually nonexistent. My head, shoulders, and chest were in my bedroom, my stomach, butt, and legs still outside. There was a flash—no, more like a beam of light shining behind me.

Uh-oh.

"Freeze!" The voice was gruff—almost too gruff.

I tried to peer over my shoulder without killing myself. I saw pavement. I saw scattered leaves. I saw grass. I saw pink flip-flops. I saw toenails with glittery nail polish.

"Happy?"

Her laugh was a dead giveaway. It was like listening to a hyena cackle after inhaling a helium-filled balloon. I dropped to the ground. "Hardy har har," I said, turning around with the most sarcastic look I could muster.

"I'm sorry. I couldn't help myself. I saw your light and then I saw you climbing out the window and then climbing back in . . . It was just too good to pass up," she said.

I crossed my arms across my chest in an effort to look huffy. "Well, you caught me. I'm running away, and there's nothing you can do about it."

"You *are*?" Happy gasped as if I'd said the most unbelievable thing ever.

"I am."

"But it's not safe out there! You could get lost, kidnapped . . . even killed! Whatever it is, I'm sure you can work it out. Please. I'll help you. You can stay at my house for a few days. My mom won't mind. Let's go wake her up. We can ask her." Happy latched onto my wrist and pulled. But I held my ground, keeping my limbs as stiff as possible. She let go. Her face was pale and blotchy. "I'm *not* going to let you do this, Pablo!"

I couldn't hold it in any longer. I coughed and sputtered and snorted and chortled. "I'm sorry. I couldn't help myself either!" I said in between fits of laughter.

It was Happy's turn to cross her arms across her chest. She was obviously annoyed that I'd gotten her back so good. But I could tell she wasn't really, truly mad by the way her lips quivered at the corners. "Okay. Okay. Now we're even," she mumbled.

"C'mon. I need to sit," I said, gesturing toward the front steps. I plopped down. "So, I was *actually* coming to see you—"

"Really?"

"Really." I peered from the side. Her skin was back to normal, and her lashes were fluttering like moths around a streetlamp. "Guess what? Miguel is going to take me to the beach again! Isn't that awesome?"

Happy's lashes stopped fluttering. "Oh . . . that's great. *Totally* awesome," she said, trying to sound all excited, except I could tell she was faking it.

"But there's more . . ." I scooted toward her. "You can come with us, Happy! My mom said you and Jem can come! You can finally see the sea! Isn't that cool?" I gaped at her, waiting for her eyes to transform into the shiny marbles I'd imagined.

But all she did was cringe and bite her lip. "Don't get me wrong, Pablo. I'm grateful. It's just that I always dreamed of going to the beach for the first time with my family . . . with my brother and my sisters. With my mom and dad." She looked down at her lap and fiddled with the ruffle of her Hello Kitty pajamas.

"Oh," I replied softly.

Happy cleared her throat and continued. "We never do anything together . . . My dad's always working, and in the daytime, when he's home, he's usually asleep or walking around in a daze. And my mom is always too busy cooking, cleaning, doing laundry, gardening, shopping. Even when we help out, it's not enough. There are just too many bills—tuition, electricity, water, food, medicines. Bills, bills, and more bills. It never ends!"

I gulped down the saliva that had accumulated in my mouth.

What was I supposed to say?

I mean, there I was unloading problem after problem after problem, and all along, she'd had her own to deal with. "I'm sorry," I finally said. "I didn't know."

"It's all right." She wiped her eyes and looked up at me. "I just don't talk about it that much. It is what it is. You know?"

I nodded. "I understand." And I really did. There were so, so many things I wished I could change but couldn't.

There was this awkward silence.

I wracked my brain.

Thinking. Thinking. Thinking.

What could I possibly say to convince her?

I thought about what Happy had said to me, about experiencing new things. I thought about Mamá, and how hard she worked, and how she encouraged me to go to different places, talk to different people, eat different kinds of food, even though I refused most of the time. I thought about Happy's parents and how they probably wished they could give her more. *So* much more.

That was it!

I cleared my throat. "Um . . . But, like . . . don't you think that your parents would want you to go, even though they can't? I mean, isn't that the reason they work so hard? So you can have a better life than they did?"

Happy frowned. I couldn't quite tell if she was upset, or simply contemplating what I'd said. "Hmm . . ."

Thinking. Thinking. Thinking.

I sat up straight and pleaded with my eyes. "So, will you come? Please?"

Happy covered her face with her hands. But then a second later, she looked at me all serious-like. "I just have one question, Pablo."

"What?"

"When are we leaving?"

I gawked at her. "What do you mean? You're coming?"

"Yes. I'm coming. You're right . . . My parents wouldn't want me to miss out. I wouldn't want to miss out either," she said, punching my arm with tears in her eyes.

FORTY

It was all set. We were going to Anawangin
Cove in Zambales, wherever that was. I never thought I'd go
camping in a zillion years. Much less camping for two days
with actual friends. Though I wasn't so sure if Jem considered herself my friend yet. I didn't really care either way.

I was *that* happy.

And Happy was *that* happy too.

The next couple of days were like a whirlwind, or perhaps more appropriately, a typhoon since we were in the
tropics. There were all sorts of preparations that included
camping equipment, first-aid kits, toiletries, and food, which
seemed to be the most complicated matter. On one side there
were the non-vegetarians—Ms. Grace, Zeus, Happy, and Jem,
who insisted on all sorts of questionable food items such
as bright red hot dogs, Vienna sausages, something called

corned-tuna, and a variety of SPAM (who knew canned lun-
cheon meat came in so many different flavors?). On the
other side, Miguel and me, the vegetarians—thank god I
wasn't the only one. Our haul consisted of soy dogs, veggie
burgers, vegetarian baked beans, instant noodles (mushroom
flavored), and lots and lots of granola bars. Thankfully, we
all agreed on one thing: s'mores. So we made sure to pack
a jumbo-size supply of graham crackers, chocolate bars,
and gelatin-free marshmallows. Because gelatin was actually
made with animal skin and bones.

Eww.

The worst part of packing, though, was my own stuff.
The stuff only I could pack. Unfortunately, I left it to the last
minute.

Good move, Pablo.

It was almost midnight. I stood in the middle of my room
debating with myself about how many different kinds of
insect repellant, sunscreen, and hand sanitizer I would need.
There were the waterproof kinds, the lotion and spray kinds,
the scented and unscented kinds, the alcohol and alcohol-
free kinds. They were all laid out on my bed. I was dizzy just
looking at them.

The doorknob jiggled. I didn't even have to look. I knew
it was Chiqui. She was holding a plate with a giant slice

of banana bread, and a glass of milk that was so full that every time she moved, the milk sloshed dangerously close to the rim.

"Chiqui!" I gasped, taking the glass away before anything disastrous happened.

She just gazed at me with innocent eyes. "Kuya Pabo, me wuats," she said, pointing at my computer.

"Not tonight. I'm kind of busy."

But she didn't seem to get it. She did her bouncy walk until she reached my desk. "Wuats! Wuats!"

I sighed. "All right. Fine. But I'm going to pack while you're at it. Okay?"

She nodded and hopped on the chair. I searched for *Speak Cartoon, Learn English for Kids, Episode Four* and clicked "Play." The obnoxious chipmunk voices began jibber-jabbering. I ignored them, or at least I tried to.

Hmm . . . How many changes of clothes am I going to need?

What if I puke? What if I puke more than once?

I opened my dresser drawer and pulled out all my shorts and all my T-shirts and a couple of sweatpants and sweat-shirts for good measure. Surely they would come in handy to protect me against the blood-sucking mosquitoes and sand fleas.

Next came underwear. Theoretically, I should only need two or three pairs. But we were going to the beach. That meant sun, sand, and salt water. Any of those variables were a formula for disaster.

Sweaty Butt + Sand = Disaster

Salty Wet Butt + Sand = Disaster

Sweaty Butt + Salty Wet Butt = Disaster?

Okay, maybe that last one was a stretch. I grabbed all my underwear, and then all my socks, and then all my pajamas, and basically everything in my dresser, and jammed it all into my duffel bag.

Except the zipper wouldn't close.

Chomp. Chomp. Chomp.

I looked over. Chiqui was chewing the banana loaf with an open mouth. It was like sirens ringing in my ear, forks scraping on empty plates, a squeegee cleaning a wet windshield. The robotic chipmunk voices seemed even louder.

"Are you ready for school yet?" said chipmunk mom.

"Yes, Mother," said chipmunk kid.

"Have you packed your lunch?" said chipmunk mom.

"Yes, Mother. Thank you," said chipmunk kid.

"Have a good day, then!" said chipmunk mom.

"You too, Mother!" said chipmunk kid.

Ugh.

How on earth was I supposed to finish packing with that racket? Maybe I just needed a break. I threw myself on the bed. Everything that was on it bounced and scattered, making an even bigger mess. I jammed a pillow over my head. I needed silence. It didn't work, though. The chipmunk voices were still there, sounding like they were gurgling underwater. And then there were the crunching sounds. Not from Chiqui's chewing, but the crunching of the pillow next to my ear. It was as if there were thousands of microscopic termites living inside it, munching on the threads and fibers.

Relax, Pablo. Breathe and focus.

The noises got a little softer. I could feel the mattress bounce. A second later, the pillow lifted on one side. Chiqui's one eye stared at me. "Kuya. Yu kay?" she asked. Her face was pinched with worry.

I exhaled and yanked the pillow aside. "I'm okay, Chiqui. Just a bit stressed out, that's all."

She must have sensed that I wasn't really okay. Instead of replying, she snuggled closer. Her face lay over my heart, and one of her tiny arms snaked across my chest. I could see crumbs on her cheek and a smudge of grease on her chin. But none of it mattered. The moment she squeezed me, I melted. I felt like one of those chocolate lava cakes—fudgy on the outside, warm and gooey on the inside.

After that, everything got kind of heavy. Hazy too.

Her breathing. My breathing. Our breathing became one.

My shoulders sank into the mattress. So did my hips and legs and feet. Slowly, really, really slowly, my eyelids drooped.

FORTY-ONE

"Pablo, mi amor. Wake up!"

My eyes slammed open. It was still dark, but Mamá was looming over me as if I'd overslept. "Why aren't you packed yet? Miguel is going to be here any minute!" she said.

The beach. Camping. I glanced at my clock. 3:45 A.M.

I bolted from my pillow. Chiqui rolled off my chest, nearly falling from the bed. She rubbed her eyes, looking confused.

"I must have fallen asleep," I mumbled.

Mamá threw her arms into the air. "Come on! I'll help you! Hurry!"

We were like two bees buzzing around and around and around. Chiqui watched the spectacle, her expression going from puzzled to curious to suspicious. There was no time for thinking, for explaining, for anything other than packing.

Mamá grabbed something. I grabbed something else. After a while I couldn't tell her hands from mine.

I glanced at the clock. 4:00 A.M.

It was a miracle. My duffel bag was packed. I was dressed with clothes that *actually* matched. Nothing was broken, and nobody was hurt.

I was ready, or at least as ready as I'd ever be. Just in time too, because Miguel's truck pulled up to the curb. For some reason my heart thumped wildly.

Thump, thump. Thump, thump. Thump, thump.

Mamá was too frazzled to notice. But Chiqui must have had supersonic hearing or something. She perched herself at the foot of my bed and glared at me with the same accusing glare as Mayari and Tala. I guess they didn't call it an "eagle eye" for nothing.

"You better go!" said Mamá as she hurried from my room.

I picked up my bag and followed her.

Don't panic. Keep calm, Pablo.

I repeated those words over and over as we marched down the hallway. The front door opened. Mamá went outside and waved at the truck. I was about to do the same, but I couldn't. Not because I didn't want to, but because I *really* couldn't. I was being pulled from behind. I turned around.

Chiqui was gripping the back of my shirt with both hands. Her face was scrunched up and red.

"Chiqui," I said in a hushed voice.

She loosened her grip. I put my hands on hers, uncurling her itty-bitty fingers one by one. When I was freed, I bent down so we were level with each other. "I'm only going away for two days. I'm not leaving you, Chiqui."

"*I'm not leaving you.*" It may not have been a lie then, but it *was* a lie. Eventually I *would* be leaving her. She just didn't know it yet.

Her eyes filled with tears. "No go, Kuya Pabo. No go," she croaked.

My heart shattered, and it felt like I'd swallowed my own tongue.

"Pablito!" Mamá called.

I could hear car doors opening and closing. I could hear bags being dragged. I could hear footsteps. I could hear Mr. Cheery, aka Miguel. I could hear Mamá giggling. I could hear so many noises and voices. But I wasn't listening to any of them.

At that moment the only one that mattered was Chiqui.

I held her face, keeping my gaze as calm and steady as I could.

You're not going to cry, Pablo. You're not going to cry.

"Two days, Chiqui. I'll see you in two days. Okay?" I

showed her two of my fingers. She sniffled and then nodded like she understood. I wanted to tell her to behave. I wanted to say goodbye. But I could feel myself choking up. So I smiled and hugged her instead.

I picked up my bag and turned my back on her.

I was a traitor.

I was a liar.

I was probably the worst person in the world—no, in the galaxy. Maybe even the entire universe.

We were piled into the truck. I thought everyone would be quiet and sleepy and moody, but it was the exact opposite. The chatter was nonstop.

"Is it too hot?"

"Too cold?"

"Is anyone hungry?"

"Does anyone need to stop at the gas station?"

Zeus never seemed to run out of questions.

"Oh, look! There's Enchanted Kingdom. It's our version of Disneyland, you know."

"Oh, look! It's the People's Power Monument. It was built to commemorate the People's Power Revolution of 1986, you know."

"Oh, look! Ali Mall is just down that way. It was one of the first shopping malls ever built in the country, and it was named after the great boxer Muhammad Ali, you know."

Ms. Grace never seemed to run out of facts.

"OMG! Look at that building. It's *so* tall!"

"OMG! Look at that billboard. It's *so* big!"

"OMG! Look at that bridge. It's *so* long!"

Happy never seemed to run out of ridiculous things to look at.

After a while the energy fizzled. Everybody conked out. As tired as I was, though, I just couldn't sleep. All I could do was watch the scenery zoom by. There was a lot of beauty. Like the sky, which changed from dark blue to gray to yellow to pink to purple and then to blue again. Like the distant mountains that touched the clouds. Like the trees with orange flowers so bright, it looked as if they'd caught on fire. Yet there was also a lot of ugliness. Much more than I cared to see. Like the piles of garbage that seemed to have sprouted by the road. Like the rivers and canals clogged with plastic debris. Like the children—too many of them—begging on the streets.

Some of them reminded me of Chiqui.

I sighed.

Why was it so hard for me to accept that she was only a guest? She would come and go just like every other person, from every other country before this one. Surely I would move on, right? Out of sight, out of mind. When she was gone, I would forget. Of course I would.

I tried to swallow past the lump in my throat. I coughed. Then choked.

Who was I kidding?

When she was gone, I would *not* move on. I would *not* forget.

Not ever.

FORTY-TWO

All of a sudden the truck exited the highway. The turn, the change of speed, the screeching brakes, jolted everyone awake.

"This is a good place to stop for breakfast," said Zeus.

He pulled into a gas station the size of an airport hangar. It was super-duper big. And there were a bunch of fast food places surrounding it, with names like Chow King, Jollibee, and Max's Fried Chicken.

I already knew it was going to be a dirt, germ, and sensory overload, so I put on my sunglasses before stepping out of the truck. Everyone was still kind of groggy and dazed and stiff except for Ms. Grace, who was somehow wide-awake and looked kind of like a tour operator instead of a chaperone. All that was missing was a bullhorn and clipboard.

"Okay, everyone! Bathrooms first. Make sure you wash

your hands and then let's meet at Pancake House in five minutes," she said.

Pancakes. My stomach grumbled at the thought of them. I'd never been to Pancake House, but surely a house of pancakes would make perfect pancakes, right?

"C'mon, little man." I followed Miguel, who was already sporting a snazzy new pair of sunglasses, and Zeus, who was walking and stretching his legs at the same time. The men's bathroom was situated down a dingy hallway next to the ATMs. I could tell just by looking at the once-white door covered in smudges, smears, and splatters that it was definitely *not* going to be a Pablo-approved bathroom.

Far from it.

I stood there itching from head to toe.

Zeus went ahead inside, but Miguel stayed with me. He was trying not to react. It was obvious by the way his face slackened, like no biggie. But I could tell he knew something was wrong. Maybe he'd been observing all along, just as Chiqui had.

"Try not to look around too much, Pablo. It's a gas station bathroom... Best we just go in and out and get it over with," he said.

Easier said than done.

But he was right. I had to pee. Though truth be told,

I would have much rather done my business behind some bushes or something. "Okay," I mumbled.

Miguel pushed the door open.

You can do it, Pablo.

I took the deepest breath I could possibly take and held it. Maybe if I hurried I wouldn't even have to breathe the air in there.

Go! Go! Go!

I dashed into the bathroom, almost crashing into some random guy who was leaving.

"Sorry," I mumbled. The guy didn't even look at me.

I followed the dirty wet tiles straight to the urinals, which were chipped and stained and looked like they hadn't been cleaned in a while. There wasn't a urinal cake in sight either.

JUST PEE ALREADY, PABLO!

I undid my zipper and let it all out. The only problem was that I'd had way too much to drink, so my pee went on forever and ever and ever. I was running out of breath. Fast.

Finally, the stream stopped. I closed my zipper and then speed-walked to the sinks to wash up. Zeus was nowhere in sight, but Miguel was standing there with a weird kind of grimace. "Um. The sinks aren't working," he said.

What?

I panicked.

I couldn't hold my breath in any longer.

Wheeeeeew.

I sucked air. The sharp smell of urine hit me. I was woozy. I was dizzy. Germs were in my nose, throat, and lungs. Everywhere. The bathroom tiles whirled around and around. Miguel grabbed me by the shoulders and pushed me through the door. Fresh air.

Inhale. Exhale. Inhale.

Miguel went into the convenience store. He came out with a mini-bottle of 70 percent alcohol. He broke the seal and squirted it all over my hands and his. They were soaked. The germs were dying. Dead. I wasn't woozy or dizzy anymore. The whirling stopped.

"Thank you," I whispered.

He patted my back. "Let's go eat. I'm starving," he said as if nothing had happened.

But I knew he knew. He'd figured it out. Surprisingly, I didn't mind, though. It was almost a relief.

Phew.

As soon as we entered the Pancake House, I felt much better. Like a thousand, million times better. I was even hungry. The smell of pancakes and syrup invaded my nostrils, erasing all traces of urine.

"What took you so long? We already ordered," said Happy.

I slid into my seat not knowing what to say.

"Oh, it's my fault. I had to buy a couple of things at the convenience store," Miguel blurted out.

The waitress popped out of nowhere. "Will there be an additional order, sir?" she asked Miguel.

He glanced at the menu for a second. "I'll have a black coffee and a mushroom omelet with whole wheat toast and he"—Miguel gestured at me—"will have an orange juice and the classic pancakes with the butter and syrup on the side. Please bring extra forks and knives and napkins as well. Thank you."

Wow. Miguel really does pay attention. Is he like a secret agent spy or something?

I was impressed—so absolutely, positively impressed that my chin dropped and there was saliva leaking from the side of my mouth.

"What's wrong with him?" I heard Jem whisper to Happy.

Happy jabbed her with her elbow. "*Anyway* . . . Can you believe this is our first time eating at Pancake House? I've been wanting to try their bangsilog since my classmate Maritess is always bragging about how good it is and how her dad brings them here *every* Sunday after church."

I had no idea what bangsilog was, but for whatever reason I had this picture of a girl in a school uniform banging her forehead against a big log. I laughed. Except of course nobody knew what I was laughing at.

Jem rolled her eyes. "It's bangsilog. I'm sure it's not *that* special."

For a second I thought Happy was going to stick her tongue out. But she didn't. Instead, she crossed her arms and sulked.

"But Miss Jem. Not all bangsilogs are created equal," said Zeus with a chuckle.

Ms. Grace nodded. "I have to agree. There are good bangsilogs, mediocre bangsilogs, and just plain awful bangsilogs."

I couldn't take it anymore. Both my hands slapped the table. "What are bangsilogs? Will someone please tell me already?"

As if by divine intervention, the waitress approached us, placing a large oval plate in front of Happy. "Here is your bangsilog, miss," she said with a smile.

At first it was crickets. Then laughter burst out of everyone's mouths. The waitress looked confused. They all kept on laughing, except for me.

I was both mesmerized *and* disgusted.

There was a whole fried fish with a runny fried egg and a mound of greasy-looking rice.

Was *that* supposed to be the famous Pancake House bangsilog? How could any reputable house of pancakes serve such a thing?

Don't look, Pablo. Don't look. Don't look. Don't look.

But then Ms. Grace said, "Personally, I think the eye and the belly are the best parts."

I looked.

Happy had a big spoon and a big fork. For a split second she looked like a surgeon with a scalpel in her hand. With the fork, she held down the fish's head. With the tip of the spoon, she poked into the fish's eyeball.

THE. FISH'S. EYEBALL.

God, no . . .

All I could do was turn away and hope no one noticed.

FORTY-THREE

The rest of the drive, all I could think about was how affected I was by that gas station bathroom, and how that bangsilog had permanently damaged my fondness for breakfast. How could anyone eat an entire fish—head, skin, tail, and all, first thing in the morning?

Ugh.

It was like a really bad nightmare that wouldn't stop. I kept on picturing the urinals sticking out of the walls like filthy open mouths. I wondered how many gallons of pee they had swallowed. I kept on visualizing Happy scooping out that fish eyeball with a spoon and popping it into her mouth, *yum-yum-yumm*ing like it was the best thing ever.

Finally, Zeus pulled the truck into a vacant lot. "We're here!" he announced.

"This is it?" asked Happy.

There were loads of tricycles and vendors and only a

slice of beach that looked more like a docking area for boats, so I suppose her concern was valid.

Miguel peered between the two front seats. He must have seen the confusion plastered on our faces, because he pointed toward the beach and said, "We can't drive directly to the cove. That's what all those bangkas are for."

"Bangkas?" I blurted out. "What the heck are bangkas?"

Ms. Grace touched my shoulder. "See all those boats, Pablo? Those are bangkas. They're outrigger canoes made out of wood. The larger ones are motorized. The smaller ones only use paddles. It's the most common mode of water transportation in the Philippines. They can also be used for fishing," she explained.

I gawked at the narrow canoes with their bamboo outriggers. They looked flimsy, like do-it-yourself balsawood boats a kid would make.

"It's the easiest way, Pablo. The alternative would be hiking through a mountain to get to the other side," said Miguel.

It felt like every gaze in the car was directed at me. White spots of panic flashed, making everything I looked at all polka-dotty. Happy reached over and squeezed my hand. "You can keep your eyes closed. We'll help you," she said softly.

"I—I don't know," I mumbled. I felt like a big baby. It was

just so humiliating. All I could do was stare at my lap—stare and stare and keep on staring until someone said something.

"You need to trust me, Pablo."

I looked up at Miguel. His gaze was warm and steady and safe somehow. I had to trust him. What else could I do? Make everyone stay in the car for two days? Demand that Zeus turn around and bring us back home?

I couldn't do that. Not to Happy. I wasn't going to ruin it for her.

Suck it up, Pablo.

"All right. I'll give it a shot."

Happy squealed and hugged me. "Come on!"

I tried not to look at anyone or anything as we got out of the truck. I was embarrassed. Ashamed. For a moment there was a bit of a commotion. Vendors began swarming around us, holding up sarongs, T-shirts, beaded necklaces, refrigerator magnets, and such. Ms. Grace held up her hand, trying her best to shoo them away. Then a couple of guys appeared, strutting like they were in charge. Zeus and Ms. Grace spoke to them in Tagalog. It kind of sounded like they were arguing. But they were also smiling, so I wasn't sure if the conversation was a good or a bad one.

Eventually, Ms. Grace sauntered back with a satisfied grin. "Okay. So the parking is 100 Pesos a day. They've also secured us a brand-new bangka to take us round-trip for 3,000 Pesos, and they're going to help us carry our stuff too."

"Sounds good. It's a deal," said Miguel.

By the time we were done unloading the truck, the vendors had miraculously disappeared. The path to the beach cleared. I could see the sea, the waves rippling, the multi-colored bangkas bobbing up and down. I was starting to feel nauseated. Happy led me to where the street ended and the sand began. She wove her fingers through mine and held on tight, as if she were my mother and I, her insecure toddler.

"Close your eyes, Pablo, and don't let go of me," she commanded.

My face was burning. I knew it wasn't from the sun. My cheeks were probably a lovely shade of beet red. To be honest, though, I didn't even care. All I cared about was surviving the boat ride.

I closed my eyes. Happy stepped forward. So I stepped forward. There was sand under my shoes. Happy stopped. So I stopped. Her breath. I couldn't hear it. I knew she was excited. But she didn't say anything. I was relieved. I didn't want to hear about how blue the water was, or how the waves frothed when they hit the shoreline, or how the clouds puffed like cotton candy. None of that would make me feel any better. In fact, I felt worse just thinking about it.

All of a sudden there was another hand holding me from the other side. I flinched.

"They're already waiting for us on the bangka." It was Jem's voice.

I was surprised. Maybe she *was* my friend after all. Or maybe she was just losing her patience. I guessed it didn't really matter much. As long as we got to where we were going. The three of us hobbled along. It felt weird. Not being able to see while my feet sank and tripped and tried to catch up.

"You're doing great, Sir Pablo!" Zeus shouted from up ahead.

After several clumsy steps, Happy and Jem slowed down. And then suddenly, we halted.

"Anong nangyari? Bulag ba siya?" said a guy's voice.

Jem's arm tensed. "Huwag ka na makialam!"

The guy snickered. "Sus. Ang taray mo naman."

I didn't really know what they were arguing about. But I figured it had something to do with how absurd I looked. *Whatever.*

They dragged me several more feet before stopping again.

"We made it!" said Happy.

I exhaled.

"Umm . . . so . . . how are we going to get him up on *that*?" said Jem.

277

I turned to where I thought she was standing. "Up on what?"

"Up on the gangplank," said Miguel from somewhere above my head.

"The gangplank? As in a pirate ship?"

Happy giggled. "Well, the bangka *is* called 'Johnny Deep'!"

I was going to roll my eyes but then I remembered they were closed. "You're kidding, right?"

Miguel guffawed. "No. Really. There's even a likeness of Captain Jack Sparrow on both sides."

I was tempted to look. I mean, it was just too silly *not* to be true. But as tempting as it was, I knew I couldn't risk it. My stomach groaned and gurgled.

"So what are my choices, then?" I asked.

"Well, you could give the gangplank a go, but I'm warning you . . . it's about six inches wide, with a bunch of notches to trip on," said Miguel.

"Hmm. Maybe you can stay behind me and hold on to my waist," said Happy.

"*That's* not going to work," said Jem.

I could practically hear them eye-daggering each other.

All of a sudden, someone grabbed me by the shoulders. "Wait!" I shouted.

But before I knew what was happening, I landed with a thud.

"Or . . . the bangka guys could carry you on board," said Ms. Grace.

Ugh.

I was beginning to regret this entire trip.

Miguel plunked me down on the safest seat and handed me a life vest. I wasn't sure what made it the safest, since the entire thing wobbled when it pushed off. As soon as they turned on the engine, every square inch of wood vibrated like it was about to fall apart.

No! No! No!

I had to keep my mind clear of such catastrophic thoughts.

The bangka was *not* going to sink.

I was *not* going to drown.

And I most certainly was *not* going to get eaten by a shark.

"You okay, Pablo?" whispered Happy.

No. I wasn't okay. But I felt like I needed to pretend.

"I'm fine. As long as I don't open my eyes, I'm fine."

"Good. They said it should take us fifteen minutes to get there."

That was fifteen minutes too long.

"You know, those guys on the beach thought you were blind." I could tell Happy was grinning by the tone of her voice.

"Well, technically, I *am* blinded, even though it's voluntary."

"Jem told them to mind their own business."

"Really?"

"Really."

"Huh."

"Hold on!" Miguel shouted.

The bangka dipped and then soared. I was suddenly weightless. Happy grabbed my arm. But her grip wasn't strong enough. My butt flew off the seat. I could hear arms and legs thudding against the hull, against one another. Voices.

"Hay naku!" said Zeus.

"Big waves! Sit tight, everyone!" said Ms. Grace.

"Pablo! I'm coming!" Miguel's voice was heading toward me.

My eyes opened just as the sunglasses flew off my face. It was a slow-motion blur of white clouds, blue water, and startled faces.

Crash.

I landed with my upper body leaning over the edge. My sunglasses were floating away. I caught a glimpse of the

Captain Jack Sparrow likeness. And then all I could see was the depths of the sea, which seemed bottomless.

I was terrified.

Someone latched on to my chest. "I've got you, Pablo!" said Miguel.

It didn't matter, though. I didn't feel safe. In fact, I still felt like I was spinning, flying, falling. A wave swelled and slapped the side of the boat like it was coming for me.

My stomach clenched, twisting tighter and tighter.

It ripped and let loose.

I vomited. I puked. I hurled.

Miguel pulled me back into the bangka. He held me tight. I closed my eyes. "Maybe we should go back," he said in between huffs and puffs of air.

"No," I croaked. "*Please.*"

Yes! Yes! Yes!

That's really what I'd wanted to say.

But I wasn't going to ruin it for Happy.

I'd made up my mind.

Everyone went quiet.

Even the sea—as if it knew it needed to cut me some slack.

FORTY-FOUR

We arrived in one piece.

Alive.

Thank god.

As soon as I got off the bangka, I turned my back on the sea. There was a long stretch of beach that curled in front of a forest with mountains behind it. There wasn't much else. It was a weekday, the best time to come, according to Miguel; the crowds preferred Saturdays and Sundays.

I stared at the rows and rows of nearly identical pine trees.

One, two, three, four, five.

I shook my head—the numbers *had* to stop. I wasn't about to stand there and count every single tree. Not after everything that had just happened.

Just act normal, Pablo.

Okay. I blinked and tried to look at everything through

"normal" eyes. The white sand reminded me of snow, that's how white it was. There were also wooden picnic tables, and huts with thatched roofs, and colorful flags on bamboo poles. Besides us, there was a guy in a hut that I think was meant to be some sort of information booth, and an old lady and her shack-of-a-store right next to it.

Miguel came up from behind, holding a bunch of camping equipment. He handed me his brand-new sunglasses. "Here, take these."

"You sure?"

"Yeah. I'm sure. I don't really need them other than for looking cool and all," he said with a wink.

"Thanks."

"Why don't you go and rest while we set up camp?"

Once again I felt like a big baby.

Wah! Wah! Wah!

But he was right. I had no energy whatsoever.

I hung my head low. "Okay."

I felt so useless, so defeated. I hobbled toward one of the huts. In the distance I could hear shouting and giggling. I didn't look. I didn't have to. I knew Happy and Jem were running around the beach. It was probably the best day of their lives. Thank goodness Bing and Lito were too young to come. Their chanting and screeching would have only made it worse.

I collapsed on a bamboo bench. Maybe I would feel better after a nap.

Thankfully there was a breeze. It blew back and forth, ruffling the hut's thatched edges. It was like listening to crinkling paper. For a while I gazed up at the pattern on the ceiling. The dried palm fronds were woven so meticulously. They were perfect. My eyes stung from staring so hard. Maybe if I stared and stared and stared, I wouldn't think about what had happened.

But it didn't work.

My mind drifted.

Whoosh. Crash. Whoosh.

I kept on picturing the waves breaking against the side of the bangka.

Whoosh. Crash. Whoosh.

Captain Jack Sparrow's eyes mocked me.

Whoosh. Crash. Whoosh.

It all made me think of the time when I was a little kid on a dock, walking toward a white yacht. The sky was like a melted orange Popsicle. Mamá held my hand tight. My father was up ahead, laughing with his friends.

"Wa-ha! Ha! Ha!"

I could feel my stomach clenching, my knees were wobbly, sweat was trickling down my face and neck.

"Pablito, are you all right?" Mamá had asked.

I nodded even though I wasn't. My father would surely get annoyed. And I didn't want Mamá and him to start fighting again. We were going on a leisurely sunset cruise just like any other family.

I wasn't going to ruin it.

By the time we reached the yacht, my father was already drinking beer with his buddies.

"*Wa-ha! Ha! Ha!*"

Laughter. Chatter. Footsteps.

The yacht was swaying. A motor rumbled. We were moving away from the dock, farther and farther. My stomach clenched even tighter. I couldn't move. I didn't want to move. Everything was spinning.

"*Pablito?*" I heard Mamá say. But I didn't see her because I was too busy glaring at my blue canvas shoes, the ones my father had insisted on my wearing. He called them boating shoes. I hated them.

Mamá was at my side, and then she wasn't. "*Cal. Something is wrong with Pablito. I don't think he feels well,*" she said from somewhere up ahead.

"*Wa-ha! Ha! Ha!*"

My father's buddies kept on laughing.

Whoosh. Crash. Whoosh.

The yacht swayed so much, it was as if the floor was rolling under my feet.

"*Hey, what's the matter with your kid?*" someone asked.

"*Cal?*" Mamá repeated.

My father sighed. And then he chuckled. I wasn't looking at him, but I knew exactly what he was doing. His shoulders were shrugging. His hands were swatting the air. His face was scrunched up as if he'd just heard a joke. "*Nah. It's nothing. Pablo's just going through a seasickness phase. He'll get over it.*"

Whoosh. Crash. Whoosh.

My insides gurgled.

Whoosh. Crash. Whoosh.

Mamá felt my forehead with her hand.

"*Do you need to throw up, mi amor?*"

Whoosh. Crash. Whoosh.

"*Wa-ha! Ha! Ha!*"

Whoosh . . .

I ran to the railing.

But it was too late.

"Pablo! Pablo! Wake up!"

Someone was shaking me.

My eyes fluttered. I was back in the hut. Happy stared at me. Her face was scrunched with worry. "Are you okay?"

I opened my mouth to reply. But no words came out. Instead, I gagged and choked, and suddenly my insides exploded.

I vomited. I puked. I hurled.

Again.

All over Happy's pink flip-flopped feet.

I didn't think it was possible to be more humiliated. But it was indeed possible. After the vomit-fest, I escaped to one of the tents. The only problem was there was hardly any air. It was so hot, the sweat was pouring out of me like water from an open faucet. My clothes were drenched, even my underwear. But I didn't care.

I was alone by choice.

"Knock-knock," said Happy from outside.

"I'm not home."

"I can hear you."

"*Obviously*," I mumbled.

"Come on. Let me in," she pleaded.

"It's safer out there. You never know when I might puke again."

Happy sighed. "So what? My dog pukes all the time. Like every day. And when the twins were babies, they used to puke whenever I burped them. Lito even puked in my ear once."

"Really?"

"Really."

I unzipped the door flap and let her in. "OMG, it's so hot in here," she said, fanning herself with her hands.

"It's not *that* bad."

"Not that bad?" She giggled and pointed at me. "You're so sweaty, you look like you've been swimming."

"Okay. Okay. You win." I left the door flap open and turned around so I was facing the opposite end.

Happy sat with her legs crossed. Rivulets of water dripped from her skin. Parts of her were coated with sand.

Ignore it, Pablo.

But I squirmed knowing *that* sand would eventually fall into *my* tent. The one I would sleep in.

"So. Are you planning on coming out sometime?" she asked.

"Eventually ... Maybe later."

"Okay. Okay. You win." She exhaled.

I rolled my eyes.

"*Anyway.* I didn't come here to bug you," she said, scooting closer.

"Oh really?"

"Uh-huh."

"So what did you *not* come here to bug me about, then?" I asked.

Happy didn't reply immediately. Instead, her gaze

dropped. For a second I thought maybe she was blushing. It was hard to tell.

Nah . . .

What would she be blushing about anyway?

"I just . . . Well . . . I just wanted to check on you. To see if you were okay . . . Because that's what friends do. Right?" she said, meeting my gaze again.

"Oh." As soon as I said it, I realized how unenthused I sounded. "Um. Yeah! Of course! Right! That *is* what friends do . . ."

She grinned. "So? *Are* you okay, Pablo?"

Was I okay?

"Yeah. I'm fine. Don't worry. I'm just a bit tired," I said, swatting the air with my hand, like no biggie. "Go on and have fun out there. I'll come find you in a little while."

"All right. Good. See you in a bit!" Happy waved, and then she crawled out of my tent.

I could hear her bare feet slapping the ground as she pranced off.

Phew.

I exhaled.

The last thing I wanted was for Happy to worry about me the entire time we were there. I wouldn't let her. She was going to enjoy herself even if it made me completely and utterly miserable.

One ... Two ... Three ... Four ...

I counted and kept on counting, wondering how long it would take for me to be okay.

Ten minutes?

Twenty?

Thirty?

Maybe never?

FORTY-FIVE

Eventually, though, I had to pee. Really, *really* had to pee.

So I stopped counting.

At least it was dark outside. Through the door flap, I spotted the girls' maroon-colored tent, and Miguel and Zeus's navy-blue one. Thank goodness Mamá had suggested I sleep by myself. She knew I needed my own space.

Phew.

In the distance, there was laughter and the scent of a bonfire. I grabbed some wet wipes and a change of clothes and then crept outside. There was a sign nailed to a tree with an arrow pointing to where the bathrooms and shower facilities were located.

Yes! Bathrooms! Showers!

I stumbled through the maze of pine trees. Up ahead, a

building materialized. I ran faster. I stopped. There it was. The supposed facilities were a bunch of rectangular stalls made of concrete hollow blocks, thatching, and bamboo. For some reason, there were faucets outside with plastic buckets filled with water. It looked like a tropical-themed prison.

Yikes.

My skin itched like crazy, like it already knew how bad it would be inside. One of the shower stall doors was open. I tiptoed toward it and peeped in. There was a wet concrete floor, an old rusty shower head *drip-drip-dripp*ing, another bucket, and what looked to be moss or mold or some kind of growth sprouting everywhere.

Ugh.

There was no way. It smelled like rotten leaves, damp earth, and stinky armpits. I stepped back. Slowly. I wasn't even going to bother with the toilets. What was I going to do?

Pablo. Think.

I didn't have much time. My bladder was about to burst. I scurried behind the row of stalls. There was a bunch of tanks and stuff, and some scraggly bushes that were meant to hide the mess. It would have to do. Better outdoors than some petri dish full of germs.

I tucked myself in between the bushes and let it all out. It must have been gallons of pee, at least that's what it felt like—gushing on and on and on as if it would never end. But finally it did.

Ahh... I exhaled.

It was time to improvise. I looked around once more. When I was sure nobody was watching, I peeled my damp, smelly clothes off until I was butt-naked.

It couldn't get more humiliating.

Just get it over with.

I pulled out several wet wipes and did a wipe-tuck-wipe-tuck method, so every time I cleaned a different part of my body I had an unsoiled section of wet wipe. It kind of worked. After using up half the pack, I had this somewhat fresh feeling. Good enough. I plucked my underwear from the pile of clean clothes. One leg. Two legs. Okay. Done. I grabbed the shorts. One leg. Two...

"Sir Pablo! Sir Pablo!" Zeus's voice echoed toward me.

A beam of light cut through the darkness. I lost my balance. I stumbled. I fell right into the bushes.

"Oww!"

How was I supposed to know they were bougainvillea bushes? I was desperate. It was dark. Of course I didn't see the thorns.

I was sitting by the campfire. Ms. Grace kneeled in front of me, pulling thorns out with tweezers while everyone else pretended not to look. Every time she dug one out, she would dab my skin with antiseptic solution. It simultaneously throbbed and stung. But I didn't say a peep, because, well, I didn't want them thinking I was a wuss. After a while I had these orange spots all over my legs, arms, and torso. I looked diseased.

It was officially the worst vacation ever.

Sizzle. Sizzle. Sizzle.

Jem, Happy, Zeus, and Miguel were holding hot dogs on sticks over the bonfire. Miguel tucked a soy dog into a bun and handed it to me. "Plain, right?"

I took it and nodded. How did he always know what I wanted? What I liked? What I needed? My stomach groaned. I hadn't eaten anything since breakfast. It didn't even matter that I was covered in orange polka dots in front of *everyone*.

I chomped down. *Mmm.* The soy dog was gone in three bites.

Ms. Grace pulled out the last thorn.

Ouch.

I must have looked super-duper relieved, because Happy smiled one of her smiles. It was hard to describe. It was kind of like staring into a rainbow while eating a big bowl of vanilla ice cream with whipped cream and a cherry on top. I wondered if she was born with that smile and that's why her parents named her Happy.

She got up and plopped down next to me. "I really think orange is your color," she said with a straight face.

I glared at her. "Ha. Ha. Ha."

"What? I'm serious."

Sizzle. Sizzle.

Miguel handed me another soy dog. "Here you go, little man. Eat up." And then he popped open a beer and sat by himself, staring at the fire like he was thinking about life and whatnot.

I nibbled on my soy dog.

Crackle. Crackle.

Swish. Swish.

The fire was spitting out embers. Happy dug her bare feet into the sand, making circle patterns over and over again.

Swish. Swish. Swish.

She stopped and looked up at me. "Thanks, Pablo," she said softly.

"Thanks for what?" I replied.

"For this . . ." She kicked up some sand. "The beach, the sea, the bonfire, the hot dogs, the tent. *All* of it. It's because of you, Pablo . . ."

I could feel the fire on my face even though we were several feet away.

"It's nothing," I said with a shrug.

Happy scooted closer. "It's *not* nothing . . . It's *everything*."

I smiled at her. But what I really wanted to do was run into my tent and hide so she wouldn't see my face melting from all the heat in my cheeks. Because what she didn't realize was that it was her—*she* was the best, most loyal, most supportive friend I'd ever had. Not the other way around. I should have been the one thanking her.

"Is it s'mores time yet?" Miguel announced.

Phew.

"Yes, please!" Happy bounced off the log with excitement.

It was mad chaos after that. We ran around in the dark searching for long sticks. It was a miracle nobody got poked in the eye. There was also the shrieking whenever an unsuspecting crab would scuttle out of the shadows. They were only the size of Matchbox cars, but for whatever reason, Jem, Happy, and Ms. Grace acted like a knife-wielding serial killer was chasing after them. Thankfully, it got quieter when the marshmallows, graham crackers, and chocolate bars came out. Before long, our sticks were loaded with white marshmallows. We had to keep an eye on them. The marshmallows turned a toasty shade of brown pretty fast. Jem scowled when hers turned black as charcoal. I tried not to laugh. I really wanted to. But I didn't. Unlike Happy, who fell to the ground giggling so hard, she forgot all about her marshmallows and got sand all over them.

Jem stuck her tongue out and said, "Ha! Buti nga sa'yo!" And even though I had no idea what it meant, I could tell just by her tone that it was something to do with karma or revenge or one of those spiteful kinds of things.

Zeus chortled.

Ms. Grace shook her head.

Miguel popped open another beer.

And I squished my marshmallows in between a slab of chocolate and two graham crackers.

Crunch! Crunch!

My munching was contagious. Suddenly, they were all gobbling their own s'mores. The feast didn't last, though. As soon as the marshmallows were gone, everyone looked real sleepy. One by one, Jem, Ms. Grace, and then Happy shuffled off to their tent. Zeus fell asleep on the sand next to the bonfire.

"You should get some rest, Pablo. It's been a long day," said Miguel.

"In a bit. I'm still kind of loopy from all the sugar."

Miguel chuckled.

Zeus mumbled in his sleep, and then he snorted so loud it scared the crap out of me.

Miguel sputtered. I sputtered. We lost it around the

same time, covering our mouths so we wouldn't wake him. I almost fell off the log—that's how hard I was laughing.

I caught my breath.

It was just me and Miguel. The last men standing.

The log I was on suddenly felt hollow, empty, lonesome. Like something was missing.

No. Someone.

I sighed. "Too bad Mamá and Chiqui aren't here . . . I really think they would have liked this place."

"Yeah. Maybe next time . . ." Miguel's words lingered. And then, they sort of just disappeared, floating like the ashes above the fire. He stretched his legs out on the sand and gazed up at the sky. There was this strange calmness about him. Or maybe he'd just had one too many beers.

"So, about Chiqui." The words spilled out of my mouth.

Ugh. Why did I just say that?

Miguel's gaze dropped. "What about Chiqui?"

I got all clammy and itchy, and it felt as if the serial-killer crabs were inside my shorts.

Great. Good job, Pablo.

"Um . . . uh . . . It's just, I was wondering if you really think another family is going to want to adopt her?"

Miguel sat up straighter. "Well, yeah. Sure. I'm pretty optimistic about it."

I gulped. But the graham crackers and marshmallows

and chocolate and soy dogs were in the way, as if they'd regurgitated back up.

Why was Miguel so optimistic?

Did he know something?

Should I ask?

I leaned in closer to him. "The thing is—" My throat clenched up. For a second I couldn't speak. I coughed. That's when it all blasted out of me. "The thing is, I'm kind of, like, happy, Miguel. The happiest I've been in a long time. I—I never really wanted a brother or a sister, you know...I guess I just didn't know what I was missing. But it's different now. Chiqui, she's like the sister I never knew I wanted... And...and it's killing me...it's killing me that she's going to be taken away..."

I hadn't planned on it. But there were actual tears in my eyes. Real ones. Not the crocodile kind. I sniffled and waited for him to say something.

"I'm sorry, Pablo." Miguel exhaled. "But this is a conversation you should be having with your mother. You *need* to tell her how you feel...She's not a mind reader. She may be a lot of things, but a mind reader isn't one of them."

"But...but...I can't...What if..."

There it was—the dreaded what-ifs.

Miguel seemed uncomfortable all of a sudden, like the

299

crabs had gone from my shorts to his. "You *can*, Pablo. You can talk to her. Whatever happens, at least you tried."

He was right. Of course he was right.

There was this moment. Neither of us said anything. We stared at the bonfire. Listened to the waves. Allowed everything to sink in until it couldn't sink any deeper.

"Okay," I finally said. "I'll talk to her."

Miguel nodded. "Good."

And somehow, I felt a bit better.

A bit relieved.

A bit braver.

A bit more . . . hopeful.

FORTY-SIX

It was weird when I woke up the next morning. Actually, it was barely even morning. I mean, technically it was, but at 5:15 it was still kind of dark, so it didn't really seem like it. Yet somehow, I was bright-eyed and bushy-tailed. What was the deal with that saying anyway? The bright-eyed part I understood. But what was about the bushy-tailed? I didn't have a tail, and if I *did*, it probably wouldn't be very bushy.

Never mind.

So anyway, when I glimpsed out of my tent, I saw the beach and the sea and the hint of light peeking from the horizon. And for some reason, I wasn't dizzy or woozy or nauseated. That was the weird part.

Obviously nobody else was awake. It was quiet. Even the waves seemed kind of quiet. That was weird too. Or maybe it was normal, and me thinking it was weird *was* weird.

Never mind.

I tiptoed to the edge of the tree line. Somehow it felt like there was this invisible border dividing the safe zone and the not-so-safe zone. The other side, where the sand never seemed to end, where the waves frothed on the shoreline, where the sky was clear of pine trees—that side was supposed to be the side I feared. Yet at that moment, it didn't seem quite as scary as it did before.

"Magandang umaga!" I heard someone say. I searched for the voice and found it several feet away. It was the old woman at the shack-of-a store, which was kind of like a mini sari-sari store in a bamboo hut. She was seated on a tree stump, drinking from a coffee mug.

"Oh. Um. Good morning," I replied.

She smiled and waved me over without saying anything. I looked down at the invisible border. I looked right. I looked left. I looked over my shoulder. Why was this old lady talking to me? What did she want?

The paranoid part of me wanted to run in the opposite direction. But the other part, the curious part, wanted to stay and see what happened.

I crossed the invisible border and approached her, stealing glances with every step.

Step one: Silver hair braided down her back.

Step two: Loose-fitting granny dress with parrots on it.

Step three: No shoes, only bare feet with calloused soles.

Step four: Crinkly eyes and shiny brown skin.

Step five: A leather twine necklace with a brass pendant.

I halted in front of her and stared at it. The pendant was triangular shaped with a single eye engraved in the middle. It was kind of creepy, but I was fascinated with it for whatever reason.

"Divine Eye," she said, rubbing the pendant. Before I could even react, she stood and reached for a small thermos in her shack. Then she poured some of the hot drink into another mug. "Here. You sit."

It was as if she was commanding me. I should have been offended, but instead I took the mug and settled on the nearest tree stump. The old lady sat back down and continued sipping from her drink.

"Nescafe three-in-one," she said after swallowing.

I lifted the mug and sniffed it. Coffee. The old lady had given me a big cup of coffee.

Nice.

The first sip was strong yet creamy and sweet. It warmed me and made the corners of my cheeks tingle. "Thank you. It's delicious," I told her.

The old lady winked. "I, Manang Lorna," she said with a

thick accent. "Kahapon, I see you, sa kubo." She pointed at the hut on the beach with the thatched roof.

The hut. Oh god. She must have seen me puke my guts out. How humiliating. My face burned. I focused on the coffee mug. Maybe she would stop talking to me if I looked catatonic.

"I think you no like beach. No like dagat . . . How you say . . . sea. Yes, you no like sea. You get sick. Make suka. Diba?"

Don't look at her, Pablo. Do. Not. Look.

Was she some kind of witch? Some kind of psychic? How had she figured it out?

She didn't even know me.

I pretended to sip my coffee, gazing at her over the rim of the mug. Manang Lorna was eyeing me with her actual eyes *and* with her eye pendant. I gulped the coffee and the giant glob of shame in my throat.

"Um. But how could you tell?" I finally croaked out.

She cackled. "No magic. Manang Lorna watch. I see people. Many people."

"Oh."

"Is bad. You scare. No normal. No good. Sea is beautiful. Is better you brave. You fight. Laban." Manang Lorna raised a fist in the air. "Laban! You fight. You win. No more scare."

For a second I felt like puking. What she was telling me—it was a slap in the face. Like she was stomping on my feet and kicking me in the stomach. It hurt. Really bad.

But it was true. It was all true.

This old lady. This stranger. For the first time in my life, someone was telling me I wasn't normal. I wasn't right. I *needed* to change.

"So . . . um. Like how am I supposed to fight?"

Manang Lorna clutched her stomach and her heart. "Scare is here and here. No there," she said, pointing at the sea. "You go. You make friend with sea. No more scare. Promise."

Huh?

First she tells me to fight, then she tells me to make friends with the sea?

What was she talking about?

Maybe she was just delusional.

That was it.

She was a deluded old lady.

"Hay . . ." Manang Lorna pushed herself up as if her bones hurt. "I rest. Mamaya, I open store."

I handed her back the mug. "Thanks for the coffee."

"Salamat is 'thank you.' You learn speak Tagalog. Is good. You stay here in Philippines," she said with a nod.

My face got all hot again. It also stung. She was right,

though. All along I should have been learning Tagalog. But it had never really occurred to me—the importance of learning the language and the culture of whatever country we were living in. It hadn't seemed worth it if we were just going to move again in a couple of months.

"Salamat," I repeated.

And then she just hobbled down the beach, leaving me alone again.

I gazed at the beach, at the water, at the sky. For a second I wanted my sunglasses. They were in my pocket. I could have easily pulled them out and slid them on. But the second came and went. I didn't need them anymore, even though the sky was changing colors and the sea was beginning to shimmer. In fact, the shimmering looked like winking.

It was as if the sea were winking at me.

You're not going to puke, Pablo.

You're not going to drown, Pablo.

You're not going to get killed by a shark, Pablo.

The sea was calm. The sea was reassuring me.

I could hear Manang Lorna in my head, "*You go. You make friend with sea. No more scare. Promise.*"

I inhaled the salty air and walked. It didn't even matter that there were bits of shell and seaweed fronds and dead funky-smelling crabs and sea urchins in my path. I just kept on going until my toes were wet. By then, the sun was a fireball at the edge of the horizon. The water was purple-y and calm. So were the clouds, which had golden beams of light shining through them. It was kind of like staring through a big stained-glass window. It was breathtaking and peaceful. So peaceful, it made me warm and fuzzy and hopeful inside.

That's *exactly* what I was feeling.

Hopeful.

Manang Lorna had a point.

I *had* to face my fears.

I *had* to fight.

When I got home, I'd talk to Mamá, just as Miguel had suggested. I would tell her *everything*, even if it made her mad or sad. She might ground me forever, or strangle me, or send me off to Abuelita's. But at least she would know the truth. At least she would finally know how I really felt about my father, about moving around so much, about Miguel, about Chiqui—*especially* Chiqui, and how she needed us, and how we needed her, and how we should never ever let her go.

I waded into the water. It was a bit cold. But I kept on going until it was thigh high. I wasn't scared, considering I didn't even know how to swim. Yes. It was true. I didn't know how to swim.

So what?

I'd seen bigger waves in a bathtub.

Splash.

I dunked my head.

Oh my god.

I was actually underwater.

I held my breath. My eyes were closed. There was fizzing and popping and whooshing as if the sea were whispering. I couldn't understand. Not really. But I knew what I wanted to hear.

Everything is going to be fine, Pablo.

Everything *was* going to be fine.

I burst through the surface. *Hwaaahh*—inhaling air.

It finally looked like morning. I stumbled back to the beach, into the forest, back to my tent. My skin, my hair, my clothes were sopping wet. I must have been quite a sight.

"Hey. You're up." Miguel emerged from behind some trees.

"Uh. Yeah," I replied.

I could tell he hadn't been awake for very long, because his eyes were still crusty and he had these wrinkle marks on his face from leaning on his pillow. He gazed at me from head to toe. "You need a towel?" he asked.

I looked down at myself. Water dripped everywhere. There was even a circle of wet sand around my feet that reminded me of an old-fashioned doughnut. "I *am* pretty wet." I chuckled.

Miguel chuckled too. But I figured he wanted some sort of explanation. I mean, part of me wanted to blabber about everything that had just happened. About Manang Lorna. About what she'd said. About the sunglasses that had stayed in my pocket. About the sea and how I'd made friends with it. I could even imagine what he'd say when I dragged him to the beach and showed him the new and improved Pablo.

"Awesome, little man! You'll be ready for surfing in no time!"

But the other part wanted to keep it secret. Keep it quiet. Keep it all to myself. That way I wouldn't jinx it.

Zip it, Pablo.

"The water in the shower . . . it was freezing. I thought it would help if I kept my clothes on," I said, trying to sound as convincing as possible.

"Ah. I should have warned you about that. We're lucky we even have showers. Never mind hot water. Go dry off. I'll start breakfast," he said with a smile. "Scrambled eggs and toast okay?"

"Yes, please."

"How about some coffee?" he added with a glint in his eye. "I won't tell if you don't."

I coughed. "Oh. I don't need any. Thanks."

Little did he know I'd already had a cup. I could feel the caffeine and sugar coursing through me. I was energized.

Okay.

Let's do this.

I'd return to my tent.

I'd change.

I'd have breakfast.

I'd make an effort to enjoy myself.

I'd go home.

I couldn't *wait* to see Chiqui.

I'd talk to Mamá.

And I'd fix *everything*.

FORTY-SEVEN

I ran up the steps and unlocked the door. I was finally home. I didn't think it was possible to miss the peeling paint, the water stains, the missing tiles, and the moldy old-house smell. But I had. I really, really had.

"Mamá! Chiqui!" I yelled.

It was quiet.

Ms. Grace sauntered in behind me, glancing at her watch. "They're probably still at the doctor's office."

"Oh. Right."

"Do you want some merienda? I could fix us some tea and cookies," she asked.

I didn't want cookies or anything else to eat. How was I supposed to have a leisurely afternoon snack when all I wanted was to find Mamá, sit her down, and talk to her? I just wanted to get it over with already.

I exhaled. "No thanks."

"I'll be in the kitchen if you change your mind."

Ms. Grace was gone. I just stood there, my limbs hanging like wet laundry. *Drip. Drip. Drip.* It was such a major letdown. I'd rehearsed my speech in my head the entire drive home. Everyone was conked out, except for Zeus, who was focused on the road listening to an '80s radio station. At one point, he started singing along to some song about karma and chameleons and I totally lost my train of thought.

So anyway, all I could do was lug my stuff to my room. That would surely kill some time.

Done.

Now what?

Unpack.

Should I do toiletries or clothes first?

Hmm.

Maybe clothes.

I was considering dumping the entire contents of my bag straight into the hamper to avoid getting sand on the floor when I noticed a truck parking in front of the house. It was a chocolate-brown UPS truck with a chocolate-brown uniformed driver. That driver was heading toward our front door, holding a package in his hands.

A package!

He hadn't forgotten. My father.

It was here! The shark tooth necklace was here!

I zoomed out of my room just as the doorbell rang. "I got it!" I shouted loud enough so Ms. Grace could hear.

Whoosh. The humid air from outside hit me. "Good afternoon, sir," said the UPS man.

"Oh. Hi. That's for me," I said, taking the envelope from his hand.

The UPS man didn't even seem to care that I was just a kid. He handed me a form and a pen, and pointed to where I should sign. Simple enough. I scrawled my signature. "Thanks," I said, closing the door before he could say anything else.

I ripped the envelope open, fumbling with plastic, tape, staples, and labels.

Ugh.

Why did they have to pack it in so much stuff?

Where was the shark tooth?

There were only papers, papers, and *more* papers.

Nothing. Nada.

This package wasn't even from my father.

Oh well. Maybe he was just too busy. Maybe it would come another day—tomorrow, the next day, the next week, the week after that. Yeah, that was probably it.

Sigh.

Who was I kidding?

Of course he'd forgotten.

Stupid papers.

I stared at them. What were they anyway? There were so many words. I recognized some names—Mamá's and Miguel's—and some other names, which sounded Filipino and maybe Swedish? Danish? German? I couldn't tell for sure.

The papers had that official kind of look to them, with signatures and stamps and all. I squinted, studying them more carefully. There were terms that jumped out at me: Temporary Guardian, Child, Adoptee, and Adoptive Parent.

My heart was pounding. It hurt. Like there was a knife stabbing me in my chest. I couldn't breathe. I was dizzy. The room was spinning.

"Pablo. Who was that?" said Ms. Grace, poking her head out from the kitchen. She took one look at me and frowned.

I couldn't talk. My throat was tight. I coughed. I choked. I dropped the papers and ran.

"Pablo!" she said louder.

I locked my bedroom door.

No! No! No!

I was too late. Someone was going to take Chiqui. Take her from us, from me.

Miguel. Why didn't he tell me?

Knock-knock-knock.

"Pablo! Pablo! Are you okay? Can we talk? *Please.* Let me in."

I ignored Ms. Grace.

There were tears in my eyes. I didn't even realize they were there until I felt them dropping off my chin. My face, neck, and ears were throbbing. After a minute I was burning all over. Then my stomach began to fizz and gurgle. I felt sick. Nauseated. I wanted to puke. But I couldn't.

All the hurt. All the pain. All the sorrow.

They were all bubbling inside me.

I felt so alone, as if the entire world had just abandoned me.

FORTY-EIGHT

I was in bed. Comatose. Not really—I mean, it was more of a self-induced numbness. That is, until I heard the front door squeak open. Mamá's boots clomped into the hallway and then behind her the *tap-tap-tapp*ing of Chiqui's sandals.

"Pablito! We're home!"

I balled my hands into fists and pushed them against the mattress. How could Mamá act so normal? As if everything was just fine? As if she had no secrets? I was beginning to think I didn't know her at all.

Maybe I never had.

Knock. Knock. Knock.

"Mi amor? Are you in there?"

The heat returned, spreading from my head to my toes like wildfire. I pounced off the bed and stomped to the door, opening it with so much force the doorknob hit the wall.

At first I couldn't see anything past the white flashes in my eyes. But then slowly Mamá's green gaze appeared, and her freckles—so many of them mocking me from her smooth, pale face. "Pablo . . . What's wrong?"

"What's WRONG?" I repeated so loud my throat hurt. My hands trembled. I looked down at my feet.

Just say it, Pablo. Say it.

I swallowed, ready to spit the words out. But then Chiqui peered out from behind Mama's legs. She smiled at the sight of me. I heaved. All of a sudden, she leaped forward and hugged me.

Ms. Grace hurried past us. "I have to go. I'm sorry. Traffic. Bye." The front door opened and closed.

I looked up at Mamá. There was something different about her—more faded, more worn, more tired. She bent down and said, "Chiqui. Please go to the other room and look at some books . . . LIB-RO . . ." She held her hands in front of her face and made them look like an open book. "I need to talk to Kuya Pablo for a few minutes."

I didn't think Chiqui understood.

She held on to my waist and wouldn't let go. Mamá tried to coax her away. But it was no use. It felt like someone was smashing my chest with a sledgehammer. My heart was fracturing. It was going to bust open at any moment. I held Chiqui's face with my hands and stared into her big, shiny eyes. "It's okay. Go on. You can come back to my room when we're done talking. I'll tell you all about my trip."

Chiqui hesitated. Then she let go of me. It hurt knowing how much she trusted me.

She *trusted* me.

And I was just going to leave her.

No! You're not going to let that happen, Pablo.

Mamá led Chiqui to their bedroom. I stood there and waited. My arms stiffened. My jaw tensed. I breathed in and out, in and out.

You can do it.

A minute later, Mamá returned. Her forehead was wrinkled with worry. I stepped back. She came into my room and closed the door.

"You saw the papers."

"I did."

"Pablo. She can't stay with us. Not forever." Mamá inched toward me. "I never lied to you, mi amor."

I stepped back even farther. "Why? Why *can't* she stay with us?"

"It's just not possible. I have too many responsibilities. And I already have you—"

"NO! Don't make this about me, Mamá!"

"That's not what I meant."

"Then what? What exactly did you mean?"

She covered her face with her hands. When she pulled them off, there were tears in her eyes, on her cheeks, sticking to clumps of her hair. "I'm alone, Pablo. It's hard for me to explain what it's like, to be a single mother doing it all by myself."

I leaned forward and stuck my chin out. "But that's just it, Mamá. You don't *have* to do it all by yourself . . . Just STOP running away from people, from places, from everything!"

She shook her head. "No, Pablo. I have to do what I have to do. Chiqui *needs* a mother, a father. She *needs* a stable home environment—"

"And what? *I* don't *need* those things?"

Mamá's face was blank, as if she hadn't heard me. "The Martens—they're perfect. Mr. Marten works for the Asian Development Bank. And Mrs. Marten is a therapist. Their son, Lucas, has always wanted a little sister. They're committed to staying here for however long it takes . . . They're exactly what Chiqui needs."

I took her hand and squeezed it. "They might be perfect, Mamá. But they're not *us* . . . Chiqui needs *us*."

She closed her eyes and breathed like she'd never breathed before. For a moment I thought maybe I'd convinced her. Maybe she would open her eyes and smile and hug me and tell me Chiqui could stay. Tell me that we could stay too. But then I saw the tears, I saw her lip quivering, I saw her hands shaking. She opened her eyes. "I'm sorry, Pablo. I've made up my mind."

I yanked my hand from hers. "If Chiqui goes, I go too. I'd rather go live with Dad, with Abuelita, with anyone other than *you*!"

Mamá didn't say anything. She just stood there. Her eyes were murky green. Her cheeks were bright red.

She was wounded. I had wounded her with my words.

I blinked.

She turned her back on me.

I blinked.

She was at the door.

I blinked.

She was gone.

I locked my door and retreated to my bed. The blanket. The sheets. The pillows. I crawled under them, over them, around them until I made a nest. The world disappeared. Maybe I could stay in there forever.

Boom! Boom! Crackle. Crackle. Boom!

Was that thunder?

I peeked through a gap between the mattress and the blanket. Outside everything was gray. Even the sky looked like it was covered in smoke.

Boom! Crackle. Boom!

Rain began falling. I'd never seen so much of it coming down so hard, so fast. It was like the sea was upside down, dropping all at once.

Boom! Boom!

More thunder.

Boom!

But for some reason, all I could hear was Manang Lorna's words: *"Is better you brave. You fight. Laban."*

I had to keep on fighting.

But how? Mamá wouldn't listen.

Boom! Boom! Crackle. Crackle. Boom!

All of a sudden, I was electrified, as if the thunder and lightning had zapped through the window into my flesh and bones. I leaped from my bed.

Think. Move. Run.

I *had* to do *something*.

That was it.

I wasn't going to sit and take it any longer.

Boom! Crackle. Boom!

I was going to run away.

I shoved my feet in the first pair of shoes I could find. A hoodie. I grabbed a hoodie from my dresser and put it on. It was inside out, but it didn't matter.

Boom! Boom! Crackle. Crackle. Boom!

The window. It would have to do. I opened it and shimmied outside.

Squish.

My feet landed in mud. There was no avoiding it. Almost immediately, I was sopping wet. For a moment I stared at Happy's house across the street. Maybe I could go over there and hide while I figured out what to do. I stepped forward.

Boom! Boom! Crackle. Crackle.

I could feel my heart against my chest, the adrenaline pumping through my body.

No!

This wasn't Happy's problem.

It was my problem. My problem alone.

Fight, Pablo!

I ran.

Boom! Boom! Crackle. Crackle. Boom!

FORTY-NINE

Too many tricycles were out on the road.
It was dark. The streetlamps were dim—even dimmer with the
buckets of rain falling, and the tree branches swaying all over
the place. There was practically a small river flowing down
the street, flooding the gutters so they gurgled and bubbled.
If there was any more rain, the cars and tricycles and scooters
would be floating, and so would the people and the dogs and
cats and roosters and cockroaches.

But I kept on running.

There were probably all sorts of vermin and germs and
bacteria and viruses in the water, flowing in and out of the
sewers. It was horrible. It was all too horrible.

But still, I kept on running.

Boom! Crackle. Boom!

It was like the thunder had banged on my skull.

I raced down the street. It was chaos. Besides the mud

and water and muddy water, there were leaves, plants, and branches. There was also garbage clogging the sewers, so even more water flooded the roads and sidewalks.

But it didn't matter. None of it mattered. I kept on going—hopping, leaping, splashing, and dashing as fast as I could. There were so many people everywhere. I didn't look one bit out of place.

I didn't even stop. Not for a moment. Not to think about what I was doing or where I was going. Yet my feet and legs seemed to know.

Go, Pablo! Fight!

Finally, the concrete ended. I paused right where the path to the sanctuary began. It was covered with at least four inches of murky water. The trees were whipping back and forth in a way that made me nervous.

What now?

I glanced at my sneakers, which were covered in sludge. My clothes were filthy and wet. I didn't even want to know what was on my skin and hair. The more I hesitated, the more I didn't care.

The wind stopped.

Run!

I ran and ran and ran until I reached the entrance. But the gate was locked. There was music coming from the security guard hut.

Clang! Clang! Clang!

I slammed my hands on the chain-link wires. "Mang Wily! Mang Wily!" I screamed.

After a few seconds, a startled-looking Mang Wily appeared; his eyes popped from underneath the hood of his blue rain slicker. "Sir Pablo? Is you?" he called out.

"Let me in, Mang Wily! It's an emergency!"

He hurried to the gate and opened it. "What happen, Sir Pablo?"

"Uh. Um . . ." It felt like the mud had somehow clogged up my throat. I didn't know what I was doing, what I was saying, where I was going. Tears dropped from my eyes, but the rain washed them away.

"Sir Pablo?" Mang Wily tilted his head and reached his hand out. "You want I call your mother?"

That's when I took off into the darkness.

"Sir Pablo! Sir Pablo!"

Mang Wily's voice faded.

Boom! Crash! Crash!

Lightning lit up the sky. Everything around me brightened for an instant. The sanctuary was different—scarier and wilder. I had a feeling that something was going to jump out at me with every twig that snapped and every plant that rustled. To make matters worse, the pouring rain and wind made it harder for me to see. I had to backtrack several times because it was just too dark. When I stumbled across an enclosure, the animals would spook. I must have looked like a hideous monster or something. The kalabaws' eyes practically bulged from their sockets. The spotted deer scurried behind some bushes. The monkeys howled above my head.

Run! Run! Run!

But where was I running to?

I whirled around, sprinting down one path and then another.

Hoohoo! Hoohoo!

The owls—it almost sounded like they were calling me.

Hoohoo! Hoohoo! Hoohoo!

The hooting got even louder. I cut through some hedges. Suddenly, the owl enclosure was right in front of me. I halted and caught my breath. As much as I wanted to keep on running, I couldn't. My mind—all my thoughts were mixed up, swirling around and around. I was sopping wet and exhausted.

Hoohoo! Hoohoo!

The enclosure—it was sheltered from the rain. Sort of. I was sure the owls wouldn't mind if I took a breather in there. At least, I hoped not. I rushed to the door and opened the latch. The owls gazed at me with round yellow eyes. I wanted to dash in there. But I knew the birds would panic. So I tiptoed through the hay, trying to avoid the twigs and crunchy debris. When I reached the other side—the side with a makeshift roof of sticks and leaves and grass—I crumpled to the floor. Even though it was warm and humid, I shivered.

I was scared. *No.* I was terrified.

Not of the rain and the wind and the thunder and the lightning.

I knew the storm would eventually pass.

What terrified me was the cold, harsh reality.

I was probably going to lose Chiqui.

I was probably going to lose all the people I'd grown to care about—Miguel, Happy, Ms. Grace, and Zeus.

I was probably going to lose the only place that felt like home again.

All the fighting, all the running, all the best-laid plans would fail me.

I curled up and cried.

Hoohoo! Hoohoo!

Maybe the owls were crying too.

I cried and cried and kept on crying for god knows how long.

Boom! Crash! Boom!

"Pablito! Where are you?" I heard someone scream. I peeped between my knees just as a beam of a light illuminated the enclosure. "Mi amor!" Mamá ran down the path. Behind her I spotted something, no, *someone*—Chiqui. She was dressed in an oversize purple raincoat and boots.

The owls screeched and flapped their wings.

Mamá burst through the door. "Dios mío . . . Thank god . . . Thank god you're okay," she said. "Are you hurt?"

I didn't say a word.

"Kuya Pabo . . ." At first it was only a whisper. But as soon as Chiqui saw me, and I saw her, she yelled, "KUYA!" and scampered toward me.

I hugged her, and even though we were both sopping wet, I stopped shivering.

Mamá froze, except her eyes, which blinked so fast, little droplets of water fell from her lashes. "Chiqui . . . She *does* talk to you . . . ," she said in a hushed voice.

"Yes," I said, meeting her gaze.

She frowned. "But . . . but why didn't you tell me when I asked you?"

"I didn't *need* to tell you, Mamá. If you'd just paid more attention . . . If you'd listened. If you'd been around more . . . you would have known."

Her lips flattened into a straight line. "You shouldn't have run away, Pablo . . ."

I sat up and glared at her. I couldn't *believe* what she was saying. "Really? *You* of all people, Mamá? Isn't that what you've been doing all this time? Running from place to place to place?"

"That's different—"

"Is it?"

It was silent. Except not really. The rain continued battering down and the wind howled and the owls wouldn't stop screeching. With every second that passed I could feel myself getting braver, bolder, angrier.

I was fed up.

I wasn't going to let Mamá's problems become my problems.

Not anymore.

"I meant what I said. If Chiqui goes, I go too."

All of a sudden, Chiqui's arms loosened their grip. She gazed up at me with teary eyes. "*Mee* go, Kuya Pabo? Ayoko! *Mee* no go!"

It felt as if my heart had jumped into my mouth.

Oh god.

What do I tell her?

I pulled her closer. "*Shh* . . . Everything's going to be fine."

Boom! Boom! Crackle. Boom!

The thunder made my ears ring.

Boom! Boom! Boom!

Chiqui nuzzled my shirt. She began to sob and heave and cough. The rain fell even harder. I shielded her with my body. *Shh.* I kept on repeating, *Shh. Shh. Shh.*

What else could I do?

"Pablo."

I looked at Mamá.

"We already talked about this," she said. "I'm your mother. Don't you think I know what's best for Chiqui?"

Chiqui trembled. She whipped around and faced Mamá. "*Mee* no go. NO go!"

"Don't worry, Chiqui. I'm *not* going to let anyone take you," I said, loud enough so Mamá could hear me. My arms throbbed and twitched. I wanted to punch something. Hard. But I stood my ground. "You *lied* ... at Heinz's house ... You told Chiqui you would take care of her. You said it. I heard you."

She exhaled and curled her fingers around her imaginary calming stone. "Everything I've done ... everything I'm doing is for us, mi amor. You'll see ..."

"For us? Don't you mean *you*? Because everything you've done is for *you*. I never wanted to leave California. I never wanted to travel the world. I never wanted any of it. Do you think I like not having a real home? Not having any friends or family around? When are you going to realize that this isn't just about Chiqui?"

Mamá gasped. "But—but why didn't you tell me?"

"Because I was scared," I said, staring at the ground. "I was scared of losing you, just like I lost Dad."

"Oh, Pablito—" Her voice cracked. Tears dribbled from her eyes. She was crying. It was the kind of crying she called ugly. But to me it was beautiful. Even with all the sadness, the anger, and the frustration—Mamá was still beautiful. "I didn't know," she whispered. "I didn't know you were so unhappy."

"That's just it, Mamá. I *was* unhappy. But I'm not anymore. I like it here. It's not perfect. But it feels right. It feels like home." I coaxed Chiqui into my arms again. "And home is you, me, *and* Chiqui. She's part of us now. We need her just as much as she needs us."

Mamá didn't move. She didn't say anything. I could tell she was giving it some real thought. Her face was blank, but her mouth was slightly puckered, as if she wasn't quite sure what words were going to come out. Chiqui looked at her, then at me, then at her, then at me again. It was obvious how nervous she was by how she breathed—shallow, erratic, fast. Still, she managed to whisper something to me.

But I couldn't hear.

I bent down. "What is it, Chiqui?"

"Sista." She patted her chest. "Broter." She patted my chest.

"Yes, Chiqui. Sister. Brother," I said with a nod.

Mamá took a few wobbly steps and dropped to her

knees. She embraced us both. Her tears dripped on my head and neck. The owls cooed softly. The rain stopped—I hadn't even noticed.

It was peaceful.

Mamá breathed deep. She cupped Chiqui's face and kissed her on the forehead. "Chiqui, mi amor." And then she pulled me closer and kissed me too. "Pablito . . . how about you and me and Chiqui go home now?"

I nodded.

Chiqui smiled.

And then we went home.

All together.

The three of us.

FIFTY

TWO WEEKS LATER

The hospital waiting room smelled like
Vicks VapoRub. Not because some person with a horrible
chest cold was sitting nearby, or because a clumsy nurse
had spilled a gigantic tub of it right in front of me. No. It
smelled like Vicks VapoRub because I'd smeared a bunch of
it on my upper lip. I read somewhere that coroners used it
at the morgue so they wouldn't have to smell the stench of
dead bodies.

Ugh.

Gross.

Anyways, there weren't any dead bodies or anything.
But I thought maybe, just maybe, the Vicks VapoRub might
make the hospital smell more tolerable. If I was going to
have to sit there for hours while Chiqui had her surgery,
the last thing I wanted was to inhale the germs and bacteria

and viruses, which to me smelled like a toxic bouquet of old sweat, farts, vomit, and bad breath.

"Kumusta? How are you all holding up?" Ms. Grace appeared, holding a big white box with green polka dots and a cardboard hot beverage holder filled with cups. "I've got doughnuts, coffee, and hot chocolate," she said, putting the stuff on a table.

Mamá squealed and pounced on the nearest coffee cup. "Gracias, Grace. This is exactly what the doctor ordered."

Exactly what the doctor ordered. We were in a hospital. It was kind of funny, actually. But Mamá wasn't laughing. She just sat there sipping her coffee. Her brow was furrowed, her freckles were paler, her hair was frizzed, and her clothes were wrinkled from sitting and standing and pacing, over and over and over again.

"Any news?" asked Ms. Grace.

Mamá shook her head. "Nothing yet."

Ms. Grace tucked herself into the seat next to her and rubbed her back as if to console her. "I'm sure we'll hear something soon."

Silence.

I looked away and started counting the green polka dots on the doughnut box.

One. Two. Three.

They said it was a routine surgery, nothing to worry about.

Then how come it felt as if decades had already gone by?

Four. Five. Six.

Squeak. Squeak. I looked up at a pair of squishy white nurse's shoes. But they only walked in the opposite direction toward some other people, worried about some other patient.

Seven. Eight. Nine.

The loudspeaker crackled. Maybe they would call us.

"Doctor Arellano, please come to the nurses' station."

Nope.

I exhaled and then inhaled. The Vicks VapoRub made the insides of my nostrils burn. I coughed.

Ten. Eleven. Twelve.

All the polka dot counting was making my eyes water. I shut them. I didn't want anyone to think I was crying. I mean, there wasn't anything wrong with crying. I wasn't sad, though. I was worried. Mortified, actually.

What if something *did* go wrong?

What if there was a complication?

What if . . . what if she . . .

Ms. Grace stood and smoothed the creases from her pants. "I'll go to the nurses' station and see what I can find out."

"Thank you, Grace." As soon as she was gone, Mamá patted the empty seat next to her. "Come, mi amor."

I didn't say anything. I just plunked myself from one spot to the other.

Thirteen. Fourteen.

The doughnut box was farther away. So I had to squint to count.

Fifteen. Sixteen. Seventeen. Eighteen.

Mamá shifted positions and cleared her throat. "I—I wanted to talk to you, Pablo."

I found her eyes, which at that moment were the same soothing green color as the peridot crystal in her grasp. She took my hand, placed the crystal on my palm, and then placed hers on top, like we were making a peridot hand sandwich.

"I wanted to say . . . I'm sorry . . . after everything that's happened. With everything that's still happening, I haven't gotten the chance to properly apologize." She leaned closer so our shoulders touched. "I've been selfish. As a mother, I should have considered the consequences of what I was doing. I should have seen. I should have known you were unhappy . . . From now on, I want you to open up to me. I want you to feel like you can tell me *anything*. Anything at all. Whatever it is, we'll work it out. Together. Okay?"

I felt a strange sort of warmth in my hand. The spot where the crystal was radiated to the tips of my fingers, radiated to my wrist, into my arm, into my chest, into my heart, into the pit of my stomach.

Inhale. Exhale.

Miraculously, I was calmer.

"Okay."

We opened the peridot hand sandwich and I gave the crystal back to her.

I smiled.

Inhale. Exhale.

My throat was clear.

"Mamá." She looked at me.

Inhale. Exhale.

And then all the words—the ones I was thinking and feeling—poured out. "Mamá. You *really* should know that I can't *stand* hospitals. Just the thought of them makes me itch all over. Sitting here feels like the worst kind of torture. Like I'm inside a septic tank filled with puss and puke and poop and germs and all sorts of deadly viruses . . . If it weren't for Chiqui, I would have already run down that hallway, out the door," I said, pointing at the exit sign.

Mama's eyes widened. "Oh, Pablito, mi amor! Madre mía! All this time you've been suffering."

Squeak. Squeak.

"Carmen. Pablo." Ms. Grace was back. This time with Chiqui's doctor.

Doctor Huang was still wearing his scrubs. He had a surgical mask hanging around his neck, so his entire face was exposed.

His smile—it was unmistakable.

"The surgery went well, very well. Chiqui is in recovery. You can go see her now," he said.

The surgery went well.

It went well!

Thank god. Thank goodness.

My eyes watered. Again. Tears. There were tears of joy, tears of relief dripping down my face. I wiped them away with my sleeve.

"She's okay, Pablo." Mamá hugged me from the side. Her freckles had somehow come back to life, hopping around from one pink cheek to the other. She took my hand and squeezed it.

"Come, mi amor . . . Let's go see Chiqui's new smile."

The door opened. At first all I saw were the pastel-purple walls and the yellow linoleum tiles and the rollaway beds and all the contraptions with tubes and lights and numbers and sounds.

Bleep. Bleep. Bleep.

There was a nurse with Minnie Mouse scrubs leaning over one of the beds. She straightened her back and smiled. "Good job, Chiqui."

That's when I saw her. The pastel-purple walls, the yellow linoleum tiles, the rollaway beds, the contraptions—they all disappeared. All I could see was Chiqui. Her eyes. Her mouth. She was trying so hard not to smile. But I could still see it hidden through the clear surgical tape, through the stitches that ran between her lip and her nose, through her tender, swollen flesh.

It *was* a smile.

And it sure was beautiful.

FIFTY-ONE

A month had passed since Chiqui came home from the hospital. It was almost June—the tail end of the Philippine summer. By then, we had managed to get through nineteen whole episodes of *Speak Cartoon, Learn English for Kids*. It was mind-numbing. Excruciating. Torturous. But it was also amazing, beyond amazing to watch her transform into an entirely new Chiqui—one who was confident, curious, friendly—almost *too* friendly. She wanted to make friends with *everyone*.

Finally, we'd reached episode twenty—the very last one. *Thank god.*

We could finally move on to something more normal. Something that wouldn't make me want to bang my head against the wall while wearing earmuffs.

As usual, Chiqui's eyes were glued to the computer screen like her life depended on it. I, on the other hand, was trying but failing to ignore the annoying chipmunk voices. You'd think I would have been used to it after nineteen episodes. But for some reason the jibber-jabbering just got worse and worse and worse.

Crunch. Crunch. Crunch.

Chiqui's new snack obsession was cheddar-flavored popcorn—the kind that was covered in neon-orange powder. I suspected it wasn't even made from real cheese. When I read the ingredients, there were all sorts of chemical names that sounded like they belonged in drain cleaner or antifreeze or that bright blue liquid to clean the toilet bowl with. I tried to tell her it wasn't very healthy. But that only made her hug the giant bag even tighter. She gave me this pouty, frowny kind of look and said, "No. No. No Kuya Pab-*low*. Dis mine."

Pab-*low*.

Ugh.

It was her speech therapist's fault.

I suppose going from "Pabo" to "Pab-*low*" wasn't all that bad, but still. I wished she wouldn't emphasize the "low" quite so much. For whatever reason, it gave me an inferiority complex.

Oh well.

Crunch. Crunch.

Chiqui went back to her popcorn and her chipmunk voices. Every other kernel would miss her mouth and fall under my desk. I sighed, retrieving the broom and dustpan I had in my closet. Mamá bought them for me at the palengke after I tried to convince her to get me one of those cordless mini-vacuums, or better yet one of those robot vacuums that went around and around the room bumping into walls and cleaning even when you weren't home. But she just shook her head like I was bonkers and told me an old-fashioned broom and dustpan would be just as good.

Whatever.

A robot vacuum was a great investment. Especially since Chiqui was sticking around for good.

Yahoo!

The process wasn't going to be a fast one. It might take two or three or four or even five years. That's what the lawyers had said. But at least the ball was rolling on the paperwork. Whatever that meant. And Miguel was pulling some strings. Lots of strings. I couldn't help picturing Chiqui tangled up in a life-size ball of yarn, with Miguel pulling and pulling until she was finally freed.

Speaking of freed.

I was *totally* off the hook.

It turned out that keeping Chiqui's real name—Tintin—a secret didn't even matter all that much. Miguel had sent an investigator to poke around. There were no records that her mother had ever given birth. No birth certificate meant that technically, she could have whatever name she wanted.

Weird, huh?

So I decided to fess up, even though I knew Chiqui didn't want me to. I figured it was okay since the adoption was already in the works. After our talk in the hospital, the last thing I wanted was to keep any more secrets from Mamá.

Phew.

Thankfully, she didn't get mad at me.

Not one bit.

Neither did Chiqui.

We ended up sitting together as a family. And with Miguel's help--because Mamá's Tagalog wasn't quite good enough—she asked Chiqui's permission to put Tintin on her birth certificate. Mamá explained that she didn't want to erase her past; it was important she not forget who she was and where she came from.

Chiqui would be her nickname.

According to Ms. Grace, who always made sure to fill me in on the facts, many, if not most Filipinos went by names completely unrelated to what they were born with.

Supposedly, Zeus wasn't even Zeus. He was Alberto.

Gasp.

Mind blown.

And Happy wasn't Happy either. She was Elena.

Double gasp.

And Bing was Susan.

And Jem . . . *drumroll, please* . . . was actually Irene.

Go figure.

So that's how it was decided.

Chiqui was still Tintin. And from then on, Tintin would be called Chiqui.

Anyways, back to the cheddar-flavored popcorn. I *had* to sweep the kernels off the floor. I just *had* to. *Geez.* There was neon-orange powder stuck in between the floorboards. An old-fashioned broom and dustpan, huh? Clearly Mamá was the one who was bonkers. I'd need some wet Q-tips and a mop to get it real clean.

Ugh.

I glanced out the window. The sun was kind of mellow for a hot summer day. There was also a breeze making the tree branches sway. It almost looked like they were waving at me. *Come out and play, Pablo,* they seemed to be saying.

Happy, Jem, Bing, and Lito ran out of their house. They placed a can on the sidewalk, and then proceeded to skip and hop and take turns throwing flip-flops at it. Even from all the way across the street, I could hear them screaming and laughing and saying, "Ikaw na! You're it!"

I couldn't help smiling and laughing too. That's how ridiculous they looked.

"Thank you for watching *Speak Cartoon, Learn English for Kids, Episode Twenty!*" the chipmunk voice said.

Chiqui slid off the chair, licking cheese powder from her fingers. I cringed. Then cringed some more when she wiped her hands on her pink dress. The dress had cheesy orange stripes. She didn't seem to care, though. Especially after she spotted the kids playing outside.

"Kuya Pab-low. We go play!" she shouted, hopping up and down. "Pleeze!" she begged, aiming her brand-new smile at me.

It was my Kryptonite. *That* smile, it was perfect even with the pink scar above her lip—the scar that her doctors said would fade but would never go away completely.

I just couldn't say no.

Sucker.

"Sige. Maglaro tayo." The Tagalog words felt weird on my tongue. Like they didn't belong there. But Ms. Grace assured me I was doing great. A quick study. A natural. Apparently, I *was* good at learning languages.

Go figure.

Chiqui grabbed my hand. "Tara!"

The big bag of popcorn was forgotten.

The mess of neon-orange powder was forgotten.

The old-fashioned broom and dustpan were forgotten.

Even the annoying chipmunk voices were forgotten.

We left all that behind and went outside.

"Mi amors!" said Mamá when she saw us. She was standing out front with Miguel and Zeus, staring at the facade of the house. Her baggy overalls were smeared with paint, and her hair was desperately trying to escape from the bright red bandanna on her head. "What do you think?" she said, pointing at the wall.

There were three swatches of paint in different colors. The last couple of weeks she'd been on a home improvement rampage—replacing broken tiles, fixing leaky windows, repairing kitchen cabinets, and painting—lots and lots of painting. I studied the swatches, squinting my eyes and rubbing my chin as if I had a beard. There was a pale yellow the exact shade of mashed potatoes, an off-white one that looked like French vanilla ice cream, and a blue one that reminded me of the sea at sunrise.

"That one," I said, gesturing at the blue swatch.

"Yes!" Mamá fist-pumped the air.

Miguel laughed.

And Zeus, well, he frowned and shook his head. "But Ma'am Carmen, white is more practical," he said.

"White is boring!" she exclaimed.

Miguel grabbed Mamá and kissed her. "Zeus, my man . . . the lady has a point."

"Kuya Pab-*low*," said Chiqui, pulling on my shirt.

We left the adults behind and stood on the curb, waiting for the tricycles to pass by. Finally, the road cleared. A gust of wind blew above us, shaking the narra trees. Hundreds, maybe thousands, maybe even millions of tiny yellow flowers showered down. It was as if particles of light were falling straight from the sun.

I held Chiqui's hand as we crossed. There was still part of me that was disgusted by the cheesy powder on her fingers. There was still part of me that wondered what bacteria, what viruses, what germs were floating in the air and oozing under our feet. There was still part of me that wanted to count every single flower on the ground, and then sweep them up with the old-fashioned broom and dustpan in my closet. But there was also another part of me that didn't care quite as much.

We reached the other side.

Jem waved.

Bing and Lito bounced up and down, shouting, "Chiqui! Chiqui! Chiqui!"

Happy smiled like she really, truly *was* happy to see us.

I blushed.

She removed one of her pink, sparkly flip-flops from her feet and handed it to me. "Ikaw na. You're it, Pablo!"

I took it, germs, dirt, and all, and flung it as hard as I could.

ACKNOWLEDGMENTS

It takes a village to raise a book baby.

Believe me, nothing could be truer.

This book would not have seen the light of day without my amazing literary agent, Wendy Schmalz, who never stopped reminding me that "Slow and steady wins the race."

Thank you for believing in me. Thank you for keeping me on track. Thank you for pushing me toward the finish line.

I finally won the race, Wendy!

To my editor, Joy Peskin—thank you for adopting my book baby and giving it the best home possible. I will forever be grateful. To my second editor, my kababayan, Trisha de Guzman—thank you for your keen eye, your sound advice, and for laughing at all my corny Pinoy jokes.

This book wouldn't have grown into what it is today without the nurturing of the entire FSG BYR/Macmillan team. Thank you for putting in all that hard work every step of the way. Special shout-out to book designer extraordinaire,

Aram Kim, for transforming my words into a book-shaped masterpiece.

To my cover artist, my kababayan, Christine Almeda— thank you for bringing Pablo and Chiqui to life with so much color, style, and attention to detail. You definitely made my cover fantasies come true.

To my mom, Helena—thank you for being the best cheerleader a girl could have. Surviving this journey would have been impossible without your love.

To my dad, Wahoo—I'm thankful for the support. Pursuing my dreams would have been a lot harder without your help.

To my big sister, Katya—thank you for always encouraging me no matter what.

There was no way I could have ever clocked in those endless hours of drafting if my husband hadn't taken over some of the child-rearing duties. Thank you, Daemon.

My daughter, Violet—you never cease to amaze me. Thank you for being my inspiration. Thank you for making me laugh, and for reminding me that I can make others laugh too. I love you, infinity fins.

To my childhood friends, Michelle, Apple, and Guada— thank you for the enduring love and loyalty. We might not see one another often, but when we do, it's like eighth grade all over again.

It's been a chaotic few years; I could not have endured them without my fellow Roaring 20s debuts and Class of 2K20 Books classmates. Thank you for taking this wild ride with me.

To my MG Squad, Janae Marks, Lorien Lawrence, and Shannon Doleski—thanks for all the laughs and for keeping it real, always.

To my time-zone buddy—Melly Sutjitro—thank you for being there and listening to all my nonsense and whining over the years. I truly appreciate you.

I am grateful to Joseph Cole for allowing me to immortalize Justice's life through Lucky the superhero dog. His memory lives on.

And lastly, to the readers—thank you for taking a chance on my book. I hope you enjoyed reading it as much as I enjoyed writing it.

GLOSSARY OF TAGALOG WORDS AND PHRASES

✑ **Ang ganda ng bahay mo**: Your house is so nice.

✑ **Ang ganda ng ibon, diba?**: The birds are beautiful, aren't they?

✑ **Ano ang paborito mong kulay?**: What is your favorite color?

✑ **Anong nangyari? Bulag ba siya?**: What happened? Is he blind?

✑ **Ate**: a term of respect used to address one's older sister, but it can also be used to address an older female friend or acquaintance

✑ **Ayoko**: I don't want.

✑ **Bangka**: an outrigger boat commonly used for transport and fishing

✑ **Bangsilog**: a popular breakfast meal consisting of fried marinated milkfish, fried egg, and garlic rice

🦋 **Buti nga sa'yo!**: Serves you right!

🦋 **Chismosa**: a person who gossips

🦋 **Dagat**: sea

🦋 **Dahan dahan**: Go slowly or carefully.

🦋 **Diba?**: Right?

🦋 **Durian**: a large, spiky tropical fruit with a sweet yellow custard-like flesh. To some, it has an unpleasant aroma.

🦋 **Duwendes**: goblins, elves, or dwarves in Filipino folklore

🦋 **Hay**: Sigh.

🦋 **Hay naku**: Oh dear. Oh my.

🦋 **Hindi**: No.

🦋 **Hindi ko alam**: I do not know.

🦋 **Huwag**: Don't.

🦋 **Huwag ka na makialam!**: Don't meddle. Stay out of this. Mind your own business.

🦋 **Huwag kang matatakot. Aalagaan kita**: Don't be afraid. I will take care of you.

Huwag kang mag-alala. Hindi kita hahayaang mahulog: Do not worry. I won't let you fall.

Huwag kang mag-alala. Punong-puno ng magagandang damit at sapatos ang mga tindahan dito. Lalabas kang isang prinsesa!: Do not worry. The stores here are full of beautiful clothes and shoes. You'll come out looking like a princess!

Ikaw na!: It's your turn!

Itatago ko ang iyong lihim: I will keep your secret.

Ito si: this is

Jeepney: a small decorative-looking bus that is one of the most popular modes of affordable public transportation

Kahapon: yesterday

Kain tayo: Let's eat.

Kainan sa palengke: market eatery

Kalabaw: water buffalo

Kapres: menacing tree giants in Filipino folklore

Kawawa naman: poor thing

Konti lang: just a little

Kumusta?: How are you?

Kuya: a term of respect used to address one's older brother, but it can also be used to address an older male friend or acquaintance

Kuya, sa palengke tayo. Salamat: Bro [slang, not actual brother], to the market. Please.

Laban: fight

Libro: book

Lolo: grandfather

Lugaw: a rice porridge, oftentimes eaten when someone isn't feeling well

Mabuhay: Literally translates as "Live!" But it is often used to welcome someone, or as a cheer when toasting drinks.

Mabuti naman po: Quite good, sir.

Magandang umaga: Good morning.

Mahal kita: I love you.

Mamaya: later

  Manang: a term of respect used to address one's older sister (someone aged forty or older), but it can also be used to address an older female friend or acquaintance

  Mangosteen: a purple tropical fruit with fragrant, slightly acidic flesh

  Maniwala ka sa akin: You can trust me.

  Manong: a term of respect used to address one's older brother (someone aged forty or older), but it can also be used to address an older male friend or acquaintance

  Merienda: afternoon snack

  Monggo: a soup or stew made with dried mung beans (similar to lentils)

  Nanay: mother

  Ngiti: smile

  Opo: a polite or respectful way of saying yes

  Palengke: market

  Pancit: a traditional Filipino dish made with rice or egg noodles and mixed with vegetables, meat, or seafood and hard-boiled eggs.

🦢 **Pasalubong**: a gift or souvenir given to a friend or relative by someone who had just returned from travel

🦢 **Pulis**: police

🦢 **Rambutan**: a tropical fruit related to the lychee and longan fruit with a hairy-looking outer shell

🦢 **Sa bahay**: at home

🦢 **Sa baryo**: at the village

🦢 **Sa kubo**: in the hut

🦢 **Sa munisipyo**: at the municipality

🦢 **Saging**: banana

🦢 **Salamat po**: Thank you.

🦢 **Sarap**: delicious

🦢 **Sari-sari store**: a small convenience store

🦢 **Sige. Maglaro tayo**: Okay. Let's play.

🦢 **Siguradong, gusto mo ng French fries, noh?**: I'm sure you want French fries, right?

🦢 **Sorbetes**: ice cream

℞ **Suka**: vomit

℞ **Sus. Ang taray mo naman**: Jesus. You're so sassy/prickly/mean.

℞ **Susmaryosep**: a contraction of "Jesus, Mary, and Joseph" to express anger, frustration, or disbelief

℞ **Taho**: a breakfast or snack food made of silken tofu, sugar syrup, and sago pearls, usually sold by a roving street vendor

℞ **Takot ka ba?**: Are you afraid?

℞ **Tao po**: a phrase used to announce his/her/their presence at an entrance of someone's home

℞ **Tara**: Let's go.

℞ **Tita**: a term of respect used to address one's aunt, but it can also be used to address a much older female friend or acquaintance

℞ **Tito**: a term of respect used to address one's uncle, but it can also be used to address a much older male friend or acquaintance

℞ **Turon**: a popular snack consisting of ripe plantain banana, brown sugar, and sometimes jackfruit, rolled in rice paper sheets and deep fried

❧ **Ube**: a purple sweet yam often used as an ingredient in sweets and ice cream

❧ **Unggoy**: monkey

❧ **Walis tingting**: a handleless broom made from the stiff midribs of palm leaves, used to sweep outdoors

AUTHOR'S NOTE

Most of us take our smiles for granted.

They just happen.

When we're happy.

When we're laughing.

When we're nervous.

Lips curled at the corners.

Teeth, exposed.

Perhaps a dimple or two, like exclamation points at the end of a sentence.

But this isn't the case for the 4,000 plus children born with cleft lips and palates every year in the Philippines. For them, smiles are a source of sadness, of heartache, of pain, of anger.

In developed nations like the United States, cleft lips and palates are, by and large, surgically corrected very early in life. But in poorer countries like the Philippines, birth defects are commonly left untreated into childhood and even adulthood, because the majority of families simply cannot afford the cost.

Like Chiqui, these children often live isolated lives, staying home rather than going to school—where they can be bullied, laughed at, and stared at. Some, in more extreme cases, may even have difficulty breathing, eating, and speaking.

Thankfully, there are now organizations dedicated to giving children with cleft lips and palates free medical treatment. With the help of donors and volunteer surgeons and nurses, they'll get their second chances—to smile without shame or embarrassment.

Lips curled at the corners.

Teeth, exposed.

Perhaps a dimple or two, like exclamation points at the end of a sentence.

A smile.

Just like yours and mine.

But *never* taken for granted.

If you would like to learn more about the wonderful work these organizations are doing in the Philippines, you may visit them online:

1. Mabuhay Deseret Foundation: mabuhaydeseretfoundation.org
2. Operation Smile Philippines: operationsmile.org.ph
3. Smile Train Philippines: smiletrain.ph

Read Tanya Guerrero's next heartfelt novel . . .

Turn the page for a sneak peek.

One

I wore my last remaining girlie shirt to the airport. It was pastel purple with a tiny frill at the sleeve and collar, and two heart-shaped silver buttons. It was exactly the kind of shirt Mom used to buy me. And the kind of shirt I swore I would never wear. Not anymore. Especially since it was already two sizes too small, but it didn't matter. I stood as straight as I could, angling my shoulders and neck the same way a ballet dancer would. I knew how because my parents had season tickets to the New York City Ballet at Lincoln Center.

The shirt. The stance. The touch of Vaseline I'd dabbed on my lips. It was my last-ditch effort to stay in New York City, where I belonged. Maybe Mom would take one look at me and change her mind.

"Qatar Airways flight 5179 to Barcelona will begin boarding first class, business class, and families with young children at gate C7 in ten minutes," a woman's voice announced.

Okay. This is it.

I fluttered my eyelashes.

Mom smoothed her silk Hermès scarf with her delicate fingers. She glanced at me. But it was like she wasn't really seeing me. Like she was skimming the newspaper with her tortoiseshell eyes.

"Well . . ." Mom stepped closer, into the light. Her skin was flawless, her lips a matte burgundy, her eyebrows perfectly arched. "I hope you take this time to reflect, Alba. To make some changes . . . I think Spain will be good for you."

I exhaled. My ballet posture deflated. "Okay," I mumbled.

Suddenly there was a mass of people crowding around us, bumping me with their carry-on bags as they lined up. A lady in a uniform the same shade as Mom's lipstick approached us. She had this ridiculous hat tilted on her head with a small gold pin of a deer or impala or whatever.

"Hello, Mrs. Green. I'm Sofia, and I'll be taking care of Alba on the flight." The lady smiled and bowed her head, and then she placed one of those sticky-label thingies on the side of my chest. I glanced at it and read it from upside down.

Alba Green
QR 5179
Unaccompanied Minor

The label made me feel like a dumb kid.

"Thank you, Sofia. May I have a moment with my daughter?" said Mom.

"Of course." The flight attendant stayed put. She half turned, focusing her gaze on the glass window with the big white airplane on the other side.

I stared at my black Converse and wondered what would happen if I dropped my backpack and ran. How far would I get before someone caught me?

"Alba."

I looked up.

"*Please*. Try not to hate me. This will be good for you. You'll see," said Mom, placing her hand on my cheek.

I stood there, speechless. No matter how Mom framed it, the bottom line was, I was being cast out. Banished. Mom had finally made good on her threats.

"We should go," said the flight attendant over her shoulder.

I stepped away, but Mom pulled me back. "Wait." She had tears in her eyes. Tears that dribbled down her cheeks, leaving grayish mascara tracks on her pale skin.

I was shocked.

I had never seen her cry.

"*Crying is undignified.*" Those were her words. Not mine.

"Mahal kita," she said, so softly I could barely hear her. *I love you*, in Tagalog. She only ever spoke it when Dad was around.

Out of habit, I scanned the terminal. But he was nowhere in sight.

Maybe she was just being sentimental.

Whatever.

I moved backward, slowly. I watched her wipe her face with the tips of her fingers. The tears were gone and so was her makeup. Under her right eye, the skin was a yellowish green—the color of a nearly faded bruise.

"Bye, Mom."

I turned my back on her, like she'd turned her back on me.

I walked off and followed the clicking of the flight attendant's high heels.

Click-clack. Click-clack.

She gave my ticket and passport to another lady with the same uniform on. And then we turned into a corridor. The flight attendant started talking. *Blah. Blah. Blah.* "I like your short hair. It's so cute. *Perfect* for summer in Spain."

I nodded and kept on walking with heavy feet.

For once, I just wanted to stay home with Mom. Even if it meant being around Dad. Not that Dad was around much. When he was, it seemed like he could barely stand being in the same room as me.

He didn't want me.

And of course Mom did whatever *he* wanted.

So I guess she didn't want me, either.

I paused at the crack between the walkway and the entrance to the plane. My breath halted for a second and then heaved, as if there was only a bit of oxygen left on earth.

"Alba?" The flight attendant touched my arm.

I flinched.

This was it. My last chance to run.

My heart pounded against my chest, creeping up my throat until it felt like I was choking. I coughed, then swallowed. But the lump of fear, of anger, of sadness, of regret, stayed put.

They *really* didn't want me.

I was alone.

I stepped over the threshold.

Because what did I have left to lose?

Nothing.

Two

I'd forgotten how small airplane bathrooms were. As long as I stood in the same spot, there was just enough room to place my backpack on the lid of the toilet, pull out my extra clothes, and change. I stuffed the purple shirt deep into the bottom of my bag.

Breathe.

I stared back at myself from the mirror.

It was me.

The *real* me. Not the me I'd fabricated for Mom's sake.

I had on my favorite T-shirt, which I'd found in a thrift store. It was faded and gray, featuring a glam-rock David Bowie with a red bolt of lightning striking through his face. Mom hated it and Dad hated it even more. It was kind of ironic, since Mom was the one who'd introduced me to David Bowie's music. I remembered it like it was yesterday, because it was the first time I'd gotten suspended from school—I'd hurled an open carton of chocolate milk at

Alexis, the sixth-grade mean girl who insisted on making my school life a living hell. We were in a cab, on the way home. Mom's lips were sealed tight. She had nothing left to say to me. All she did was sit stiffly on the other side of the seat, as far away from me as possible. Once in a while, I'd steal a glance at her as she glared through the window, unmoving. But then a song came on the radio. The cab driver turned the volume up.

> *But I try, I try . . .*
> *Never gonna fall for (modern love) . . .*

All of a sudden, I noticed Mom's fingers tapping to the beat. Seconds later, the tip of her high-heel shoe joined in. Then she began mouthing the lyrics.

I was surprised. More shocked, really.

I couldn't remember having ever seen her bopping to a song before. *Huh.* I scooched a bit closer and then mustered the courage to speak. "This song . . . It's cool," I mumbled.

Mom jumped, as if I'd spooked her out of a daydream. But then her lips unsealed themselves, curling into a slight smile. "It's David Bowie . . . an icon. I used to listen to him when I was your age."

As soon as we got home, I looked up David Bowie online, and I've been obsessed ever since. Somehow, his music made me feel closer to Mom, even though in reality she was far away—distant and cold.

And now she *literally* was far away. Pretty soon, an entire ocean would come between us.

Just forget about her, Alba.

I grabbed a tissue and wiped the gloss off my lips. Then I splashed cold water on my face and ran my wet fingers through my hair. "Boy hair," Mom liked to call it. She always put on a judgy voice whenever she said it, as if short hair wasn't a girl thing. As if short hairstyles were exclusive to lesbians. I'd heard Dad say that once when he thought I wasn't listening. Except he'd used a different term for it, spitting it out like a curse word.

Whatever.

I went back to my seat in economy. Mom and Dad always flew business class. But I guess I wasn't good enough for that, either. Other passengers were milling along the aisle. They looked like happy, fresh-faced tourists—families with kids on summer vacation, couples going on their honeymoons, backpackers excited to explore the world. And then there was me—poor, pathetic me. I was probably the only twelve-year-old kid onboard being sent off against her will to live with her estranged grandmother. Any second someone would whip out the world's tiniest violin.

"Honey, please fasten your seat belt. We'll be taking off shortly."

I glanced at the flight attendant. "Okay," I said, making a big show of snapping my seat belt together.

She went away. I was alone again. Not completely alone,

but sort of. The seat next to me was empty, but in the seat next to that, there was an old guy with *really* thick glasses reading a *really* thick book. Every once in a while, he'd glance at me. I knew the look. It was the same one I got every time someone was trying to figure out if I was a boy or a girl.

I was *so* over it.

I just ignored him and stared at the tray table in front of me. The flight attendants were doing their safety demonstration. *Blah. Blah. Blah.* I wasn't paying attention.

Finally, the engine rumbled. I closed my eyes and waited for the surge.

A minute, maybe two, maybe five passed.

Then . . .

Whoosh!

The airplane thrust forward. For some reason I coughed. I choked. My heartbeat *thump-thump, thump-thumped.* It felt like I was running. Farther and farther. From Dad's angry gaze. Mom's screaming. Faster and faster. My arm hurt. Someone was squeezing it.

"Let go!" I thought it was just a voice in my head, but then I heard a gasp. My eyes snapped open. The old man with the book. His hand was touching my arm.

"I'm sorry," he said. "I didn't mean to scare you . . . Are you all right?"

I nodded, but I wasn't all right. Far from it.

The man took his hand away with this bewildered look. He went back to his reading.

Now that the plane had leveled off, the passengers around me were relaxing. Some flipped through magazines; others watched movies on the screens in front of them.

But I was too tense for any of that. My shoulders were stiff, my chest tight, as if there was a giant rubber band stretched across my rib cage. I tried closing my eyes. Maybe I could just sleep the entire way there.

Right.

If only.

Wishful thinking.

Instead, I peered out the window. We were already high up in the air, flying above the trees and buildings and roads and people. They became smaller and smaller, turning into little Lego trees and little Lego buildings and little Lego people.

We flew into the clouds. They made me feel kind of better.

Like *maybe* this wasn't the end of the world.

Whatever was up ahead, wherever I was going, couldn't possibly be as bad as what I was leaving behind.

Right?